LONA CHANG

By AshleyRose Sullivan

Superhero Tales

Awesome Jones: A Superhero Fairy Tale

Lona Chang: A Superhero Detective Story

Other Novels

Silver Tongue

LONA CHANG

BY
ASHLEYROSE SULLIVAN

 SEVENTH STAR PRESS

Cover art and illustrations: AshleyRose Sullivan
Cover art in this book copyright © 2017 AshleyRose Sullivan

Editor: Karen M. Leet

Published by Seventh Star Press, LLC.

ISBN Number: 978-1-941706-64-0

Seventh Star Press
www.seventhstarpress.com
info@seventhstarpress.com

Publisher's Note:
Lona Chang is a work of fiction. All names, characters, and places are
the product of the author's imagination, used in fictitious manner. Any
resemblances to actual persons, places, locales, events, etc. are purely
coincidental.

Printed in the United States of America

First Edition

Dedication

For Scott, who always believed in Lona Chang.

With thanks to Kristin, for the DPNs.
And everything else.

PREVIOUSLY IN AWESOME JONES: A SUPERHERO DETECTIVE STORY...

After years spent in mediocrity, Awesome Jones finally lived up to his name and his potential. He fell in love with the charismatic Lona Chang, befriended Captain Lightning--Arc City's stalwart hero-- and discovered that he had super-powers of his own.

Awesome needed those powers, honed with the help of an ancient league of crime-fighters known as the Guild, when the creature who murdered his parents—the Echo—came for Awesome and Lona.

Awesome won the battle but it left scars.

AWESOME JONES AND Lona Chang stood before the judge.

"You ready?"

Lona smiled.

"Of course."

BANG! BANG! BANG!

Dust fell from the ceiling. Alarms blared. Awesome and Lona exchanged a glance.

HOURS EARLIER, AS dawn broke over Arc City, Lona Chang awoke in the familiar bedroom of their little house. She had been dreaming. In the dream, she saw herself and Awesome Jones back in the Guild Hall just where they had sat two months before. She listened again as Sharmilla spoke.

> "You have violated one of the Guild's most sacred rules and used lethal force against the Echo. You are hereby excommunicated from the Guild. You are forbidden from wearing a cape— forbidden from practicing as an Agent."

The implications of her words hung in Lona's memory. Awesome was forbidden from following in his father's footsteps. Forbidden from chasing his dream and living up to his potential.

Sharmilla's voice--speaking what they knew to be Pythia's decree— echoed in her head. Calm and cool.

Lona had awoken with a start.

As the memory of that night drained away, gold dust, a manifestation of her newfound ability, erupted in the air. She breathed deep. Remembered Neima's training.

The dust swirled through the room, slipped into the closet, and nestled in the pocket of a light, yellow blouse.

"It's today."

Arc City's newest hero—who had completely ignored Pythia's decree--was snoring softly beside her. Lona watched him breathe, watched the rise and fall of his chest. She laid a soft hand on the muscle of his shoulder and felt the warmth of his body before she leaned forward and kissed his cheek. His gray eyes opened and she said again,

"It's today."

"Today?"

"The courthouse. I'll make breakfast."

Awesome grabbed her as she tried to scoot from the bed. His arms, wrapped around her waist, were still getting bigger, stronger, tougher. Bruised knuckles flashed before Lona's eyes as he swept her backward. She cackled as he kissed her.

"I love you."

Over and over he kissed her.

"I love you."

She laughed and squirmed and caught her breath and almost escaped the bed but a warm tongue was lapping at her toes and she laughed again and looked toward the foot of the bed where Tulie rested her muzzle and pouted. Lona patted the covers for her to jump up. Their knee-high, brown and white, spotted mutt bounded onto the bed and panted warm breath onto their faces before following Lona into the kitchen.

Lona moved a pile of bills from the countertop and reminded herself to pay everything that afternoon. They had both elected to give their severance packages from Akai Printing Company to Mr. Sprat's family—as a thank you for all their former boss had done for them.

Since then, Lona had finally tapped into the trust fund left for her by her father, Humphrey Langdon. It was more than enough, each month, to cover their expenses but, to Lona, it still felt like taking money from a stranger. She wished her parents could be there today but, in the same thought, she realized how grateful she was to have the family that she did. She remembered that she was lucky and happy and she swept her messy hair behind her ears as she started breakfast.

They ate. The scent of French toast and strawberries with crème permeated the room. Lona showered while Awesome did the dishes and filled Tulie's food and water bowls. She slipped into her yellow blouse and blue skirt and stood in front of the bedroom mirror smoothing the fabric with steady hands. She listened as Awesome called Andy and got no answer. Then Roy, who was working. Then Julia and Neima, who would meet them at the courthouse.

When Lona was finished, she called Pop and her adoptive parents—the Changs. They were thrilled, of course. Lona gazed out the kitchen window as she spoke. Spring had arrived and the air was crisp and cool. The morning sun shone on Awesome's pots. Some had been brought in. Some given away. Some held budding flowers—white pansies with violet hearts and tall, yellow tulips. Lona listened as Mrs. Chang fluttered in the background and Mr. Chang said they would be there. She hung up.

Lona stood in their bedroom doorway and watched Awesome button a plain, cotton shirt over his uniform. The sleek, high-tech uniform had mysteriously arrived at their door two months ago and so far it had served Awesome well as Arc City's new *Baron*. It hadn't taken a single rip or tear and it fit perfectly, in spite of Awesome's still-changing physique.

"No one will ever know you went to the trouble of wearing a suit to your wedding."

"You will. That's all that matters."

That smile.

"I'm so proud of you. *My Baron.*"

Granite columns stood like stoic soldiers guarding the Arc City courthouse. The building had begun to show its age. The copper dome on top was a mix of orange and green. It reminded Lona of a leaf resisting the fall.

Awesome and Lona held hands and climbed the steps together. Inside, they found Julia and Pop waiting on opposite sides of a crowded hallway. The Changs were chattering away as they assessed a mural of Arc City's past heroes.

ARC CITY'S FINEST

A throng of people moved through the hallway, their shoes clopping on the pale, marble floors. A news crew with microphones held aloft swept past them. When the crowd thinned, Lona saw Roy standing outside a set of huge double doors at the end of the hallway.

Awesome stared at Roy. His black, Assistant Agent uniform had been replaced by a new, Guild-sanctioned suit. Now he was covered in a charcoal fabric that shimmered when he moved and, in place of his old prism, he wore a new symbol.

His mask was the same—the plain, black, domino style—and his dark hair, rather than hanging shaggily over his eyes, was cut short and swept back. Awesome nodded to the man, the friend, the hero. Roy nodded back, curt and sharp, all business.

Lona took Awesome's hand as she watched the exchange and the crowd pass between them.

"What's going on?"

Awesome shook his head but Julia approached.

"It's a big trial. You didn't see it in the paper?"

Now Awesome remembered. One of the bigwigs from the Under Arc crime syndicate was being tried today and a key witness—a man who had rolled over on the whole group—was being brought in from Guild Secret Protection to testify against him.

Awesome looked around again. There were regular courthouse employees, lawyers and their assistants; there were the city police; there was Roy. And then there were about ten Suits. The black

9

started with their hats. Their suit coats concealed their Guild-issue phones, stunners, and badges. The black continued down their legs to Guild-issue, rubber-soled shoes. There was a time when Awesome had hoped to be good enough just to try for his Tie. Now, he was wearing his unsanctioned Baron uniform under his wedding clothes.

Was this better?

His thoughts were interrupted as Julia handed Lona a little bouquet of spring flowers. Julia seemed almost the same as the girl he'd first seen scuttling around the Guild Hall cafeteria. Her eyes were still black and shining and her fingernails were still colored with chippy polish but her bouncy braids had been shorn off into a short afro and her smile wasn't as free and easy as it had been then.

Lona hugged her friend and felt the warmth of Julia's body. She remembered the words Julia had said when she left the Guild and she and Awesome had helped her move into the apartment she shared with Neima--

"It's like every projection of me is a reflection—a mirror—and when the Echo killed one of me, he broke that mirror. It's gone now. There were five. Now there are four. That part of me died and it can't ever come back. I'm not a part of the Guild anymore. I'm not sure I ever was."

Lona had held Julia's hand in Neima's cabin and watched as her friend got a little better with time. "Better" was not "well," though, and Lona wished that she could do more for her. Though, she supposed, Julia even leaving her apartment was a triumph after what she'd been through.

"They're from the flower shop under the apartment."

Lona looked back down at the irises and daffodils all clustered together.

"They're so beautiful, Julia. Thank you."

Lona Chang

Neima came from around the corner and beamed as soon as she saw Lona. Her face, now, was a little paler, and the lines around her eyes and mouth showed a little more clearly. Lona's mentor had lost her lifelong partner and, with him, a part of herself. Still, she had taken care of Julia since the night of Awesome's birthday. Julia had stayed with Neima until she was well enough to be moved and, when they were ready, they had come to Arc City together.

It was Neima who helped Julia get a job at the Arc City Museum and Lona just happened upon the listing for an apartment right next to the museum.

They would get well together, help each other heal. At least, that's what Lona told herself.

"Hello, Neima. Thank you for coming."

"Of course, my girl."

"How are you?"

"I'm alright, I think. Tired, you know, but I'll be alright."

Lona looked over to where Julia was admiring the superhero mural and congratulating Awesome on the big day.

"And Julia?"

"She's--well, you know, she's coming along. Getting better every day."

Pop approached them, along with the Changs, who wrapped their adopted daughter in their arms.

"Mama."

Mrs. Chang smothered Lona in kisses and went about smoothing back Lona's curls and squeezing her cheeks as Mr. Chang shook Awesome's hand and then Pop's. Awesome's grandfather kissed Lona's cheek.

"You look lovely Lona, just lovely."

"Thank you, Pop."

They all moved down the hall together and Awesome glanced back, over his shoulder, at the entrance. He hoped Andy might still, somehow, make an appearance. It was Andy who had known his parents, had watched over him, had brought him into the Guild, had protected him. He was still their best friend. But he wasn't answering his phone. He was distant lately. Distracted.

Awesome and Lona missed him. Missed his presence.

A few minutes later, they found themselves before the judge.

"You ready?"

Julia stood beside Lona, holding one of the irises from Lona's bouquet. Pop was ready beside Awesome Jones with a little, silver band.

Sunlight filtered through the high windows. Lona inhaled the scent of irises and daffodils. She looked around at her little family and—even though a couple of members were missing—she was undeniably happy.

"Of course."

BANG! BANG! BANG!

Lona watched dust fall from the ceiling. Men and women stampeded down the hall. Alarms blared.

A huge man with flinty, hard skin stomped after the crowd. He roared, pulled up chunks of the floor, and threw the gigantic handfuls of concrete and marble after them.

Awesome stared after the man.

"That's Ironhide."

Lona nodded to her fiancé.

"Go get him."

He started toward the empty judge's office then suddenly stopped with a panicked look on his face.

Lona realized what had happened and opened her bag. She withdrew a folded, black scrap of cloth and threw it to him. He caught it in the air and rushed off.

Julia nudged her.

"What was that?"

"His mask. I saw it as we were leaving this morning and grabbed it just in case."

Lona looked around at them all. The Changs were huddled under an archway. Pop stood with the judge at one of the windows. Neima held her back against one of the walls, massaging her temples.

"Are you alright?"

Neima squinted at Lona, in obvious pain.

"It's a terrible time for a headache, isn't it?"

Lona frowned back at her.

"When it rains it pours, I suppose. Can you walk? Everyone's evacuating."

"Yes. It's clearing up. I'll be alright."

Clearing her throat and straightening up, Lona addressed the room.

"We need to get out of here. Let's stay together and we'll be alright."

She led them all through the hallway. Their ears throbbed from the noise of the alarms. The cratered floor shook beneath them. Somewhere in the building, Ironhide roared again. Julia screamed. Lona took her under an arm. Her friend was pale and shaking.

They heard fast-falling footsteps behind them and turned.

It was the Baron. The *new* Baron.

He was different from the Baron who had saved Lona when she was a little girl. This Baron—*her Baron*—was long and lean with dark, waving hair and gray eyes. Rather than a tuxedo, he wore a suit that moved with his quick, lithe body. And now, he called to her as he thundered past.

"Get everyone out!"

She nodded and took up Julia's arm again. She and Pop traded a look as he helped with Julia and they all rushed down the hall.

Outside, a crowd was gathering. Everyone who had been evacuated was standing at the base of the steps. They watched the courthouse. Across the street, people streamed out of the bank and onto the sidewalk where they gawked at the courthouse.

Lona led her group onto the courthouse lawn. A flicker of green dust caught in her periphery. She turned her head toward the dust but lost it as Julia pulled away from her.
"I have to go. I'm not staying here."

"Ok, but don't you need to rest first? You look like you might faint."

A thunderous crash came from within the courthouse and Julia covered her ears and ducked. When she straightened, she looked feral. Her eyes were set and dark, her fists clenched.

"No. I have to get out of here."

She pulled away and ran off. Neima gave Lona a reassuring look and followed after her. Lona watched Julia make her way through the crowd, to the sidewalk. When she was out of sight, the dust caught Lona's attention again. It quivered like a match flame.

Another crash. Lona turned back to the courthouse. What was happening in there?

Inside, Ironhide stormed down the hallway, his huge feet spitting up chunks of the floor as he ran. Awesome trailed behind him. Over the noise of the chase, Awesome heard Ironhide's voice. Was he saying something? Mumbling? It had a rhythm, a cadence.

His thoughts were interrupted as Roy caught up with them and shouted over the crash of Ironhide's thumping footsteps.

"You can't keep doing this!"

"I don't think this is really the time—"

Roy shot Ironhide with a blast of light as he ran. The big man screamed, turned, stopped and ducked. He grabbed Roy by the foot and yanked. Roy's head slapped the floor.

Awesome tackled Ironhide and brought a hard elbow down on his forehead. Ironhide grunted but otherwise ignored the blow and got to his feet as he threw Awesome back. Awesome flew twenty feet through the air and rolled to a stop. When he settled, he saw Ironhide turn the corner, toward the stairwell. Awesome glimpsed something in Ironhide's giant fist. *What was it?*

Roy groaned.

"He's going after the witness."

"Photon—"

"Just go on."

Awesome nodded and charged after Ironhide. He skidded to a stop at the stairwell and looked down. Ironhide had jumped. He was already on the first floor, pulling himself out of the crater his landing had created. Suits were swarming and, above that, Awesome heard the echo of Ironhide's gruff voice.

"249. 248. 247."

"Counting down. He's counting down."

Awesome wracked his brain to think what it could mean. What could he be counting down to? A bomb? A breakout?

He jumped.

246. 245. 244.

The elderly woman, Eleanor, counted in her head. She hummed as she did so. She had a sweet, raspy voice when she asked the man at the desk to be let into the vault at Arc City Savings and Loan. Now, she stood by herself, tapping her foot on the tile floor.

The walls around her were full of little metal boxes, decorated with numbers. She, however, was not interested in the boxes or the numbers. She stared ahead, at the back wall and the iron-barred door which guarded the bank's money.

Canvas bags and stacks of green bills lined the walls of that second, smaller room.

199. 198. 197.

She brushed a strand of mouse-gray hair behind her ear and approached the bars.

BY THIS TIME Awesome landed on the first floor, every single Suit had been taken out. He looked around. The Suits were groaning or grumbling. It seemed that one was dead. *What is he doing?*

"Baron..."

One of the Suits rubbed her shoulder and struggled to get up.

"He's gone after Montgomery. He's on this floor. 103. You can't let Ironhide get him."

Awesome took off, following the trail of chipped marble. Roy caught up with him.

"My laser barely made a dent."

"Same with the Suits' stunners."

"It's that skin."

Ironhide had been around for at least twenty years. He wasn't a high-profile criminal. For as long as Awesome could remember, Ironhide had only ever been part of burglaries. He was the muscle, not the brains, and he wasn't the type to put his neck on the line for some star witness. *Was he hired by the syndicate?*

"75. 74. 73. 72."

Ironhide's voice rumbled out from around the corner.

"What is that? What's he doing?"

"I don't know."

Awesome watched the numbers on the doors as they ran by. 101. 102.

They turned the corner and watched as Ironhide kicked in the door. Stunner shots from the Suits hit the wall beside Awesome's head as he vaulted into the room after Ironhide. The shots ricocheted off the man's hard skin. Roy barely ducked to miss one. He opened his hand, aimed, and let loose another laser blast. Again, Ironhide roared but didn't go down.

Instead, he completely ignored the little man Awesome recognized as the key witness, Montgomery, cowering in the corner behind three Suits. Ironhide continued counting down as he leapt through the window that overlooked the front lawn.

"55. 54. 53."

47. 46. 45.

Eleanor finished tinkering with the little, brassy box she had withdrawn from her bag. She adjusted two small dials on the side until they were just right, humming all the time. It was an old song. Something about a shepherd girl.

43. 42. 41.

Reaching through the bars, she set the box on the floor and pressed a silver button on its backside. The box eased open.

Bright, blue light filled the room. A ripple swept out from the box, over the little room that contained the money. The air became hot and dry. Then, all at once, the money vanished. The stacks, bags, and even the shelves and carts, were all gone.

Eleanor peeked through the bars one last time. The box was gone. The room was empty.

"19. 18. 17."

Awesome Jones, Photon, and a few Suits finally had Ironhide surrounded on the courthouse lawn. Awesome knew Ironhide couldn't fly, not with all that bulk, but he could probably jump. And, like a rhino, he could charge through all of them but him. Awesome stood his ground.

"7. 6. 5."

Roy shot Ironhide again with his laser and again Ironhide rushed the young hero and knocked him back. Blood streamed from Roy's nose as he struggled to get up. The Suits were helpless.

Ironhide started in the other direction but Awesome launched forward, wrapped his arms around the giant's legs, and they both thudded to the ground. He breathed hard as he crawled up Ironhide's back and reached for his huge wrists.

What can I even cuff him with?

"3. 2. 1"

Ironhide started to convulse. At first, Awesome assumed he'd been hurt. But the man was laughing. A silent, shaking laugh.

As Awesome reached for Ironhide's wrist, the giant stood and easily shook him off.

"Time to go, little men."

Awesome remembered what he'd seen in the man's hand—the box. Now he saw it again. Ironhide clicked it open.

"No! Roy! His hand!"

Roy saw and shot—a straight, perfect blast at the thing in Ironhide's palm. A bright crackle, the smell of ammonia, and now the little box sizzled and popped and fell to the ground.

Ironhide cracked his knuckles with a sound like a junkyard crusher and sneered at them, obviously annoyed at the destruction of his toy.

"If you two are the best the Guild has to offer then this city's in trouble."

Ironhide started his rush at Awesome Jones but was interrupted by another noise—the tremendous crack of thunder.

Captain Lightning appeared in the sky. He held out his hands and a lightning bolt, quick and white and glorious, broke through the air and caught Ironhide straight in the face. He went down, his considerable, dead weight sinking into the lawn. His eyes fluttered and he groaned.

Landing without a sound, Captain Lightning pulled a pair of X-cuffs from his bomber jacket and slapped them on Ironhide without ceremony.

"You two look terrible."

Roy dragged an arm across his nose and his high-tech uniform absorbed the blood. Awesome gave an exhausted laugh.

"Thanks."

Lona approached. She turned and pointed toward a diminutive

woman with gray hair and red, plastic glasses. She wore stylish flats and a pink scarf and, while everyone else was staring at the courthouse or at Ironhide, she paid none of it any mind and walked instead to her car.

"This was never about the courthouse, Baron. It's about her."

ELEANOR SMILED TO herself as she watched the Suits crowd around Ironhide.

"Idiot."

She dropped her leather bag into the passenger seat, started the car, put it in gear, and eased onto the gas. Nothing happened. Her tiny foot pressed harder. Still nothing. Finally, she looked into the rearview mirror. The Baron was holding the back of her car a foot off the ground. A tap came at the window and she rolled it down.

It was the Captain, his uniform's silver lightning bolt shining in the sun. He stared at her through dark goggles and smirked.

"Ma'am, we need to ask you a few questions. Please step out of the vehicle."

"YOU MADE THE front page again."

Lona smiled and pushed the paper toward Awesome Jones as he entered the kitchen. Awesome took in the familiar scene. Tulie was curled up around Lona's bare feet under the cluttered table. Lona wore one of his old work shirts and a tired, frustrated look. A pencil held her curls in a messy bun on the top of her head and she rested her cheek on the heel of her palm as she stared at her father's open journal. Notebooks, library volumes and old comics lay open next to it. He knew her handwriting filled the notebooks cover to cover but she wasn't any closer to deciphering her father's coded entries.

"How's it going?"

"Hmm?"

She shook her head and took the pencil from her hair, toppling the amber tangles, and scribbled something next to one of Humphrey Langdon's cryptic illustrations. The only legible words in the entire journal were his name. The rest of the tattered pages were filled with coded paragraphs and sketches of objects and symbols she didn't understand. Occasionally, there were dates. Or, at least, Lona thought they were dates. They went back hundreds of years so it was hard to tell.

"I'll clean up and make breakfast."

Awesome yawned and walked over to the coffee press they'd brought from the cabin.

"No, it's alright. Keep working. I'll make some grilled cheese."

Tulie jumped up and padded over to Awesome, her nails tapping on their tile floor. She wagged her tail against his leg as Awesome took the butter and a block of hard cheddar from the refrigerator and then pulled Lona's cast iron pan from its hook.

"I'm not any closer to understanding this stuff."

Lona sighed and stared at the book. She wondered where it had come from. Both the book and Awesome's Baron suit had been mysteriously delivered to their door, the brown paper packages they had come in gave nothing away about their source. Awesome's uniform was perfect for him. Other un-registered heroes made their own costumes with whatever they could find—a lot of it coming from the underground super science market. Awesome's suit was different. It wasn't cobbled together out of scavenged or questionable parts. It fit perfectly and moved with his body. The ultra-light fabric was as tough as any armor and his mask gripped to his face so well he couldn't even feel it. It was perfect. So where, or who, had it and Humphrey Langdon's journal come from?

Lona peered back down at her father's familiar handwriting. She remembered the way he had scribbled in the margins of the huge, old tomes in his library. As a young woman, she had traced the slanting letters with her fingers and wondered what kind of man her father had been. She wondered, then, if he really had died cold and alone in the Arctic Circle. But, more than that she wondered what he would say to her if he had been alive. She wondered those same things now and found herself running her fingers over those same letters, configured in an as-yet illegible pattern.

She closed the books and moved everything from the table to the little metal bookshelf Awesome had found and set up next to the kitchen table for her work.

Lona Chang

The plates thunked lightly as Awesome set them down. He poured their coffee and held his cup under his nose as Tulie re-claimed her spot at Lona's feet.

Lona took her first bite and glanced at the paper lying open on the counter.

"Did you read it? Did you see who you caught?"

"You mean who *you* caught."

"It was nothing. I didn't even have to use my ability. The bank was glowing, sort of, so I knew there must be something going on. But she was the only one not paying any attention to Ironhide's commotion. The only one. I can't believe she was the Alchemist."

The Alchemist had been a major super science figure when Awesome and Lona were children, just as the science boom was beginning. No one knew where she'd come from but she crashed onto the scene when she not only turned one of Arc City Park's granite gargoyles to pure crystal, but subsequently stole it. The statue was never recovered and she was never apprehended. Until now.

"I wonder how long she's been partners with Ironhide."

Lona shook her head.

"If they even *were* partners. She might have just hired him. He's never worked with the same group for long. Didn't he do time in Claymore a few years ago?"

"Yeah, for knocking over a drugstore downtown with some group of rich teenagers who wanted to be super criminals."

"Oh, yeah. That's right."

"Did you hear her counting when she came out of the bank?"

"No."

After the Alchemist had been taken into custody, she told Captain Lightning that it always took Guild operatives at least four minutes to arrive on scene in that quadrant of town. And she had been right. If Awesome hadn't noticed the device in Ironhide's hand and Roy hadn't destroyed it, the man would've escaped before Captain Lightning could arrive. And, if Lona hadn't noticed the little old lady walking to her car, the Alchemist would've been in the wind. Instead, they were both in custody and Awesome and Lona's wedding was postponed.

"Do you want to try again at the courthouse?"

"Tomorrow?"

She shook her head.

"No. Let's wait for the right time. The real right time. I'm glad we were there yesterday, though."

"Me, too."

She helped him clean up then leaned against the counter stroking Tulie's head as Awesome did the dishes.

"Did Roy say anything to you?"

"He warned me again."

Sighing, Lona thought about the frustrated Double A and how his promotion had given him a new confidence. She wished there wasn't such a clear separation between him and Awesome now. She wished the rules were different. Ever since she'd found out about the Guild, she'd wished the rules were different.

"You don't think—you don't think he'd ever actually bring you in, do you?"

Awesome shook his head.

"No."

But he didn't sound sure. Being an unregistered hero wasn't technically *illegal* but it did go against Guild sanctions. They played by a long list of rules and operated within a bureaucracy that Awesome didn't really understand. Unregistered heroes caused collateral damage. They often scared citizens. They got themselves and others hurt. When Guild heroes did that, they sent a team of Suits to clean up the mess.

But no one came in the wake of people like Awesome. No one was there to pick up the pieces and Roy had told him more than once that Pythia wanted Awesome off the streets.

"At least, I don't think so. Has Julia spoken to him lately?"

Lona handed him a clean dishtowel for drying and together they put away the plates and coffee cups.

"I think they're on the outs. She says he can't risk losing his Agent status by being with her. And, I think now that she's left the Guild, she feels like she's not part of his world anymore."

"But that's—"

Awesome was interrupted by the sound of the police scanner screeching in the living room. It reported a burglary in progress on Brewer Drive. No supers—so far.

"That's only about a mile away."

Awesome rushed into the bedroom and came out a few moments later dressed with everything but his mask. The speed with which he had changed was nothing short of amazing. Of course, he had been practicing.

"I can be there in about five minutes if I run."

Lona nodded and kissed him.

"Be careful."

Awesome nodded and pressed the mask to his face. He paused at the door, where his father's cane leaned against the wall, looking for all the world like a regular walking stick and not a solid cylinder of steel and iron. Looking for all the world like it wasn't a deadly weapon.

Awesome took it. He had lived to regret facing Ironhide without it. Still, as happy to receive this cane as he had been, he'd come to feel more and more that it was his father's weapon and not his own.

Lona watched him duck out into the back alley. She knew he would stay in the shadows until he got closer to Brewer Street. She knew he was getting fast. Really fast. But it wasn't quite enough. He wanted the ability to traverse the city more efficiently. But what could he do?

LONA DROVE ANDY'S truck to the downtown branch of the Arc City library. She renewed two of her cryptography books and then wandered through the stacks searching for one she hadn't tried. She focused and refocused, hoping her ability might spring to life and give her some sign of a book that might help. She closed her eyes and imagined a glowing flicker of dust on the shelves but when she looked again, nothing had changed. There was no clue. Book after book. Numbers across their spines. Nothing special. Sighing, she pulled an ancient tome off the shelf and studied the title—*Codes and Cyphers Through the Centuries: Cryptography from Ancient to Modern Times.*

Lona flipped through the pages and scanned the small print then shoved it under her arm. She walked it to one of the long, wooden tables and clicked on a green, glass lamp. She sat down, opened the book, and began at the beginning. After a few minutes, a librarian pushed a cart by her and stopped at the end of one aisle.

Lona rubbed her eyes and looked again at the cartful of books. Paperbacks and hardcovers filled the metal shelf of the cart but, between two large-print novels, were miniscule sparks of gold dust. She stood and approached the cart, careful not to lose the trail. The dust was so faint she wasn't even sure whether she was truly seeing it. Finally, she laid two fingers on the book the dust had fallen from and slid it out.

r

"Oh, I love that one."

Lona directed her attention to the person who had spoken. She was a plump young woman with red, Cupid's bow lips and bright brown eyes. Her nametag said, Jolie.

"Oh, yeah?"

"Yeah, have you read any of the Kraker mysteries?"

Lona shook her head.

"Kraker?"

"Irene Matly wrote a ton of those. Twenty-three, I think. That's the fourth one. If you like, I could get the first three for you."

Lona looked back down at the flimsy paperback in her hands and watched as the dust popped like fireworks at the frayed edges of the cover. Directing her attention back to Jolie, she smiled.

"Ok, sure. Thanks."

Lona left the library with a bag-full of cryptography books and detective novels. She stopped by the store. She bought the following items: orange juice, lamb, rosemary, shallots, and apples.

The maket had been rebuilt after the Echo's rampage through the neighborhood. The one Esmerelda and Lona had witnessed together. Lona had looked for Esmerelda when she returned to Arc City. But, Esmerelda no longer worked at the market. Esmerelda had left Arc City.

Lona went home. She found that Awesome was still not there and she went outside to meditate as Neima had taught her. Her mind, though, was hectic and she couldn't settle. Tulie nosed the patio door open, lay down on the warm stones, and nuzzled her nose against Lona's bare ankle. Lona stroked the speckled mutt's muzzle and closed her eyes again.

Dust swirled. Lona breathed deep.

ACROSS THE ROOM there was a giant man. The giant man breathed deep.

Through bleary eyes, Ironhide could see the giant man's chest moving. Ironhide was confused. He was not accustomed to being a smaller man. A weaker man.

He had been arrested many times. So many times he had lost count. And yet, this time, he wasn't at the police station. He wasn't in jail. He wasn't being transported to the Icebox or Claymore or even Onyx Island. He had been knocked out and now he found himself in a little black room with black walls and a black table. Little pinpoint lights, embedded in the ceiling, provided the only light. He felt inexplicably, horribly, terrified.

Then the door had opened. Two men in black scrubs had come for him. He had followed them, his wrists still bound, his head still clouded.

Now he was in the big room. The big room was a circle and there were no windows. On the floor, there was a picture. What did they call it? A *mosaic*. The mosaic formed a likeness of the heavens and, at the center of the room, was the earth. This is where Ironhide was brought and where he now sat—strapped to a metal chair.

A woman emerged from the shadows and stood, across the room, at the center of six other robed figures. This woman wore robes as well but hers were a deep indigo. She drummed her fingernails on a high judge's bench as she read the charges against him in a clear voice while the giant man, standing off to the side, breathed in and out.

"…arson, burglary, damage to public property…"

She named the number of times he had been apprehended, rehabilitated, and released back into society.

She pronounced his sentence. The giant man moved forward. He lumbered, haltingly, toward Ironhide. His joints made a mechanical sound. His black robes touched the floor and his black hood covered his head. Still, Ironhide tried to meet the man's eyes. Instead, through the hood's eyeholes, Ironhide found a green, electric glow.

The men in scrubs stood beside him. One jabbed a syringe into his neck. The other prepared a diamond-tipped needle.

He was woozy again. The lights above were fading. His body seemed far away and the world was growing dark.

AWESOME JONES ARRIVED home about an hour after Lona—just as she was making lunch. He kissed her as she slid boiled egg halves into a salad nicoise.

"Everything ok? How'd it go?"

"Good. It was just a couple of thugs."

"Oh?"

"I handed them over to the Suits."

"No Roy?"

"No. And no Andy either. Just Suits. I actually recognized one of them."

They took the plates to the kitchen table and Awesome washed up. Lona poured tall glasses of lemonade and told Awesome about her trip to the library. They ate and then Awesome took a shower while Lona got back to work on her father's journal. By the time he was done, though, she was out on the patio with Tulie, reading the first detective novel in the Kraker series.

That night they took a walk, as they always had. They strolled down their street, past the market, and through the park. They tried not to notice the shiny blackness of filled-in potholes where the Echo had torn the streets apart. Tiny, closed rosebuds dotted the newly green bushes. Moist air gathered into a fog as they rounded the bend where Frank, the flower vender, had once been.

No one had taken his place.

The spot stood empty. He had been murdered. Stabbed. His blood had spilled onto the sidewalk where Lona now stood.

She tried not to think about it.

And, she forced herself to think about it.

They went home. Lona took a bath. Awesome read the classifieds to her.

She inspected his scrapes and scratches from the day's work. They made love.

> "I love you, Jones."

> "I love you, too."

> "Goodnight, Jones."

> "Goodnight, Lona."

They went to sleep.

And this was how Awesome Jones, Lona Chang, and Tulie the dog spent their days and nights.

IRONHIDE AWOKE IN a dim, sterile room on a hard, metal bed. His body felt strange. Delicate.

Before he fully realized why, he began to cry. Tears slid off his cheeks and dotted the paper-wrapped bed. Tap. Tap. Tap.

How long had it been since he had cried? Since he even *could* cry.

He brought his hands to his face and cried all the harder at the sight of soft, pink flesh where there should have been cool, dark iron.

ON A THURSDAY morning, just after sunrise, Lona knocked on the door of a little downtown apartment. The scents of the flower shop downstairs floated up to her all at once. Roses, gardenias, lilies. She stood smiling at the fragrant air as Neima opened the door.

The woman's hair hung in a loose braid at her back and she wore an apron over her linen pants and shirt. It had taken Lona some weeks to get over seeing Neima outside of the woods and the quaint cabin. Speaking to her here, in this high-ceilinged building with black and white tile floors, felt strange and foreign.

"You look well, my girl."

"You too, Neima."

Lona wrapped her mentor in a tight hug as Neima kissed her cheeks. When they pulled away, Lona studied Neima's amber eyes.

"Any luck? Is there still a wall?"

"It is ever-present."

Since the night of Ben's death, Neima had been shut off from her ability. As she described it, there was a wall between her and the psychic stream of time and space she had always been able to access.

"I meditate daily but I suspect my own grief is to blame. It's not unheard of. Psychic power is sometimes temperamental and fragile. I can still sense some thoughts, can still feel the ripples of psychic energy around me but…the vast part of the world that I have always been able to access is blocked from my view. At least for now."

Julia entered from the kitchen with a fresh cup of tea for Lona and the three women settled down on the wooden floor. Pale sunlight gradually colored the room in rose, then cream, and finally white. All the while, Lona, Julia, and Neima meditated together. Their breath and hearts moved in sync.

Lona focused on the manifestation of her ability—the shimmering dust. In her mind, it swirled. She watched it move with her inhalation of breath. It shifted in color like the wings of a hummingbird and was just as erratic in its movement. Green. Gold. Red. Fuschia. Violet.

She thought of Awesome and the dust was gold. She thought of her father's journal and the dust was blue. She thought of the Echo. Red. Rust Red.

She shook her head. Shook out the thoughts. Breathed deep. Focused.

Silver. The dust was pure silver. It washed like ocean waves over her. Surrounded her. Enveloped her body and penetrated her skin. She felt cool. Almost chilly. And, as soon as she was aware of the feeling, the dust vanished.

Lona opened her eyes. She peeked at the clock on Julia's living room wall. A black and white cat twitched its tail in accordance with the seconds that passed in its stomach. An hour had passed.

Neima had already left the room and gone out to the balcony. She stood at the railing, eating fresh blueberries from one of Awesome's terra cotta bowls. The morning light cast a glow on her cheeks—paler than usual.

Lona remembered seeing her in much the same light in the cabin.

Lona Chang

Often, Lona wished they could all go back to that time. To that place. Before Ben. Before Julia. Even that time, though, had been borrowed. Even then, they had lived under the ever-present specter of the Echo.

"How is it coming with your father's journal?"

Lona took the hand-full of blueberries Neima offered and answered.

"No luck."

"You should consider showing it to your parents."

"Do you think the Changs knew something?"

Neima watched the foot traffic below. A man across the street was opening his bagel shop. A woman and her son were stocking the shelves of their newsstand. Captain Lightning comics filled the shelves. Several covers sported illustrated versions of his encounter with Ironhide. Lona made out the silver lettering of *Arc City's Finest* from three stories up.

She met Neima's eyes again; the creases around them grew tighter as she smiled.

"I would be surprised if they did not."

"I'm afraid of telling them anything about this. My ability. Awesome. I'm afraid they'll get hurt. What we do is so dangerous."

"Talk to them. They raised you, after all."

Lona nodded and glanced through the glass door at Julia, still sitting on the hard floor.

"How is she?"

"Mending. She's mending."

"Has she officially quit the Guild?"

"No. But you know how they are. They barely even acknowledged her existence to begin with."

A horn honked in the street below as a grocer pushed a dolly of oranges across the street, in front of a delivery truck. The grocer jumped at the sound of the horn. Several oranges spilled onto the asphalt, bouncing their way to the gutter.

The door slid open as Julia joined them.

"Wow, you guys look serious."

She sniffed and took a drink of water. Lona offered her some berries but Julia put up a hand.

"No thanks. Have you made any progress on your dad's journal?"

Lona shrugged and answered Julia's question with another question.

"How's the job coming along? Do you like it?"

"Varun's the best. I get to wear archival gloves and I've been helping him catalogue a bunch of stuff that just came in from Borneo."

Varun was an old friend of Neima's and head of the Arc City Museum's Asian Antiquities Department. He had given Julia the assistant position based solely on Neima's recommendation.

"Maybe he could help you with the book."

"Oh, I don't know."

"He's crazy smart. And, he speaks about nine languages."

Neima broke in.

"Show it to the Changs first, Lona. They should know about this. You aren't in the Guild. It's up to you to decide whether to talk about your abilities with them but they didn't just raise you—they also raised your father. They should know that you have his journal."

Lona nodded.

"Alright, ladies. I need to get to work," Julia said, heading back into the apartment.

"I've got to get going too. I'll walk you down."

SOME YEARS AGO:

A door opened.

One man spoke to another man.

"More war orphans?"

The other man nodded. He was younger than the first man. He had olive skin and brown eyes. He preferred to avert his gaze from the older man.

The older man spoke again.

"When will it ever end?"

The younger man shrugged and mumbled something about the length of the war as two little boys were escorted into the room. Their eyes were sunken and rimmed in red. Their pale skin and gaunt faces told a too-familiar story.

The older man knelt before the taller boy. This boy met the older man's eyes and the younger man admired him for that.

"I see you were sent to us by way of Geneva. Do you know why you are here?"

The boy didn't hesitate. He walked to the heavy, oaken desk the older man had been leaning against, and easily lifted it with one hand.

"What are your names?"

The taller boy said that his name was Marcus and the younger man scribbled the name in a form on his clipboard. The shorter boy stared at the floor. He had stared at the floor since he entered the room. Still, he didn't look up. Instead, he reached out and took Marcus's hand.

The younger man tried to peer beneath the boy's dark, dirty curls, tried to catch the boy's eyes. He saw a flash of hazel before the boy moved closer to his friend and buried his face in the stronger shoulder.

"He don't talk no more. But we call him Sunny."

"And why is that?"

Marcus nudged the smaller boy.

"It's alright, you can show him."

The smaller boy, Sunny, dug into the inside of his tattered jacket and pulled out an even more tattered soldier doll. The younger man recognized it as "Sunny the Soldier Boy" they'd been selling in Britain since he was a child. He explained this fact to the older man.

"Ah. I see."

The younger man watched the older man study the children.

"Ah, well. It doesn't matter. You won't need your old names here."

The younger man wrote something on the clipboard and depressed a silver button on the wall. Moments later, a woman in white appeared, took the piece of paper he held out for her, and motioned for the boys to follow her.

The older man cleared his throat when they had gone.

Lona Chang

"Good specimens, don't you think?"

The younger man averted his eyes, shrugged, and mumbled something about them being fine young men.

MR. CHANG OPENED the door to the little apartment above Chang's Antiques Emporium. Lona and Awesome took their shoes off in the foyer and were met by Mrs. Chang in the parlor. The fastidious woman was flustered by their sudden visit and scrambled to start a pot of tea and assemble a few cakes on a platter as Awesome and Lona attempted to assure her that it wasn't necessary.

Mrs. Chang ignored their protestations and thrust a little pink, frosted cake into Awesome's hand as Lona reached for the pack strapped over her back.

"I just wanted—well, I wanted to see a few of my father's things. I have this journal. I don't remember it at all and I can't read a word of it. I think my father wrote it all in code and—"

She took the journal from her pack and Mrs. Chang gasped at the sight of it.

"I thought I'd never see it again."

"Where did you find it, Lona?"

With shaking hands, Lona's adopted father took the tattered book from her and opened it to Humphrey Langdon's name.

"You recognize it?"

"Your father kept this journal for many years. He took it on every expedition and, as far as I know, kept a record of everything he found and did."

"Can you read it?"

He cleared his throat and held the book out to Mrs. Chang.

"No, dear. But this book wasn't meant for me. In fact, I think it was meant for you."

"What?"

"Follow me."

Lona and Awesome followed Mr. Chang down their well-appointed hallway, where the portrait of Awesome's mother still hung, to a door at the end of the hall. The door opened into a room full of strange antiquities. A curio cabinet stood against one wall and featured an old, brass lamp, a snow globe filled with lavender snow, the skull of an animal Lona didn't recognize, a framed photograph of a woman clad in animal skins, and several other oddities. Mr. Chang opened a little drawer in the cabinet and withdrew a brown envelope.

"Your father kept this in that book for years. After he left for his last expedition, we found it next to his desk. It must have fallen out."

His hands were steady as he opened the envelope and slid from it an old photograph.

Lona's eyes widened as Mr. Chang slipped the picture into her hands.

She touched a fingertip to her own, much younger face and smiled.

"I remember this."

"There's something on the back."

Awesome pointed to the back of the picture and Lona turned it over and saw her father's familiar script.

"He knew. Jones, look. My father knew."

Mr. and Mrs. Chang exchanged a look. A cuckoo leapt from the clock in the room, its body a herky-jerky shimmer of blue as it proclaimed the hour to be four o'clock. Lona peered into the curio cabinet. The oddities contained therein were both familiar and new to her. Lucky? What she understood of her father's life suddenly felt like such a small bit of information. Father. Husband. Explorer. Millionaire.

Lucky? How had he known about her ability?

"Mama? Was my father—did he have—Mama, what was he doing?"

"Humphrey was very special, Lona. But, everything he did—even who he was—he kept close. Betty was closer to him than anyone but even she wasn't privy to absolutely every part of his life."

"Why?"

"To keep us safe, I think. Even you. The way we adopted you, the way all of his wealth was locked away, it was all part of Humphrey's explicit instruction should he ever not return from one of his expeditions. He said it was all to keep us safe."

Lona thought about Harvey Sprat, her boss. Frank, the flower vender. Julia. Ben.

"I understand."

She sighed and again read her father's words.

"But, Baba, Mama, did he have an ability? Was he a hero?"

"Why? What's happened?"

Dust burst from the curio cabinet and swirled around the book, the photo, and Lona's hands. It glimmered and glowed an iridescent purple.

"It's me. I have an ability. I thought maybe—"

"Your father had it as well?"

Lona nodded. The purple dust shimmered as it swam around her fingertips and up her wrists.

Mr. Chang and Mrs. Chang both gaped at Lona then traded looks before Mrs. Chang's thin, red lips curved into a smile.

"What is it?"

"Is your ability at work presently, dear?"

Lona swallowed hard and looked again at her hands then back at her adopted mother.

"Yes, why?"

"Just the look on your face. It's just the same as Humphrey's when he could see the secrets."

"The secrets?"

"Your father, when observing the world around him, could *see* secrets. I can only describe it the way that he told us. He said that he might not always *know* the secret. But he could always tell when one was present and, usually, what kind."

The dust swirled up her arms and across her chest. The Changs may not have been able to picture it but Lona could. The manifestation of her ability was so difficult to explain and yet she felt, instinctively, that she knew exactly what her father had seen.

"He was a true detective."

"Did he call himself that?"

Mrs. Chang looked to her husband, who nodded.

"Others did. Occasionally."

"Who?"

"Honestly, dear, we never knew who any of your father's associates were. But, over the years you hear things. We answered the door or the phone and, occasionally, someone would ask for the Detective."

"Was he a Cape?"

"A what?"

Awesome had spoken without really thinking that the Changs weren't part of the Guild's world and he blushed and tried to recover.

"A superhero. Was Humphrey a superhero? Did he wear a cape?"

Mr. Chang let loose a long, loud series of laughs.

"Oh no. Humphrey might have worn a cape—fashionably—at some point but he was not a superhero. No one wrote comic books about him or news articles. He didn't patrol the city or save little children from burning buildings. He, of course, loved Betty's art, which always featured those things. But he… he didn't want to be a part of that world. He wanted to keep things—"

"Secret."

Mrs. Chang nodded.

"Did my mother know about his ability?"

"Of course."

"And yet I was never told?"

Mr. Chang answered,

"Your father expressly asked that we not inform you of his ability unless you first questioned us. We didn't suspect you to have followed in his footsteps."

Mrs. Chang was frowning now. Tears came to her eyes.

"Mama? What's wrong?"

"I should have seen. You are so much his daughter. I should have seen a long time ago."

"Oh, Mama…"

Lona took the small woman in her arms and hugged her tight.

> "You couldn't have known. I didn't even know until last year. It's only since then that I've been able to really access my ability. And, I'm still learning. I'm sorry I didn't tell you sooner."

Mr. Chang patted them both on the back.

> "Come now, no harm done. Let's go into the parlor and have some tea."

THE NEXT EVENING Lona stood in the patio doorway holding a mug of warm tea. This tea was not so strong as the variety the Changs preferred. This one smelled of lemon and spearmint. Lona wore one of Awesome's old, threadbare sweaters. She remembered him wearing this one at the cabin. She remembered him coming in from the forest with Ben, both sweating and smiling and so alive.

Now she watched Awesome. He threw a lump of red clay against the surface of the wheel and worked his thumbs into the center. The slick substance slid through his fingers and, with deft precision, he pulled the object upward.

Tulie lay at his feet watching a bee flit between the potted flowers.

Lona sighed into her tea and her breath displaced the steam, pushing it up, onto her cheeks. She thought about the journal. The rest of her father's words were coded—they wouldn't reveal themselves on their own. It was up to her. She felt that she was being tested.

"I feel more confused now than before I saw them."

"Because your dad had this whole other life?"

"Yeah. I mean, why the secrets? And, the Detective?"

She shook her head and leaned heavily against the doorway watching Awesome shape the clay in silence before continuing.

"And this book? I mean, what on earth am I supposed to do with it? There's no key. There's nothing. I'm not like him, Awesome. I'm not a detective."

He shrugged and looked up at her as the clay spun between finger and thumb.

"Not yet."

Lona laughed. She glanced over her shoulder at the kitchen table where the Kraker detective novels sat in an untouched pile.

"And I suppose those dusty paperbacks are my homework?"

"Why not? Comic books were mine. You never know what you'll get out of those things."

"Did you learn anything today?"

Awesome Jones let the wheel come to a stop and sat there looking at the little red cylinder he had made. He pulled another small lump from the mound at his feet and shaped it into a coil.

"As a matter of fact—I did. I learned that even if you have a uniform and a weapon and super strength, sometimes they get away."

He mashed the top and bottom of the coil into the side of the cylinder until it held steady. Now, it was plainly a mug. It matched the one Lona held in her hands but it was a little rounder at the bottom and the brim was a little wider.

"It's for Andy."

Lona nodded. She sat at the patio table and listened to the story of his day. Awesome had joined a fight between two petty—but powered—criminals. They were drunk and brawling their way through the arts district. They had already crashed through two storefronts and a gallery before Awesome arrived.

"As far as I could tell, one was just big and strong. I mean, stronger than a normal human but he was a brawler. No training. The other one had body elasticity."

"A stretchy guy? Really?"

"Yeah. But by the time I got there, they had already crashed the place and were on their way out. I chased them down a few alleyways but I lost track. Then, out of nowhere, I saw another guy. He just sort of dropped out of the sky but he wasn't flying. I have no idea where he came from."

"Another brawler?"

"I don't think so. I think he was an Unregistered Cape. But I think he was also too late. He turned a corner ahead of me and I lost him, too."

Awesome shook his head and slid a wire between the clay and the wheel to release the mug.

Later, as the sun set, Lona stood at the stove watching catfish sizzle in the skillet while Awesome read the paper aloud to her. Tulie stayed underfoot, licking her muzzle every time Lona stirred, chopped, or flipped anything.

Lona cocked her head to the side and closed her eyes. She smiled when she opened them and pulled another dinner plate from the cabinet. The fish hissed and she turned the stove off.

Suddenly, light blasted through their window from the patio. Lona slid a fried green tomato onto the third plate. Awesome got up to open the patio door for Andy Archer—still dressed as Captain Lightning.

The white lightning bolt on his chest stood out against the pale blue of his uniform but it was a little charred from, what Awesome assumed, must have been a fight earlier that day. Andy pulled off his gloves and slid them into the pockets of his leather bomber jacket before Awesome took it into the hall closet.

"It's so good to see you."

Lona pulled him into a hug.

"You, too. Sorry to just drop in like this."

Awesome laughed.

"It's no trouble at all, Andy. You know that."

He gestured to the food on the counter.

"Besides, Lona made your favorite."

They sat around the little kitchen table of Awesome Jones and Lona Chang. Andy dug into his catfish, fried green tomatoes, and cornbread between glugs of iced tea. Tulie sat at his feet ready for the moment a crumb might come tumbling to the floor.

He told them about his day. About how he had to fly sixty miles outside of Arc City to deal with a kid who had fallen asleep in the hay loft of his parent's barn and woken up on fire. The hay burned. The barn burned. But the kid hadn't burned.

"His parents were terrified. All his clothes were singed off but he was physically fine. Once he calmed down the fire went out but he said he'd had a nightmare and I guess that's what triggered it. He's fourteen. That's about the usual age. Not with you guys but then you two don't go about most things the regular way."

"What happened to him? Did he stay there?"

Andy shook his head and sighed.

"Couldn't. He's too dangerous. Until he can control it he'll be moved to Hartwell."

"Hartwell?"

It was a few seconds before Andy answered and Lona got the impression that, like many of the things Andy told them, they weren't supposed to know.

"Sometimes when a person's ability emerges and it's too dangerous to control, they're taken to this facility where they work with Guild specialists until they're able to get a handle on what they can do."

"And should do? Does the Guild use it as a recruitment facility, too?"

"If the person shows promise."

Lona crossed and uncrossed her legs under the table.

"What about the kid's family? Do they know where he went?"

"Yeah. They do. But, any time something like that happens they're asked to sign a non-disclosure agreement. They'll get regular visits and the kid can go home whenever he wants but…"

"What?"

Awesome guessed.

"But the facility changes them. They don't want to go back do they?"

"Not usually. Not if they're young. They get there and get around other people like them and it's hard to go back to plowing fields and doing math homework."

"Were you at Hartwell, Andy?" Lona asked.

"Ha! No, ma'am. I came at the Guild sideways."

He looked left of Lona's shoulder at the little shelf and pointed his fork at her stack of books.

"Any luck on your daddy's journal?"

Lona shrugged and Awesome took their plates as she got up and poured them all cups of coffee. As she sat down, Awesome put out a plate of fresh sugar cookies she had baked earlier.

"I talked to the Changs today. Apparently my father had a secret ability. Or, I guess, an ability for secrets."

He nodded and took one of the cookies.

"Secrets?"

"The way I can see… opportunity? Luck? He could see secrets."

"Do you think that's what's in the book? His secrets?"

"I don't know. I'm beginning to think all his secrets couldn't fit in one book."

"Lona, whatever your daddy did, whatever he did or didn't tell you was for your own protection. You were a little girl when he passed, he couldn't know exactly who you'd grow up to be but it looks like he prepared for you—like he wanted you to follow him and know whatever it was he knew."

"You're right, Andy."

She paused, took a long look at the blackness of her steaming coffee and thought about how suddenly getting closer to Humphrey Langdon only made his absence more obvious.

"I guess I just wish he was around to tell me his secrets in person."

"I do, too. I wish both your parents were still here. Not a day goes by that I don't wish Sam was here to guide me."

He ran a hand through his pale blonde hair and Lona was reminded of the first time she had seen him. How he had sat in that very spot less than a year ago and drank lemonade and seemed so tired. Now, the skin below his eyes had a blue tint and new lines seemed to have been drawn at the corners of his eyes. He didn't just look human and tired—he looked spent.

Awesome had noticed the change in Andy as well. It seemed that he hadn't been the same after their encounter with the Echo. But, of course, no one was the same. Nothing was.

Still, Awesome had noticed Andy's reticence to talk much about his work. Had noticed how busy he'd been lately. Had noticed how distracted and strained Andy always seemed to be. And now it was Awesome who asked, not for the first time, what was on his mind.

"I'm sorry, Awesome. I can't tell you—at least not yet. I have to be sure."

It was the same answer they had heard before.

"It's ok. I just wish we could help with whatever it is."

Andy half laughed and his open mouth spread into a yawn. He took another drink of his coffee and held the cup out to Lona who was pouring another for herself.

He asked Awesome to tell him about his day, and Awesome told him about his chase through the arts district and that he might have seen another unregistered hero.

"I hate that I couldn't get them and I—"

"What is it?"

Awesome hesitated but finally continued.

"When I saw that unregistered hero—I mean, his gear, it was all mis-matched and didn't really fit right. In the seconds that I followed behind him—I felt sort of, uh, ashamed. And then I realized how much quicker he was than me, how I couldn't tell where he had come from or where he went. And, in the end, neither of us caught up with those two brawlers. I don't know, I just... I hope I'm doing the right thing by being out here. Without the Guild, should I still be putting on the suit?"

Andy sat back in his chair. He sat that way for a long time and he regarded Awesome and Lona with a mixture of emotions that seemed a lot like amusement and hope. And love.

"You know, Awesome, I had a conversation a lot like this with your daddy a long time ago. Miranda had just died. Without The Tempest, I wasn't The Kinetic Kid anymore. I didn't know who I was or who I wanted to be. I felt like I'd flown over the same ocean she did but I'd never made it to shore. Like I got swept up in the storm of her death and I felt like I'd never be the same. I felt guilty because I'd wanted to quit as her Double A and work with your dad. I felt ashamed that I wasn't there when she was shot. I felt confused about what I was supposed to do next. I didn't want to go back to the Guild. I didn't want to go back to West Virginia. I didn't want to go try to live a normal life somewhere. I was an honest-to-God mess.

I went back to England to Miranda's funeral. Like most Capes, it was private. She went to the grave as Miranda Storm, not the Tempest. And Sally Jordon moved up from Double A-ing in Cape Town to take her place and her name. Anyway, your daddy came to London with me. He went out that morning and bought blue roses for me to put on her casket. He took me to an old pub in Oxford and sat there and listened to me go on about how my world was falling apart.

I said I didn't know what to do anymore."

Andy sighed and peered into his dark coffee—through his coffee—into that day, that pub, that glass of dark beer with his best friend sitting next to him.

"Sam wasn't like anybody else, Awesome. He was a Guild man, but, more than that, he was a hero. And that day he told me what that meant. Sam had grown up good. Your grandparents were good people. They raised him well. Not much money but that was alright. Then, he met your mother. Evie had escaped war. Poverty. Starvation. Abuse. He met all those other carnival folks and half of them had come through pure hell only to travel this country in its worst time. He saw little kids going hungry, he saw men and women choking on dust, he saw a lot of terrible stuff. And he said it was his job to do something—anything—about it. He wasn't rich. He wasn't some kind of genius. But he was strong and he was tough and when a couple of Suits showed up and said he might could change the world, he took them up on it.

And he *did* change the world. But not because he stopped bank robberies or fought bad guys or any of that stuff. And that stuff *was* important. But what he really was was a symbol. They teamed him up with Betty and they put out the first comic book and sold 'em for ten cents and suddenly all those kids and all their parents had someone real they could look up to. He was a good man. He would've changed the world no matter what he did but, by putting on the suit, by fighting publicly for people who couldn't fight for themselves, he showed everyone that there was someone out there who cared about them and, he figured, for as long as he *could* do that, he would do it.

Sam told me, all those years ago, that being a hero isn't about who's in charge of you. It's not about the cape or the name. It's about the people. That's who you're serving. As long as they need you, and as long as you're doing right by them, that's all that matters.

On that day, in that pub, across that ocean, I could've decided to just disappear. Or go back to West Virginia. Or throw away my cape. But I didn't. And I didn't when Sam died. And I didn't when Ben died. I kept going. Because, Awesome, in the end, it's not about the fights. It's not about the individual arrests or the guys we put away. It's about the people we protect and, more than that, it's about the way we can inspire hope."

Now Andy leaned across the table and took a long breath. He folded his hands together and looked into Awesome's eyes. His voice was level and direct when he spoke again.

"You chose to put on a uniform like your daddy's. Why?"

Awesome ran his hands over the smooth table and thought about the uniform hanging in the bedroom. The sleek suit in black and red. So much like his father's.

In the end, Andy didn't wait for an answer.

"You did it—you put on the suit and called yourself the Baron because this city— this world—needs to know that the Baron exists. That's what's important. They need to know that someone is looking out for them because this world is darker and uglier than we realize. When Sam wore that uniform and his face was on every newsstand he became more than a man. More than a hero. He was a beacon of hope in a world that needed it. And they need it now, Awesome. Maybe more than ever."

"Why? What's going on, Andy?"

He shook his head.

"When I know, I'll tell you. I promise."

They sat in silence for a long time. Andy's words hung heavy in the air. The coffee had grown cold. Eventually, the quiet was broken by Tulie as she stretched and yawned and got out from under the table and walked in a circle around the kitchen before pawing at the door.

"I'd better take her out."

Andy stood and put his hand on Awesome's shoulder.

"Listen, Awesome, I know it's hard. Without Guild support, it's even harder. But you did the right thing. And you still are. You're a good man, Awesome. Trust yourself."

Awesome nodded.

"Thanks, Andy. Thanks for everything."

"It's no problem at all. Can I take some of those cookies with me?"

Lona Chang

Lona was already wrapping some up for him.

"See you again next week?"

"Sure thing. I think Roy's on his own again next Thursday. We'll see how it turns out. You know how it goes."

"Tell him we said hello. We miss him."

"I will. It's tough for him. But he'll come around."

Lona and Awesome walked out through the patio door with Andy and Tulie following. Tulie nuzzled at Andy's leg as they walked and she panted happily as he knelt down and roughed her up behind the ears and down her neck. Finally he stood and put on his jacket and gloves.

Lona glanced over the back wall to the street where Andy's old, blue truck was parked.

"You sure you don't want your truck back, Andy?"

"Nah. You all keep it. I hadn't really used it in years."

Lona hugged Andy and gave him the cookies, which he slipped into his pocket.

"Keep working on that journal, Lona. You'll get it in the end."

She nodded and then laughed as he pulled her in tighter.

"You be careful. It's late to be flying."

Lona and Awesome took Tulie by the collar and stood back as Andy knelt on their back patio. The air around him sparked and expanded and, as quickly as he had landed, he was off, in a streak of light.

SOME YEARS AGO:

Marcus and Sunny were well fed now. Marcus's blonde hair took on a pretty sheen and loose wave and his cheeks were round and pink.

Sunny's hazel eyes were brighter now—vibrant and fierce. He had recovered his voice but only used it to parrot back whatever was said to him. And, still, he clung to Marcus as if they were real brothers. He wished, in fact, that they were real brothers—that he had real brothers.

Marcus and Sunny were allowed much time to play and explore the grounds and they encountered several other children. Many had wandered out of a war that was bigger than all of them and most didn't speak the same language. Yet, they all found they had something in common and they played as only they could.

Marcus was a quick favorite. His easy way and bright smile won everyone over and Sunny found solace and safety in his shadow.

Then, one morning, the older man in the white coat came to the room Sunny shared with Marcus. Sunny expected that he wished to speak to Marcus but instead the older man stood over Sunny's bed in the bright light of dawn and spoke to him alone.

"Sunny, we have come to realize that you are not like your little friends."

"Friends?"

"You have shown significant ability."

"Ability?"

"You are going to a new facility. We will accompany you. You are special, Sunny, and we want to make sure that your unique talents are not wasted. You must be shaped, cultivated. You are important."

Sunny would never forget the old man's words. They echoed in his head for years. After the testing. After the pain. After the dismissal that was worse than pain.

But that time was yet to come. On that morning, the older man visited Sunny and said that, more than Marcus, more than all the other children, he alone stood above the rest. He alone was important.

Sunny stared at Marcus. Still asleep in his bed the boy cast no shadow. Sunny rose and stood in the morning light with the old man. He looked back at his own bed, at the little soldier boy doll, still lying among his twisted blankets, then turned and walked away, following a step behind the old man.

FROM: *LITTLE RED:* *A Kraker Mystery*

M. Denevue and Dr. Snow were still conversing when Kraker entered the parlor. Dr. Snow was possessed of utter despondency as he addressed Kraker.

"I can't make heads nor tails of it M. Kraker. I simply cannot see a solution."

"Why, the solution is simple, Doctor," Kraker said in his usual cavalier manner. He seated himself in one of Snow's velvet chairs and stretched out his spindly legs before withdrawing a cigarette from his silver case.

"Kraker, you cannot possibly mean you have solved the murder," the Doctor said, aghast.

"Why, I shall eat my hat!"

"But, of course," said Kraker dreamily. Gray smoke blew through his nostrils and he grinned like a cat.

Alex cleared her throat and Lona snapped the book shut. She had been sitting outside the pottery classroom in the Arc City Arts Center, waiting for her old ceramics teacher to arrive. Alex carried a ratty backpack over her shoulder and pushed her glasses higher on her nose as she addressed Lona.

"More pottery from Mr. Jones?"

"Yeah, a mug for a friend of ours."

"Cool," Alex unlocked the classroom and led Lona inside, "What're you reading?"

Lona realized she still had her thumb stuck in the little paperback.

"An old mystery novel. Irene Matly."

"Is it a Kraker?"

"Yeah, *Little Red.*"

"Oh, that's a good one. And you don't know how it ends?"

Lona shook her head as Alex opened the door to the kiln room.

"It's a pretty famous ending. Is this your first Matly novel?"

"Yeah."

Lona took Andy's mug out of its little box and handed it off to Alex. She admired the workmanship.

"Cool. So, I'll just send it on to your house when it's done. Oh, and did you want a clear glaze like usual?"

"Yeah."

Lona watched Alex mark up a slip of paper and then set the mug on it before letting her gaze drift up to the wall of glaze samples.

"Same address for you guys?"

"Yeah, actually, could you put this glaze on it?"

Lona took a clay sample off the wall. It was a speckled light blue and, when Lona touched it, it seemed to shimmer.

"Sure thing."

In the truck, a few minutes later, Lona pulled the Kraker novel from her bag and held it in her hands. She thought about the detective. About the word, "detective," and then about her father. About the word, "father." She put the book back in her bag and took out Humphrey Langdon's journal.

She flipped through the pages and stopped at a drawing.

She ran her fingers over the old ink and then over the old coffee stains on the page before putting the book away. Finally, she turned the key and the truck rumbled to life.

It began to rain as she drove through town and, as she passed the museum, she slowed to a crawl and pulled off the road into the underground parking garage.

"Lona!"

Julia's mouth sported a rare smile and Lona was instantly glad she'd decided to stop by. She mentioned that she was hungry and thinking about eating in the museum and Julia offered to tag along, though she'd already had lunch. Lona tugged the bag higher on her shoulder and walked along with Julia to the museum food court.

They got in line behind a couple of tourists and waited their turn for a plate of goat cheese ravioli, rosemary rolls and a bottle of cream soda. They found seats next to the cafeteria's tall windows and Lona watched the rain stream down the glass.

The women sat in relative quiet for some time. The cacophony of museum goers drowned out the rain and the soft piano music the museum piped in. Julia informed Lona that Neima wasn't feeling well today. That she'd stayed in bed all morning with a headache and didn't even come out to meditate. Lona volunteered to check on her but Julia insisted that she had been exceedingly clear about not wanting anything but sleep.

Lona hoped Neima would be alright. The strain that came from her blocked ability, she thought, must be great.

"How's the journal coming?"

"It's not much better."

"Can I see it?"

Lona took the heavy book from her bag and opened it on the tabletop. Julia turned it around and ran her finger along the jumbled letters.

"I still think it's probably some kind of shift code."

Lona had read about shift codes in her library books and she nodded. Julia looked up from the book and tapped her lips with two fingers for a minute as she thought. Then, she caught sight of someone in the crowd.

"Hey, there's Varun. The one I was telling you about. He should look at it."

"Oh, I don't think—"

Lona shifted in her seat and reached for the book but the man was already headed for their table. Varun appeared to be in his forties and carried a leather briefcase over his shoulder. He wore a turtlenecked, paisley sweater and tweedy slacks. His dark curls and beard were streaked with silver and he smiled when Julia introduced them.

"Lona's father was—uh—really into codes. And he left her this book. Can you look at it?"

The man took a chair from an empty table and sat down at theirs. He studied one page, and then another. He flipped to a further page and studied that as well before he finally spoke.

"It looks like a shift code—but most likely more complex than a mono alphabetic substitution."

"So, it takes a keyword?"

Varun nodded and continued flipping through the book, which made Lona nervous. Her father's secrets might be coded but she didn't want a stranger looking at them. Andy had even discouraged her from sending pages to the Guild's analysts.

"Yes, although… how many languages did your father speak?"

"Why?"

"There are maps, diagrams, and drawings in here from all over the world."

He slid the book around for her and pointed at a sketch.

"This isn't a portrait. It's a—quite accurate—sketch of a piece in our collection. It's in the Ancient South East Asia exhibit. In fact, it surprises me to see it in a book this old."

"Why is that?"

"Well, because the artifact was just put on display about three years ago. It sat in storage for several years. We only had room to put it, and several other pieces from storage, out after we finished the East Wing. Here, if you're interested I'll mark the exhibit on your map."

He took Lona's complimentary museum map and circled a little, purple rectangle in blue ink.

"But, what I was saying before, if your father spoke several languages, the key word or phrase might be in any of those."

Lona looked back at the book thoughtfully as another museum employee approached their table. The woman in the museum-branded cardigan mentioned something about a new exhibit being ready for reception and Captain Lightning having escorted the cargo to the loading bay. Varun promptly rose.

"I'm sorry ladies, I must be going. It was lovely to meet you Ms. Chang."

Lona nodded and watched him hurry off.

"I'd better get going, too."

Julia stood, tugged her oversized sweater on and wrapped it tight around her body.

"Thanks for your help, I appreciate it."

"Of course. Come back again. I usually eat lunch in the apartment but I didn't want to bother Neima today. Anyway, just let me know and we'll do this again."

"Of course!"

Julia lurched forward and hugged Lona around the shoulders. Her fluffy hair brushed Lona's cheek. She smelled like flowers. Julia sniffled and, when she pulled away, she had tears in her eyes.

"Are you alright, Julia? Do you need to go home?"

She shook her head and wiped at the tears with the backs of her hands.

"No, I'm fine. I'm fine. It's like this sometimes, lately. It's ok. I just need to wash my face. By the time I get back to our offices, I'll be fine."

Lona took her by the shoulders and looked into Julia's huge, dark eyes.

"You sure?"

"Promise."

"Alright. Well, call if you need anything. Awesome and I are always happy to come by. Whatever you need, ok?"

She nodded.

"Alright, feel better."

"I will."

Lona left the museum and stood under the awning, watching the rain. She had the thought to go across the street and buy some fresh bagels for Awesome so she dashed through the downpour and into the shop. She took her time selecting one each of blueberry, sun dried tomato, and poppy seed. She thanked the woman at the counter, tucked the little paper bag into her backpack, and turned back to the door.

Through the glass, she saw the flower store across the street, above which Julia and Neima lived. A shadow stood at the window, just behind the curtain. A little too tall to be Neima, Lona thought, but a car horn blared and the shadow moved and Lona assumed it to be a trick of the light, or the rain. She went back into the spring shower, found and started the truck, and drove home where, a little while later, a perfectly crisp bagel popped out of the toaster just as Awesome came in from the streets, soaking and exhausted.

AWESOME HAD SPENT several minutes chasing a report that came across the police scanner but, for the third time that day, he was late. When he rounded the corner, Guild Suits were already cleaning up the area. Rain dripped off one Suit's fedora as he photographed a broken boutique window. Another Suit held an umbrella over himself and the boutique owner while he took her report.

Awesome ducked into an alcove and thought about going home. Lona wouldn't be there though, he thought. She'd said she would probably be out all day. He hoped she would be alright, driving in this downpour.

"Psst!"

At first he thought he'd imagined the noise but then a woman stepped out of the shadowed alley across from him. She wore a black hood over violet hair and a cape that brushed her ankles. Her black boots settled in a rainbow puddle.

Awesome held his cane at the ready but the woman laughed and it was clear that she wasn't here to fight him. She was an unregistered Cape.

"Late to the party, Baron?"

He nodded and tried to place her accent. Irish?

"You need to talk to Stargazer. He'll set you up."

"Who?"

She looked both ways before stepping across the alleyway toward him. When she was only two feet away he could better see what he'd thought were light blue eyes. They were milky white. Instead of an iris and pupil, faint shimmers of orange and blue streaked the orbs.

"Who are you?"

She apparently decided to ignore the second question and go with the first.

"Stargazer can help you get around the city better. It can't be easy when you're a marked man."

"What?"

"Everyone knows Photon's gunning for you."

"Everyone?"

"He's usually at the clinic."

"The what?"

A siren blasted in the road behind them and Awesome turned in time to see the lights of an ambulance flicker by. When he turned back, the woman was gone.

He ducked into a dry doorway and switched on his portable police radio. In a few minutes he heard another call for assistance. But, again, by the time he arrived, Captain Lightning had already come and gone.

Finally, at around four o'clock, when Awesome was hungry, wet, and dejected, he headed home.

He was happy to see the truck parked in front of the house and, as he turned his key in the door, he smiled at the sound of Tulie's joyous barking. The smell of fresh, toasted bagels filled his nose as he entered the kitchen and found Lona standing at the counter with a steamy mug of tea.

She kissed him and turned back to the kettle.

"You want a cup? You look exhausted."

"I am. I had the strangest day."

She took Awesome's favorite mug—one from the cabin—off its hook and filled it with steaming water.

He took the tea and then noticed a note on the counter, pinned under the key bowl.

"It was on the mat when I got in."

Andy had a habit of slipping notes through their mail slot. They didn't usually seem this urgent, though.

Lona took out the butter tray and a knife and set them out on the table then sat down and watched Awesome pluck the bagel halves out of the toaster as she spoke.

"I hope everything's alright. Did you see him today?"

He told her about constantly missing him, missing everything.

"Everywhere I went, Andy had already been there."

And then he told her about the strange girl he'd met and the name she mentioned.

"Stargazer? I've never heard of him."

"I know. Me neither."

She frowned and took a sip of her tea.

"How strange."

"I feel like there's so much about this stuff that we don't understand."

Awesome leaned back, staring at the ceiling and Lona reached for his hand. Her fingers were warm on his and he relished the feel of her closeness.

"We'll figure it out. It'll be alright."

He'd been trying to tell himself the same thing all day but it always sounded false. Finally, when she said it, he really believed it.

"Ok."

SOME YEARS AGO:

Sunny ate tinned meat off a green, plastic tray. He ate alone now. There were no other children here. Only people in white coats.

He had never spoken to them, though. He had only spoken to the younger man and the older man.

Sunny shivered when he thought of the older man.

The older man had always been civil to Sunny but something about his manner was unsettling.

Sunny carried his tray to the dishwashing window and left it there.

Sunny was used to this. This was Sunny's every day.

Back in his room, which was painted all in white, he took out his packet of crayons and paper and began to draw. He drew a dragon and a knight. He drew a tower in which lived a princess. He drew a horse for the knight, and a sword.

As he colored in the gray stones of the tower, he noticed the little purple points in the crook of his arm—the tiny bruises left by needles. They took his blood twice a day.

He looked out the window. A field. A path. A wall.

91

A knock came at the door. It was the younger man. Sunny was relieved.

"It's time to go, Sunny. Are you ready?"

Sunny nodded.

"Ready."

The younger man led him down a long, white corridor and into another room where a nurse strapped electrodes to his head, chest, and palms. The younger man turned on a hand-held machine, which beeped before printing out a thin strip of paper.

Sunny was used to this. This was Sunny's every day.

He stood again and was led down another corridor and into another room. In this room, a man was manacled to an iron chair. He had a black bag on his head, which swished from side to side as the man attempted to spit out the gag in his mouth.

The younger man went into another room—connected to this one by a door and a window—and gave the machine to the older man who adjusted a few silver dials.

The younger man's voice came over an intercom.

"Ready, Sunny?"

"Ready."

The man squirmed again and, suddenly, his palms glowed blue. A strange cold filled the room. Icicles formed on Sunny's eyelashes.

Sunny didn't flinch or shy away.

Sunny was used to this. This was Sunny's every day.

THE RAIN STOPPED early in the evening. Lona took a bath and listened to the last drops tap at the windows. Awesome read the paper. They waited for Andy's usual visit until they were dozing off in the living room. At last, they wandered into the bedroom and fell asleep.

All was quiet.

Until lightning split the sky. Thunder, like no thunder before, cracked.

THUD. CRASH. CRASH.

Something had hit their roof.

Awesome was standing, his cane in hand, before Lona had even sat up. Tulie barked and ran through the house at his heels. Lona sprang out of bed after them.

She watched as Awesome threw open the patio door.

There, among the bits of broken pots and flowers, among the dirt and rainwater, lay Captain Lightning.

Andy Archer.

Their friend.

Awesome dropped his cane. It clanged against the concrete.

Lona rushed to them and dropped to her knees. She put her hands to his face.

He was freezing.

In the pale patio light, his green eyes fluttered open.

"Lona?"

Tears rushed to her eyes.

"You're going to be alright, Andy. You're going to be fine. Let's get you inside."

She looked up at Awesome.

"Yeah, come on, Andy. I can carry you inside."

Andy held up his gloved hand and waved off Awesome.

"No. No. It's too late."

He coughed.

Blood speckled Lona's cheek.

"No, Andy. No. It's going to be alright."

Her tears streamed down and diluted his blood and dripped into the silver lightning bolt on his uniform. She did not notice. His eyes began to close.

A siren in the distance wailed to life. Red lights flashed. Awesome leapt to his feet and ran in their direction.

Andy's eyes popped open. What was it Lona saw there?

Alarm?

No.

Fear and remorse together. Grief.

"Someone's coming. Awesome will get them."

"No. Lona, listen. It's Grayston. It was always Grayston."

"What? Andy, what is it?"

He grabbed hold of her and, with all his strength, pulled her close. The flesh under his collar was turning a mottled gray and the color was creeping up his neck.

"I'm sorry. I'm so sorry. I couldn't stop them."

Awesome was back. He skidded to a stop in the spilled dirt and pottery shards and fell hard beside Andy. He took the man in his arms.

"Andy, it's alright. They're coming."

Andy shook his head weakly.

"No. It's you now. I was just holding your place."

He was gone.

Captain Lightning.

Andy Archer.

Their friend.

Awesome held his body close. Lona leaned into the fallen hero and the new one. She was still holding Andy's hand.

Tulie howled and her mournful baying blended with the sirens and, as if all at once, the street was alight. Every house came to life. Every neighbor came outside and stood in barefeet on wet sidewalks.

Lona looked at Andy again, in this new light. His uniform was dirty and wet and covered in dark spots—but they weren't dark spots. As Lona leaned closer, she realized the little circles dotting his uniform were holes. They ran cleanly through his body and she could see the patio beneath him—through him. She felt sick but tried to focus. She knew that whatever Andy had attempted to tell her was important and she tried, desperately, to collect as many details as she could.

His glove had fallen off in tatters. And, when Lona saw it, gold dust exploded from the cloth palm and the little holes that ran all the way through it.

Voices now. People were approaching.

She grabbed the glove and shoved it toward Tulie.

"Clean up."

Tulie took the glove in her mouth and ran into the house, returning a few seconds later to put her head in Lona's lap.

Now a new set of footsteps. Agent boots.

Photon.

Photon was leading three Suits through their back gate and onto their patio. When he saw Captain Lightning's body, he gasped and rushed forward. Awesome did, in this moment, see his friend. He might be wearing a new uniform and he might seem more composed but, under it all, this man was still Roy. He was still Awesome's friend.

"He's…?"

Awesome answered with a nod.

"What happened?"

"We don't know. He landed on our house. Where was he? Was there a fight near here?"

Roy shook his head. He opened his mouth but just as soon closed it. He seemed dumbfounded. He looked as if he were staring at something he knew to be impossible. He wiped at his mask. His tears were repelled by the waterproof material. He ripped it off and buried his face in his hands.

He whispered Andy's name.

Andy.

Andy.

He punched their patio with a hard fist.

More Suits streamed in. Then more. Roy mashed his mask back onto his face.

There were mutterings. Conversations. Men and women entered and exited and talked on tiny phones.

The neighbors approached, peered in, and walked away crying or silent or didn't walk away at all.

News trucks pulled up outside and reporters streamed out of the back with microphones ready.

"We have to get him back to the Guild."

A stretcher was brought in and set down. Awesome shook his head.

"Come on, Awesome. You have to."

Awesome would not, could not, relinquish the body of his friend. He brought his palm down to rest on Andy's chest. The lightning bolt and the person under it were still warm. But there was no movement. No beating of the heart. No life.

Awesome wiped his eyes and looked to Lona, who still grasped Andy's hand. Her eyes were red. Her cheeks were speckled in blood. She sat there in her underwear and one of his old t-shirts, covered in dirt and rainwater, and tears, and she had never seemed stronger. She nodded.

He let go.

"Goodbye, Andy."

GUILD OPERATIVES TAPED off their patio. They put little flags on the ground where Andy had landed and broken the pots. They put flags in spots of his blood. It reminded Lona of an empire claiming a foreign land. She hated it.

She watched from the kitchen table where steam from hot tea drifted up to her face and Tulie licked at the dirt and blood on her knees.

Awesome was talking to Roy. He was still wearing his mask. He stood in their kitchen with a silver-haired Guild Squire at his side, taking down everything that was said.

"But I want to help. I want to help you investigate."

"It's in the Guild's hands now, Awesome. You can't. They have their own Inspectors. A whole team of them. And, obviously this will be their first priority. It'll be *my* first priority."

Awesome was leaning against their counter with his arms crossed. He stared at Photon's Guild-issue, black boots. Had Roy ever stood in this kitchen? He tried to remember. He remembered Roy in the cabin. He remembered Roy in the Guild Hall. He remembered how he probably wouldn't have made it through that time without Roy's friendship.

"I just want to help."

"Help by telling me exactly what happened."

Awesome told him that they had been asleep. That they had gone to bed around 11:30. That they were awoken by a loud crack when something hit the roof. That he had run through the house to find Captain Lightning on their patio. Still alive. That he had heard sirens and had run to find them and that he ultimately did and directed them to the house.

"And when you returned?"

Awesome slid his hand over his face. His palms were covered in dirt and blood and smudges came away on his cheeks. He looked at Lona. She had always seemed so soft, so delicate and yet, over and over, she continued to prove how resilient she was. Now, though, she stared out the window as Guild operatives worked on their patio. No emotion crossed her face. Was she listening to this conversation? Was she a million miles away? Awesome only knew that he wanted this all to be over. He wanted to shut the door and lock away the world and feel Lona in his arms.

"Awesome?"

"What?"

"When you returned, was Andy still alive?"

Another long pause. But this time, Awesome was trying to figure out what to say, or, how to say what Andy had said to him. He felt awkward, embarrassed.

"He said, 'It's you. I've just been holding your place.'"

"What?"

The color drained from Roy's face.

"I... Roy... I don't know what to say. What do I do with that? How am I supposed to be Arc City's hero? I can't even serve under Guild law. What can I do?"

"I don't know, Awesome. I don't know. I don't know what any of us are supposed to do without him."

He sighed, long and hard, and Awesome was reminded of the dejected sidekick practicing every day on the Training Floor and going nowhere.

Roy took a drink of the tea Lona had poured for him. He coughed, surprised at its strength, and finally directed his attention to Lona.

"Did he say anything to you, Lona?"

Lona was still staring at the patio. Flashbulbs went off. Over and over. What were they photographing? She felt a hard pit forming in her stomach and was suddenly very glad she had told Tulie to hide Andy's glove. She wasn't even sure why she'd done it. Only that she knew she must.

"Lona? Are you ok?"

"What?"

Roy was talking to her but she directed her attention to Awesome. Then, Roy was speaking again.

"Yes. I'm fine. I'm sorry, what did you ask?"

"I asked if Andy said anything to you while Awesome had gone for the police."

Andy's words rushed back to her. One word in particular flooded her mind—Grayston. It reeled around in her brain and she felt dizzy. She closed her eyes. Dust swirled through darkness. Gold and green spiraled around the word—no, not the word, the *idea*. She opened her mouth to speak the word and the dust vanished.

She opened her eyes. Still dizzy, she grasped her mug of tea with cold hands and pulled it close to her face.

Finally, she shook her head.

"No. He was unconscious. He didn't say anything."

"Alright. Thank you, Clarkson"

The Suit snapped his notebook shut and slid his silver pen into his breast pocket before taking his hat from the kitchen counter.

"Sir. I'll be just outside."

"Alright. I'll be along shortly."

Clarkson nodded to Awesome and Lona and positioned his hat onto his head before slipping out to the patio. When he was gone, Roy sighed.

"I'm so sorry Awesome. I know what he meant to you."

"You, too."

Roy bowed his head and Awesome spoke again.

"We'll get through this. We have to."

Roy nodded finally, and shook Awesome's hand.

"We'll find whoever did this, Awesome. I promise. We'll figure out what happened to Andy. The Guild will handle it, ok? Trust me."

"Ok. I do. I do, Roy."

Lona stood and Roy hugged her. For an instant, Lona remembered the boy that had visited their cabin with his girlfriend in tow. Two young misfits—maybe a little tired of their trappings but still optimistic about the world—just waiting for their lives to begin. She stared into his big, brown eyes now. Was that boy still there? She was looking at the man now. The full Guild Agent. Photon.

She wondered where Julia was at this moment. Neima. Pop. The Changs. Lona was soon filled with worry about their little family. Slices of it were being cut away and it seemed there was nothing she could do to stop it.

"I'll come by again soon, ok? I'll come by more often."

Lona nodded and reached up to brush a strand of hair away from Roy's mask and back into his sleek hairline.

"Ok."

Lona slid into the crook of Awesome's body and he wrapped his arm around her. They sat up together while the Guild swarmed around their house for several hours.

Eventually, Lona fell asleep on the sofa. Awesome opened the chest in the corner of the room and took from it a quilt they had brought back from the cabin. He spread it over her and, in her sleep, she pulled it up until blue and yellow triangles touched her chin.

Awesome went back to the kitchen with Tulie, made a new cup of tea and watched the Suits work until, one by one, they had all gone. Their tape was gone. The flags were gone.

Andy was gone.

SUNDAY MORNING CAME quick. And it came slow. But, in the end, it came.

Lona stood in the bedroom and stared at her reflection. She thought she should have a nicer dress. When was the last time she bought a nice dress?

She smoothed the dark fabric with cold, shaking fingers.

Tulie whined at her side. She licked Lona's palms until Lona knelt and let the dog nuzzle into her face and shoulder. Finally, Lona sat on the floor and leaned back against the foot of the bed. She gazed at the ceiling and felt Tulie rest her head in her lap.

Eventually, Awesome wandered into the room. Without a word, he sat beside Lona. He, too, leaned back and let his gaze drift to the ceiling.

They were quiet. The house was quiet. It seemed the whole neighborhood, the whole city, maybe the whole world was quiet.

Finally, Awesome looked forward again, at his reflection. Eventually he spoke.

> "I feel like I should have something nicer. Like I should wear something nicer."

Lona smiled. It was a sad smile but it served.

"All that matters is that we're there."

He nodded.

They drove to town in Andy's truck. Wordless. Everyone they passed wore black.

They parked in the museum's parking garage and walked up to Neima and Julia's apartment. They embraced one another. Neima poured coffee, which grew cold on the counter.

Eventually, they left. They walked two blocks, to Main Street, and stood near the cemetery gates.

Awesome remembered when he and Lona visited the graves of their parents'. He remembered the flowers. He remembered that Andy had left some. He looked at his empty hands. Why were they empty? Why hadn't he brought flowers?

He remembered the broken flowers on their patio. He remembered the crushed irises scattered around his friend. He remembered sweeping them up. Throwing them away. He remembered regretting it. He should've saved them. Dried them. Then they're just dead flowers, though.

Here, they were surrounded by life. The street was full of mourners, as far as he could see.

All of Arc City had turned out for the public funeral of Captain Lightning. His was not a death the Guild could cover up. They couldn't slide some other hero into his uniform. They couldn't pretend heroes never died.

Captain Lightning had been a citizen of Arc City and that is how he would pass from the world. Of them. With them. For them.

Lona, Awesome, Julia, and Neima stood with the throng of people on the west side of the street. It should be so noisy, Lona thought.

Main Street usually bustled but today it had been hushed. No one spoke. They all stood together—waiting.

Finally, slicing through the silence, was the peal of bagpipes. The sight soon followed the sound. The pipers walked first. Followed by the city police, the fire department, the EMTs. Then—the Suits. Hundreds of them. The men and women walked in step behind Arc City's public servants and, though they always wore black, they had never looked so somber.

Guild Agents and Assistant Agents came behind them. Their capes fluttered in the breeze. Enkidu. The Quintessa. Green Bolt. Mercury Man. Phantasm. Artemis. Marvelous Man. Rama. Shade. Supersonic Sleuth.

They went on and on. The music played. The heroes marched. And, as they marched, Awesome and Lona noticed the black band around all their arms. Black with a silver lightning bolt in the middle.

Awesome instinctively touched his own arm.

Then, there was Andy's coffin. Black with silver.

It was borne, of course, upon the shoulders of heroes. The Blue Buckler. The Combustible Constable. Pisces. Photon.

The procession split before the cemetery. The pipers stopped at the gate and the police officers and firefighters went to each side. The Suits stopped as well and then split off to each side.

Only the Capes would be permitted in the gates and, last among them, the pallbearers with Andy's coffin.

Two Suits closed the gates behind them but all of Arc City crowded around the iron fence and watched. It didn't matter that most of them couldn't see into the grounds. They all bowed their heads in reverence to the fallen hero.

The Blue Buckler's lips moved as he said words only the heroes could hear. Photon, Pisces, and Combustible Constable stood to the side, silent.

Awesome and Lona pressed as close to the fence as they could. Their hands reached out and found one another.

The heroes remained standing as five among them stepped forward: Saturnus, Rama, Skadi, the Combustible Constable, and Prisma. They stood side-by-side next to Photon and, as he raised his hands, they followed.

Even from here, Awesome could hear Roy's voice. It cracked as he shouted.

"Fire!"

Light, fire, and snow blasted into the air above the heroes in a beautiful display. The light shone perfect and colorful through the ice crystals and dissipated as quickly as the blasts had been shot.

The six heroes stepped back into the crowd.

Then, they all turned their faces skyward. The crowd of mourners did the same.

Above, Awesome and Lona watched as four Agents flew in a V formation then, abruptly, one of the heroes shot ahead.

Julia wiped at her face and Lona looked over at her. Tears slid down her cheeks.

"It's missing man formation."

"Oh."

Lona looked back into the sky and watched as the heroes disappeared from view.

SOME YEARS AGO:

Sunny sat on the edge of the cot, studying lines on his palms, the length of his fingers. Sunny observed that his hands were much larger now than when he'd first arrived. He was almost grown now.

A cool breeze blew in from outside and he could hear the rustle of trees across the field. He stood and went to the open window.

Moonlight bathed the field, the parked cars, the road, and the high fence in silver light. Two floors below, he watched as a man in a white coat got into his car, started the engine and pulled away. It was that time of day. Before long, it would just be Sunny, the older man (who never seemed to leave) and the men who always guarded them.

A knock came at Sunny's door and then it opened. It was the older man. The younger man followed close behind.

"Sunny, I'm afraid we have some bad news."

Sunny's eyes moved back and forth between the older man and the younger man.

"Our superiors believe that this project isn't moving along as well as they'd hoped. They would like for you to return to them so that your new fate can be decided."

Sunny's heart raced. He wanted so much to argue, to shout, or scream. He wanted to show them that he *could* be as powerful as they hoped. Instead, he only nodded.

"Sunny, do you understand."

Sunny breathed at the floor.

"Understand."

The younger man moved to lay a hand on Sunny's shoulder but stopped at the last second, recoiling as if he were afraid of his young subject. He left the room briskly and it seemed that the older man would leave as well but, just as he laid a hand on the doorknob, he turned back to Sunny.

"Sunny, I still believe in your abilities. But—I feel that, to unleash them, will take a stronger catalyst than we have given you thus far."

"Stronger catalyst?"

"Yes. I feel that our work is too important to set aside. But I must make some inquiries. It's alright if I contact you, yes? Where you are going?"

"Where I'm going. Yes."

The older man finally left the room and Sunny behind. Once more, Sunny looked out the window at the sky. Gray clouds shifted before the moon and Sunny was cast in shadow. In the darkness, he moved back to his cot and sat down. Sunny was afraid of leaving this room, this place, these people. This was his home. He knew, in that moment, he would do whatever he had to to come back—to prove that he could be great.

FROM *THE DIAMOND SLIPPER*: *A Kraker Novel,*
by Irene Matly

"I think I am not wrong here," Kraker said, frustratedly rubbing his finger along the rim of his miniscule espresso cup.

"I do not doubt it, sir," said Abbot. The aged butler watched as Kraker lifted the mug to his lips only to set it down again.

After some considerable minutes, Kraker finally threw his espresso back in one drink and stood. He straightened his waistcoat, withdrew his watch from his pocket, and stared at its face.

"Good god, man! Do you realize—it's the trains?"

"Sir?" Abbot had already taken up the empty saucer and cup. "The trains, sir?"

"Precisely!" Kraker said and, gathering his hat and walking stick, fled from the room.

Tulie's bark preceded the patio door sliding open and shut. Lona slipped an Arc City Library bookmark between the pages of the old paperback. She'd been reading all morning. She had read six Irene

Matly novels in the last week. She had slept often and ate little. She had ignored her meditation and neglected visiting Julia and Neima. She split her days between reading and napping or, rather, lying in bed and petting Tulie while she closed her eyes and wondered if there was anything she and Awesome could've done to save their friend—wondering what might happen to Awesome, wondering where he was at that moment.

She was so proud of Awesome but she also found herself missing their days in the Akai Printing Company. These thoughts, of course, always led to Mr. Sprat and the way she had watched him die. The way she held his head in her lap as he bled out. What happened that night propelled them to the cabin. She remembered the cabin fondly but couldn't help thinking of Ben. Of his kindness and his love and his death. She sighed and listened as Awesome padded through the kitchen with Tulie at his heels.

Awesome entered the living room carrying a sack of groceries and kissed her on the cheek. She put down the book and slid off the sofa and together they put away the cheese and vegetables and bread and so on.

"Still reading Kraker?"

"Yeah. It's the last one I have."

"How many are there?"

"Twenty-three Kraker mysteries. She wrote some others, too."

"We'll, we could go to the library tomorrow."

Lona hadn't left the house since Andy's funeral. Now, she looked out the window at the blue truck parked in the street.

"We could take the bus like we used to. Maybe go out and eat."

"Did you see Roy today?"

Awesome had been out on patrol since six o'clock when the police radio went off and woke them up.

"I did. He looks exhausted."

"Did he say anything about Andy? About what happened? Do they have any idea?"

"Not really. He said the Guild is looking into it but he doesn't have any information yet."

Lona thought about the word, "Grayston." She had thought about it over and over since the night Andy died. And yet, when they had seen Roy after the funeral, something had told her again not to mention it to him—to keep it between herself and Awesome.

"Blue Buckler's helping out for now. But Linus said he won't be around for long."

"You got to talk to him?"

"Yeah, actually."

Awesome blushed and brushed his hand against the back of his head.

"He said I looked good—said I looked like my dad."

Lona touched her palm to his cheek.

"Even better."

Awesome didn't want to break up this rare moment of real happiness. He didn't want to say that the Blue Buckler had also told him that Pythia wanted him brought in—that he wasn't just an Unregistered Cape but an excommunicated member of the Guild.

But, in the end, he told her anyway. He couldn't not.

Still, the Blue Buckler's compliment had had a positive effect on their evening. Lona inspected the groceries, sniffing the new peppers and popping a snow pea into her mouth.

"I'll make some dinner."

"You want some help?"

"No, I'm fine. But—"

"Yeah?"

"Stay."

"Alright."

He was going to anyway. He sat at the table with Tulie leaning against his legs as he read to her from *The Diamond Slipper*. They neglected the newspaper.

"I wish we had known him longer."

Awesome nodded.

"I wish we had known him better."

"I wonder if that would've even been possible. Andy was…I think we were as close to Andy as anyone ever was. Maybe that's why he came here that night."

They ate dinner and took a walk.

Spring was in full force now. Cherry blossom petals blew in swirls on the sidewalk before them—miniature pink twisters. Tulips bloomed in beds beneath green trees. In these moments, the world seemed right. As if nothing had gone askew.

Tulie stopped at a hedge to watch a squirrel scurry up a maple. Her head cocked to the side and she whined when her polite nature kept her from barking.

Lona stood with the leash loose in her hand and breathed in the cool, outside air. She nudged closer to Awesome and he put his arm around her shoulders.

"It's going to be alright. We're going to make it."

She watched as a new breeze picked up the cherry blossom petals and carried them down the street.

"Yeah. I think you're right."

LONA AND AWESOME sat toward the back of the bus and watched Arc City go by. A somber mood still blanketed the city like snow. The streets were quieter, the conversations on the bus muted.

Eventually they came to their stop and exited the bus. They walked up the stone steps and into the Arc City Public Library where Lona dropped off all her books at the front desk.

"You're not renewing the code books?"

Lona shrugged.

"I think I just need a break from it. Maybe clear my head."

They went in search of the mystery section and were soon standing in front of nearly thirty Irene Matly novels. Lona pulled a few off the shelves and started flipping to their first pages.

"I wonder if I should read them in order. I mean, they aren't really serialized but it just seems like the thing to do."

"Yeah, I get it. What's the first one you've found?"

She handed him a thick hardback.

Awesome started sliding books off the shelf to check the publication dates but they were soon interrupted by the librarian Lona had encountered on her last visit.

"Oh, hi there! I take it you enjoyed those Krakers."

The young woman grinned and pulled strands of her brown bob behind an un-pierced ear. Lona realized she hadn't spoken to anyone besides Awesome since Andy's funeral and felt her cheeks redden.

"I, yeah, thank you."

The girl thrust out her hand and Lona took it.

"Jolie."

"Lona."

"Jones."

They all shook hands and Jolie pointed to the Kraker novels again.

"When I was a little girl, my grandmother gave me a set of these things. I read them whenever I was down. Something about them, you know? Escapist literature, I guess."

"Do you know what order they came in?"

"Oh, yeah. Do you want to start at the beginning? What have you read so far?"

A few minutes later, Lona had six books piled up in her arms as she listened to Jolie talk about Irene Matly's other, non-Kraker novels and some of the other detective fiction that came around her time and before.

After a while, Jolie started back to her book cart and, at the last second, Lona called her back.

"I have a question—a research question. Could you help me find something?"

"Probably. What is it?"

"All I have to go on is a word."

"Ok. Shoot."

"Grayston."

AWESOME AND LONA listened to the rush as cars passed. Main Street, at least, was coming to life again. People brushed by on their way home from work. And here, at the newsstand, Lona and Awesome stared at the papers. Images of Photon with optimistic headlines were plastered over the front pages.

Awesome scooted over and cut into the crowd on the other side of the newsstand. At least twenty men and women were gathered around that end, chattering and flipping through pages. And, when Awesome made it to the shelves, he understood why. There were shelves and shelves of Photon comics.

He grabbed one and maneuvered through the crowd back to Lona. They stood on the sidewalk thumbing through the pages of *PHOTON: Fighting Crime at the Speed of Light*. Inside, the 2D version of Roy fought a non-existent super villain called Mirror Monster—shooting a constant stream of laser beams through the Monster's reflection until he hit the real one—disabling him. It was a villain designed specifically for Roy, Awesome realized.

Awesome reached back through the crowd and grabbed five other *Photon* comics, paid for them, and, together with Lona, walked down the street to a lonely, little cafe.

They opened each issue and read in awe.

Photon jumping on his Photo-cycle and speeding down Main Street.

Photon outsmarting a hyper-intelligent alien who very much resembled a polar bear.

Photon defeating an army of robots.

And, in *Photon: Saying Goodbye*, assisting Captain Lightning as he saved a children's hospital that had been teleported into space. Lona and Awesome read along until they came to the last page—the last panel—in which Photon held Captain Lightning as he passed from the world. Captain Lightning uttering his final words—*It's you now. It's you. I was just holding your place.*

Awesome and Lona stared at the panel for a solid twenty seconds and then at each other for another thirty.

"What—what is this?"

Lona read the panel again.

"I—why did he do this? What's going on?"

Awesome shook his head. He paused as a server set down their coffee and then waited for him to get out of earshot before speaking.

"The Guild is trying to push Photon on Arc City. They're trying to make everyone feel alright about Captain Lightning being gone. They're saying they have everything in hand—that we should stay calm."

Lona stared out the window at the city they loved so well, the city she had grown up in, worked in, met Awesome and fallen in love in. Traffic whizzed past. Men and women strode up and down the sidewalks. People trudged into the cafe with newspapers and *Photon* comic books and sour looks on their faces.

"Then why do I feel so worried?"

SOME YEARS AGO:

"You're sure there's nothing more you can do?"

The woman stood with her arms crossed for several seconds. The older man was taking his time in consideration of her question. This time, she looked at him. His black hair was going gray and deep lines gave parentheticals to his mouth and everything he seemed to say, for he never seemed to say anything that didn't have some additional meaning.

"Not without killing him."

"Absolutely not. That is not how we work."

The older man peered down at his former subject. Studied him again now, in his sleep. He was barely recognizable.

"He should be moved. Taken back to the Icebox."

"Can you continue your work at the Icebox?"

"No, but—"

"Then it makes no difference. This is the best facility we have. You, yourself helped design it. It has everything you need."

"It's not safe."

"I will assign a guard detail."

"Still—what needs to be done—it will kill him."

"Find another way. This project is too important to stop. He is our most promising subject. He will stay. And so will you."

"But—"

"Or would you like to return to the Icebox yourself?"

The older man scowled at her. He took a pen from his white lab coat and began scribbling on a pad of paper from the desk. When finished, he tore off the top sheet and thrust it toward her.

"I will need these items if I am to continue."

She waved the paper away.

"Give it to my assistant."

And she left.

Her assistant appeared and took the sheet and then disappeared down the hallway.

Back in the room, the older man opened a silver briefcase on the desk and withdrew a vial of green liquid and a syringe. He looked down at the man in the bed—barely recognizable now—and raised an eyebrow.

"Well, Sunny, what now?"

Sunny was, in fact, very far away in the deepest, darkest, parts of his own mind. He was alone at times and, at others, he was quite overwhelmed by the presence of others. But, deep inside the cave of his thoughts, he was sure he could make out the voice of the older man. And, in that cold, dark space, he shivered.

THEY SAT IN a little Kurdish place with plates of food and a short, glass vase of violets between them. Their waiter brought out a pitcher and poured fresh water into their glasses. Lona slid an olive between her lips and Awesome swiped a piece of lamb through oil and spices.

It had been some time since they'd gone out for a meal and Lona thought it might bring a little cheer into their lives.

Julia had had some kind of depressive relapse and Neima had even turned Lona away from their morning meditations until Julia was ready. Lona missed them both desperately but kept her distance.

"I just can't understand it."

Awesome sighed and put down his fork absentmindedly.

"Roy?"

"I've called him four times. What was he thinking?"

She shook her head.

"I'm so sorry, Jones."

But her words seemed lost on him. He was staring past her, a look of alarm in his gray eyes as he said,

"That can't be good."

She turned and watched the street outside the window. Five men, the area around their eyes smeared in black, their bodies clad in a mixture of gray leather and black market armor, sauntered down the sidewalk carrying an assortment of dangerous-looking implements. A club, a baseball bat, a tire iron, a machete.

Awesome tugged at his shirt collar.

"Go. I'll meet you back home."

He nodded and rushed toward the back of the restaurant.

Lona took out her wallet and left enough money for the meal and a tip and was getting up to leave when she saw another woman leaving her own table. She wore a black t-shirt and jeans and had long, white hair in spite of her obvious youth. And, as she extended a thin cane and slid a pair of violet-lensed glasses up her nose, Lona realized the woman was blind.

The woman tapped her way toward the door but Lona touched her shoulder.

"Miss, you shouldn't go out."

The woman jerked her arm away.

"You really shouldn't. There's—"

But as Lona spoke, the biggest man—the one carrying a sledgehammer—swung his weapon through the glass of the jewelry store across the street. The alarm rang instantly but the thugs across the street simply crunched over the broken glass and into the store where they smashed up the display cases.

Awesome bounded onto the street, his mask firmly in place, just as the man with the machete was grabbing hand-fulls of glass and diamonds and jamming them into a black bag.

The clang of a metal security door caught his ear and he checked to see the Kurdish restaurant had closed up. Lona was safe.

He turned his attention back to the goons. Five to one. They were all armed. He wasn't—yet.

He breathed out the word, *Five.*

Awesome crunched his way into the store and, as soon as the thugs saw him, they split and fell into a circle around him. Baseball Bat ran in first, swinging. Awesome caught the barrel of the bat in his right hand and directed a jab into the man's nose with his left. The man's head snapped back and forward and, as blood gushed from his nostrils, he went down.

Four.

As the first man was still falling, Awesome flipped the bat and caught it again by the grip. He shifted toward the man at his front right— the man with the spiked club—and used the bat like a fencing foil. He thrust. The head of the bat collided with the man's face and then again with his gut, right at the liver. He gripped at his side and fell on the floor, writhing.

Three.

Crowbar (the littlest man) and Machete (the meanest looking) were to either side of him. They both rushed. Awesome dropped at the last second—falling flat to the floor and rolling backward—as Crowbar swung and Machete slashed. Blue ropes and a gush of red followed the misplaced machete swipe and spilled from Crowbar's belly as Awesome sprang to his feet.

Two.

Machete and Awesome both swung. Both dodged. Machete slashed, Awesome ducked. Machete swiped and Awesome blocked with the baseball bat. Machete grimaced when he realized the blade caught in the bat. It was wrenched from his hand. Awesome tore the machete out of the bat and held both.

Sledgehammer finally stepped forward, now that his pack was full. He growled at the smaller man.

"Go on. I'll clean up here."

One.

Machete ran from the store and into the alley next door where an engine rumbled to life. Club and Baseball Bat followed. But Awesome didn't have time to go after them as a huge hammer careened toward his head.

He ducked, swung his bat at Sledgehammer's knee. The goon growled and his knee crunched but he wound up for another swing.

Sirens blared now and mixed with the jewelry store's alarm.

Sledgehammer swung again and Awesome rolled again, through gems and jewels and glass. Sledgehammer raised his weapon for a hard swing and caught, instead, a face full of glassy sand. Awesome sprang to his feet. The hammer was heavy but the bat was quick.

The hammer cracked the pretty, tiled floor as Awesome slammed his bat into the big man's back. The bat made a sound like a thunderclap as it shattered.

Sledgehammer let out an *Oomph* but pulled himself up straight.

A hearse, with Machete driving and Baseball Bat in the passenger seat pulled up outside. They waved for Sledgehammer to join them. Awesome considered going after them and, in the half second he looked away, he heard the unholstering and cocking of a gun.

Awesome rushed Sledgehammer. The gun fired. Tires screeched outside. A burn like a bee sting bloomed in Awesome's ribs. Sirens blared louder. Awesome watched as the gun he had tried to take slid across the floor.

Sledgehammer ran for it, past Awesome, still gripping his hammer with his right hand. Awesome noticed the crowbar at his feet and grabbed it. The heft, the heaviness was familiar in his hand.

He swung. At the same time, Sledgehammer spun and swung. Sparks flew as metal met metal.

In that moment, though, Awesome was exactly as strong as he needed to be. He heaved and Sledgehammer toppled backward. Awesome jumped and pinned him from behind, pulled his cuffs from his belt, and slapped them on the man's big wrists.

The sirens grew closer and were accompanied by the roar of a motorcycle.

Awesome looked out the smashed window to see Roy skid to a stop and jump from his bike into a battle stance.

"Take it easy, Photon. It's over."

Roy's mix of exhaustion and surprise was clear.

"Awes—Baron? What happened?"

"I'd ask you the same thing. Here—"

Awesome lugged the big guy from the floor and shoved him toward Roy. Several armed Suits swarmed the store. One snapped on latex gloves, knelt by Crowbar and shook his head. They dragged Sledgehammer from the scene and began tallying up the damages. Two employees emerged from the back room and surveyed, with horror, what had been done to the store.

Roy took Awesome by the shoulder and led him out of the store and into the alleyway.

"Listen, Awesome, I—woah, did he shoot you?"

"What?"

Roy turned Awesome toward the light and tugged at something in the fabric of his suit. He came away with a flattened bullet between his gloved fingers.

"You're lucky. Your uniform caught it."

He let the smashed lead drop into Awesome's palm. Awesome said nothing. He looked at the metal, thought of how careful he needed to be, how he hadn't expected the man to have a gun, how even the crooks in Arc City never used to carry guns.

"Awesome, listen, about the comic—"

"So you did get my calls?"

"Yeah, I just… Awesome I'm so embarrassed. And I'm so sorry. I never approved the comic, I never meant for them to use Andy's words like that."

"Then why did you tell them?"

Awesome was shouting now. He could feel his cheeks burning, his heart racing. He hadn't been this worked up in the fight. He hadn't even fully realized how angry the comic had made him until this moment.

And Roy saw it, too. He backed away.

"It was in my report."

"Your report? That was *personal*. Why was it in your report?"

"You don't understand. You have to file *everything*. Every single thing. And Clarkson was right there the whole time. If it hadn't shown up in my report, it would've shown up in his. Everything goes in."

"Not that, Roy. I told you that as a friend. And because I'm terrified. And I don't know how to do what Andy wants me to do. I just got shot! And I didn't even realize it! And where were you, anyway?"

Roy leaned against the brick wall of the jewelry store and buried his face in his hands before finally answering.

"I was across town. I've been doing this all day. Low-level thugs have been hitting high-end places all over the city since dawn. All the other Agents have gone back to their home cities. We have a couple of Assistant Agents around but they're stretched too thin. The Suits can't keep up with the calls. And, I can't keep up. I just go where they tell me and hope I get there in time."

His voice was quieter now. He would've sounded calm if he didn't sound so defeated.

Awesome sighed. He stood beside his friend and put a hand on his shoulder. They were quiet a long time but it was Roy who spoke again.

"I'm sorry, Awesome."

"It's ok."

The sun moved lower in the sky and Awesome peered out and upward. Across the street, on the roof of the Kurdish restaurant, he saw the girl in black and violet. Her cape swished in the wind.

"Roy, do you know who that is?"

But, by the time Roy looked, she was gone.

A few minutes later, Roy was gone too. Awesome turned back down the alley. As he passed the dumpster, he tossed the smashed bullet in and listened to it clang against glass bottles.

"HE LOOKED EXHAUSTED."

Lona sighed.

"It's what he's always wanted."

"Not like this."

Awesome sat on the toilet lid while Lona applied alcohol to a cut on his neck. He hadn't realized he'd been clipped, probably by the man with the machete, until he got home and took off his uniform.

She applied butterfly stitches one at a time.

"Did he say anything about Andy? About the investigation?"

"No."

She sighed.

"Maybe I should've said something about Grayston...or the glove. I'm not getting anywhere with it."

He shook his head.

"No, you need to trust your instinct."

Awesome put a light fingertip to the cut and hissed at the pain.

"I'm glad you're alright, Jones. I couldn't see anything once the owners of that restaurant dropped their security shutter."

She told him about the blind woman leaving ahead of her, through the back. She told him about how when she got out there she saw a homeless man picking up Awesome's discarded clothes. How she left by herself down the alley and brought the truck home on her own.

"I can't believe those goons were out in broad daylight."

"They were underlings for The Ashes."

"The Ashes? That's one of the Under Arc gangs. Since when are they so bold?"

But, in that instant, they both knew the answer.

No one felt safe since Captain Lightning died.

"COME IN, MY GIRL."

Neima wore an embroidered shawl over her black, cotton dress. A few wooden bracelets click-clacked together on her wrists when she wrapped her arms around Lona and spoke softly into the younger woman's ear,

"It seems an age since I saw you last."

She pulled back now but grasped Lona's shoulders with firm hands,

"How are you?" Neima asked.

"I—I think I'm going to be alright."

After everything that had happened, it was a comfort to be in Neima's company again. The woman's gentle strength and confidence soothed Lona to her very core. Neima had seen heroes, friends, and her dearest love pass from the world and yet, here she was, still so ready to help her young friend.

Neima led the way into the kitchen where she poured coffee into two, blue and white china cups. A third was still half-full and sitting on the counter next to the sugar bowl. Lona supposed Julia had forgotten to empty it before leaving.

"How's Julia?"

Neima shook her head.

"She's about as well as we all are, I think."

Something about the way Neima answered her question made Lona hesitate. She had been about to inquire further into Julia's recovery. Instead, she changed direction and focused on the real purpose of her visit.

"Neima, do you know the word, 'Grayston'?"

Leaning against the counter, Neima stared down at the irregular pattern of flecks and spots in the granite. Her brow knitted together.

"*Grayston*. I don't think so, Lona. Why?"

Lona took a moment before she spoke. She hadn't told Roy about Andy's last words. Should she tell Neima?

"It's just something I've been looking into. But so far, I haven't come up with much. Grayston could be a lot of things, apparently. It's an island off the coast of Maine, a glass making company, a dead philanthropist, an airplane engineer, an abbey in Scotland, and an old sanitorium in the mountains."

"Hmm. It doesn't sound at all familiar—oh!"

Neima doubled over and pinched the bridge of her nose.

"Are you alright?"

"It's just a headache. I'll be alright. Need to lie down."

Taking Neima's arm, Lona led her to the sofa and helped her get situated. She poured a cold glass of water and set it on the coffee table and then closed the heavy curtains in the living room.

"Is that better?"

"Yes, thank you."

Lona Chang

She pressed her hand to Neima's forehead.

"You're burning up, Neima. You should go to the doctor."

Her mentor waved her off.

"I'll be fine. It's just a headache. Julia will look after me, don't worry."

"Julia's at work, Neima. Remember?"

"That's right."

She nodded, her eyes closed. White and strawberry hair was matted to her forehead with sweat.

"I should stay."

Neima opened her eyes, took Lona's hand and smiled up at her.

"It's alright dear. I'm just tired. I've been meditating so much lately… with so little reward. I just need sleep."

"Are you sure?"

"Yes. Of course. I just need rest and quiet. I'll be fine after a nap."

Lona tried to argue but, in the end, Neima won. Lona let herself out.

Still, she was determined not to leave her mentor suffering alone in the apartment without at least letting Julia know. She descended the stairs, came out of the building by the flower shop, and turned into the museum.

By now, Lona was familiar with the layout but didn't have the desire to wander about, looking for her friend. Instead she went to the service desk and asked for them to call Julia. An older lady with bright red lipstick made the call and soon handed the receiver to Lona. Julia asked Lona to meet her in the Chinese pottery gallery where she was working.

"What's going on?" Julia asked a few minutes later.

Julia stood up from where she'd been adjusting a piece of ancient pottery. She locked the case and took off her gloves.

"I was just over at the apartment. Neima's sick. I just wanted to let you know. She wouldn't let me stay."

Julia sighed.

"Her headaches are getting worse."

"What's happening? Has she seen a doctor?"

A couple passed, arm in arm, between them. Cameras hung on rainbow straps around their necks. Julia moved around the case and closer to Lona where she spoke in a low voice.

"No. The more she tries to access her power, the worse it seems to get."

"Can this even happen? Can you just wake up one day and lose your ability?"

Shaking her head, Julia led them out of the exhibit and down the corridor.

"I don't know. It seems like she's getting weaker every day but I don't know if it's some kind of sickness, or if it's because she lost Ben, or if…"

Julia trailed off but Lona knew the words she'd left unsaid—*if she's just getting old, if she's dying.*

Lona didn't want to think about it. Wouldn't think about it.

"She just needs rest, I'm sure. Has she gone to the Guild Hall? Tried to see their doctors?"

"She doesn't want to."

"Did she say why?"

Lona knew Ben and Neima's split from the Guild hadn't exactly been amicable but, as far as she knew, she was still on speaking terms with Pythia.

"She just said she wants to be left in peace. I think, whatever this is—whatever she's fighting—she wants to fight it on her own."

Lona was hurt. She wanted to help Neima—wanted to be there for her no matter what the problem was. And, she knew that Neima was letting Julia into a part of her life that Lona couldn't access. Her feelings must've shown on her face.

"Lona, Neima lets me in because—"

She paused and took a deep breath before continuing.

"—because we're both broken. You and Awesome walked away from that forest with each other and with newfound abilities and came back to Arc City with uniforms and books and all this promise. Neima lost Ben. I lost a part of myself and then I lost Roy. And now Andy's gone. Neima and I need each other. I don't mean to push you away and neither does she. I think we just need time. I'm sorry."

They stopped in front of the double doors that led to the offices. Lona had her arms crossed in front of her chest but now she let them go. As much as she wanted to be jealous of Julia's newfound closeness with Neima, she understood that this simply wasn't about her. It was about them.

"Oh, Julia, I'm so sorry. I know you and Neima need each other. I just miss both of you. And I feel selfish because I also need you. Both of you."

To her surprise, Julia smiled. It was a quiet, gentle smile and Julia opened her arms to Lona.

"I miss you too. I think we're all just so overwhelmed. Last year, I was waitressing in the Guild Hall. I had a ridiculous crush on my best friend. And I wanted more than anything to just have a real conversation with one of the Capes I saw every day. Now, after all that's happened… you know some of it's better, Lona? It really is. But it's also a lot more complicated."

"I know. I understand. I do."

And she did. A year ago, Lona was working as a secretary and only paying passing attention to the Capes that flew around her city. But she had been so lonely. She had craved family and friendship and now she had that. Her new, strange little family was precious to her. She wanted to guard them but, one by one, they seemed to be slipping away.

Finally, they separated. Neither had been able to say all that they wanted or needed to say but, in the end, they both felt some sense of repair. It was a start.

Lona started toward the galleries and turned back in time to see Julia go through the doors and down the hall. Bright dust flickered around her, as it had nearly every time Lona had seen her lately, but Lona still couldn't understand what it meant.

She passed the recent discoveries gallery, slipped through the rooms full of Minoan and Cycladic Island art and wandered through the Greek vases gallery. She paused to view a lekythos showing Hercules and a lesser, unnamed hero. It occurred to her, as she leaned in closer to view the red and white figures worked on black, that she had never seen the statue from her book. She dug through her bag and found the map Verun had marked for her then left the vase gallery.

Lona's fingertips rose to touch the plaque near the statue: *From the H. Langdon Collection.* Her father's name was here, in this museum. Had he found this sculpture? Had this been the result of one of his expeditions? She felt a renewed sense of optimism toward her father's journal. She stood there for several minutes, reading and re-reading the plaque and then sat on a bench and observed the statue, imagining her father finding it, sending it here, recording the find in the journal she carried with her even now. Museumgoers came and went and she listened to their voices echo and their footsteps clack against the floor until, finally, she rose to leave as well. She glanced back at the unknown goddess one last time, as if saying thank you and goodbye, before leaving the museum.

THE TRUCK WAS parked three levels down, in section C-13. Lona took the stairs, as she always did, and clip-clopped down them thinking that she would be glad to get home and tell Awesome about the statue while they ate dinner. She thought about dinner. Maybe pork chops? She wondered whether they had any rosemary.

Lona came out the heavy metal door and into section C. The top two levels had been full when she arrived and now this level was full as well.

She passed car after car and finally saw the top of the blue pickup ahead but, as she got closer, an eerie feeling pressed in on her. Her heart thumped. Footsteps were following close on hers. She slung her bag around to her front and thrust her hand in for the keys. She brought them out and fumbled with them as she picked up speed toward the truck. She broke into a jog and the footsteps picked up.

Lona heaved a deep breath as the footsteps suddenly passed her. They belonged to a young man who ran on to the next car ahead. He jumped into an open convertible and brought it to life. He flashed Lona a handsome smile as he put his arm over the passenger seat and began to back out. She smiled back, blushing in relief and jingled her keys as she approached the truck.

BAM!

Lona's head hit the glass of the driverside window and her body pressed into the cold metal. There was a man behind her now. She could feel the heat of his body, the heaviness of it, as he twisted her wrist behind her back. She struggled and he pulled her back and rammed her harder against the truck.

She saw his reflection, dimly, in the window. Tall, ski mask, blonde hair poking out the bottom. Brown coat. Red t-shirt.

"Drop the bag and the keys."

She hesitated.

"I said, 'Drop it!'"

Somewhere in this garage, somewhere in or around one of these hundreds of cars, there had to be another human being. She thought she saw a glimmer of dust—gold dust—in her peripheral vision. Someone *must* be there. Her heart raced. She screamed. With all the voice she could find, she screamed as loud and long as she could.

Now she felt the hard metal of a gun on the back of her head. The *pop-snick* as the man pulled the hammer back.

"No, *you* drop it."

This was another voice. A new voice. Fabric whipped, bodies clashed. The gun came away from her head. She dropped and rolled under the truck, to the other side, grabbing her keys as she went. When she came back up, she saw both men. The man who had assaulted her tried to block the shot from the other man.

This new man wore a hooded sweatshirt and moved so fast she couldn't see his face. With fast, vicious strikes, he wailed on the mugger relentlessly. The mugger went for the gun. The hooded man, staying tight like a coiled snake, suddenly lashed out and this time, when he punched, his fists glowed with a hot, blue, sparking electricity. The mugger hit the cement floor with a smack and groaned. The man in the sweatshirt gave him another jolt of electricity then pulled a zip tie from the pocket of his pants and bound the mugger's wrists behind his back.

He lugged the big mugger to his feet and shoved him in the direction of the exit.

"Let's go, buddy."

Then, he shouted in her direction.

"You'd better get going, ma'am. It'll be dark soon."

Lona unlocked the truck from the passenger side and got in, then immediately locked the door and slid over to the driver side. With shaking hands on the wheel, she felt she could finally breathe again. After a few, long seconds, when she was sure no one was there, she opened the driver side door and leaned out to pick up her bag then jerked back in, started the truck, and pulled out.

AWESOME SAT ON the tub and wrapped Lona's wrist with one of the ice packs they kept for him. Finger-shaped bruises were forming on pale skin but it wasn't broken. When he was finished, he brushed the curls away from her forehead where another bruise was taking shape. Her knees and palms were scraped. Her skirt was torn.

Tulie sat at Lona's feet, looking back and forth between her silent masters, whining. Finally, Awesome spoke and she attended him.

"I should've been there."

Lona shook her head. Her neck was sore. She winced.

"No. You're a hero, not my body guard."

"The city's getting more dangerous every day. Maybe you shouldn't be going out on your own."

"I can't do that. I'm not just going to sit in the house all day. I can't."

Awesome nodded. He knew he was being absurd but he wanted to keep her safe. How could he leave the house every day to protect a bunch of strangers when the person he loved above all else might be hurt?

Awesome thought about it. He watched as Lona leaned forward and stroked Tulie behind the ears. Lona was so kind and amiable but Awesome knew, more than anyone else, how tough she was. He knew what they ought to do.

"I'll train you."

Her eyes met his.

"What?"

"You'd keep training with Neima. You need to hone your ability. But, I can teach you to fight—or at least how to defend yourself—Arc City's going to take some time to get back on its feet and you can't hide in the house all day until it does. I'll train you."

"Ok. Let's do it."

He helped her from the bathroom and, as a spring shower started, he made tomato soup and grilled cheese for them both and they sat in the kitchen making a plan for the new training sessions.

LONA STARED AT the shredded, silver glove.

She looked from the glove to the sketch of the glove she had made in her notebook. She penciled in a few more circles to represent the holes then looked back at the original.

Lona told herself to focus. She breathed in and out. Closed her eyes. In and out. Swirls of dust emerged in her mind. Green, gold, and silver swirls danced in the darkness. Slowly, she opened her eyes. The dust bloomed from within the glove like lilies—red and gold. It flowed in and out of reality and Lona felt that—

BING-BONG!

The doorbell. Tulie followed quick on the sound. Barking and racing through the house to the door. Lona jerked as if coming out of a trance and stood, her heart racing. It was the mailman.

"Howdy, Miss Chang. Just dropping this off for you. Didn't want to leave it out front."

She took the little brown package from him. It was stamped all over with *FRAGILE*. She knew immediately what it was.

"Thanks, Hank."

"Not a problem Miss Chang. Better be going. Don't want it to get dark on me before I finish my route."

She nodded and closed the door and nudged back Tulie who was nosing all over the package.

"Careful, girl. Sit."

She did.

"It was for Andy."

Tulie whined and leaned into Lona's leg at the sound of the name.

"I know."

Lona opened the package and took the mug, wrapped in brown paper, from within. It had a note.

Lona Chang

Alex had been right. The mug wasn't how Lona had pictured it. The kiln temperatures must have been a little off. Crackles of silver like micah were embedded in the glaze which ran from white at the top to blue at the bottom.

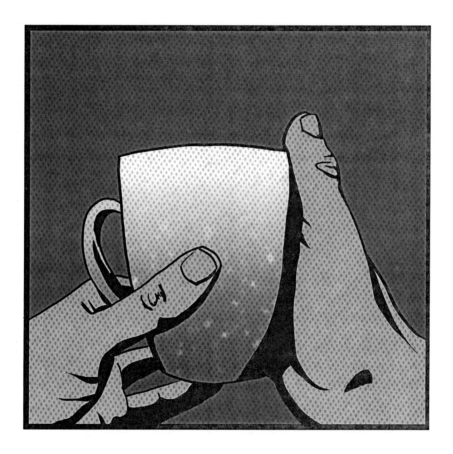

A few hours later, when Awesome got home, he took the mug in his hands.

"It's perfect."

"I think so, too."

"He would have loved it."

Lona nodded and stirred the zucchini and shallots with a wooden spoon.

"Jones, do you think the Guild are really doing all they can about Andy's death?"

He'd been wondering the same.

"I don't know. I mean, a Cape can't just get involved in the kind of battle Andy must've been involved in and no one notices."

"Exactly."

"But, if the Guild is investigating, and they're onto someone, it's not as if they're going to tell the general public about it. And that's what we are now. We might know Roy but we see him less and less and Julia and Neima seem to want nothing to do with the Guild these days."

Lona went to the table and took another glance at her notes. Then, she picked up Andy's glove. The material was weightless but durable. State of the art. Not even bullets could penetrate the fabric. So what had created the holes? Holes that left no blood, no trace of violence—only mottled skin and death.

Lona again read the list of *Grayston* possibilities and wondered what Andy had meant. Was it part of a specific message or had he been delusional? Why come to Awesome and Lona? Why fly to their house when he must have known he was dying?

Lona sighed and shut the book. She put it on the shelf and Awesome took the glove back into the bedroom closet. When he returned, Lona was sliding barbecue chicken and sauteed zucchini onto two plates and Tulie was licking a glob of sauce from the floor.

"If I see Roy, I'll ask him again. But, with everything that's been going on, I guess he's spread pretty thin."

Awesome hadn't actually spoken to Roy since the jewelry store smash and grab and he'd only seen him at crime scenes twice. Both times, Roy was off on his motorcycle before Awesome could talk to him.

"Do you miss it, Jones?"

Lona took a sip of water and looked across the table at him.

"Miss what?"

"Do you miss being part of the Guild?"

He half laughed.

"Was I ever really part of it?"

Awesome poked at his food for a few moments before he continued.

"I was only ever there because of who my parents were. And, I think if Andy hadn't been backing me, Pythia never would've let me in. No one would listen to me about how my ability worked and, the whole time I was there, I felt like the best chance I had was to maybe *someday* try for my tie and become a Squire. I don't miss that part. And I didn't like their attitude toward people who don't have super powers."

"Regulars."

Lona smirked when she said it.

"Yeah. But, I do miss Roy. I miss feeling like I was going to be part of something bigger. I miss training with Ben. I miss the idea that I was part of the same line as Andy and my dad. But being an Agent with the Guild isn't worth not being able to be with you or follow my own instincts."

He paused again and thought before he continued.

"I don't regret what happened with the Echo. I don't regret putting an end to him."

Lona nodded.

"I love you, Jones. And, I'm proud of you. You're an amazing hero. It doesn't matter whether you have all the power of the Guild behind you or not."

"AGAIN."

Lona got into position, Awesome behind her, gripping her wrist. Lona moved slowly through the steps.

Drop.

Lona dropped into a lower stance.

Break.

She moved her arm in, at an angle, against his to create leverage. Breaking through at the weakest point in his grip—the meeting of finger and thumb.

Go.

She spun out of his reach.

"Good."

She nodded.

"Now you just need to do it enough that it's muscle memory."

"So I don't panic and forget."

"Right."

"And after?"

"After?"

"I want to learn offense, too. I want to be able to fight back."

"Alright. Let's do it."

They practiced Lona breaking Awesome's wrist lock several times before sitting down to plan a hand-to-hand combat training regimen.

After a while, the police radio came to life and Awesome hustled out of the house. Lona made a cup of tea and sat on the patio, reading *The Emperor's New Gun*.

FROM: The Emperor's New Gun

Really, I couldn't begin to fathom just what Kraker had got up to. I might have aided my friend all of these twenty-odd years, but I often felt that I knew him no better than I did that first morning in the train station. He was polishing his shoe just now. Looking, as ever, completely engrossed in the task at hand. And yet, I knew he must be planning some fantastic feat. I knew his mind was working furiously for, if it did not, an innocent girl would die tonight.

Lona snapped the book shut and looked around at the patio.

"Come on, Tulie. Let's go for a walk."

Tulie and Lona walked together around the block. They walked down to the park and through the rose gardens. Tulie stopped to point at squirrels and sniff flowers. She watched other dogs and other people but stayed close to Lona who smelled edgy and nervous. Any time they crossed a strange man, any time someone jogged from behind and passed them, Tulie felt Lona tense. She smelled her cold, anxious sweat. Tulie eventually decided to lead her master back toward home.

As they approached their house, Lona stopped to look at her own roof. Andy's impact had left a wound there. Shingles were cracked or smashed. Some had slid down into the gutter.

"The Guild should've fixed that."

Her voice was quiet. She spoke only to herself. She was surprised the Squires missed it in their damage report. She wondered how well they ever mended what was broken.

Lona led Tulie inside and locked the door behind her. She was surprised to find Awesome in the shower. His uniform was lying on the bathroom floor. A strong, alcohol scent filled the air.

"Everything ok?"

Awesome laughed from behind the shower curtain.

"A bunch of thugs robbed the White Rabbit brewery. I'm covered in bourbon stout."

"Did you get 'em?"

"Yeah."

"Good."

Lona slipped out of her jeans and t-shirt.

"Be careful."

"Huh? Why?"

"I'm coming in."

"I SAW ROY TODAY."

Awesome stood at the counter, throwing the scraps from Lona's cutting board into the trash. Mussels simmered in the pan with garlic, onion, white wine and tomato puree.

"Yeah?"

"He said the Guild is onto a suspect for Andy's death."

Lona stopped stirring and looked at Awesome.

"Did he say who it was?"

"No. Just that they should have someone in custody soon."

Awesome was quiet for some long seconds. He was tense, Lona thought.

"What's wrong? Did he say something else?"

Awesome sighed and watched as Lona moved the pan from the burner.

"He said if I don't stop wearing a cape, Pythia will have me brought in."

"What else is new?"

He shook his head and stood against the counter with his hands in his pockets and his head down.

> "He sounded different. He sounded serious. He doesn't want to do it but—"

> "But he's a Guild man."

> "Yeah."

Lona slid the mussels into shallow, earthenware bowls and Awesome carried them to the table. Tulie smacked her tail into their legs as she trailed around after them with her nose in the air and, once they sat, she resigned herself to her own food bowl before finally curling around Lona's feet.

AWESOME LOOKED AT the bookshelf behind Lona's seat. He knew she had almost completely stopped working on her father's journal as she tried to search out the meaning of Andy's last words to her. He realized they were fighting battles on multiple fronts. He, in the streets of Arc City, and Lona in the secrets of their predecessors. He wondered how much of their separate battles were, in fact, connected—whether they would course into the same sea.

FROM: *Goldilocks and the Bearskin Rug*: A Kraker Mystery, by Irene Matly

"But, my god, sir, I didn't recognize you!" Abbot said, throwing a gloved hand over his breast.

"Of course not, you would never recognize me in the guise of the elusive Mr. Gold" Kraker said. He seated himself on the divan and peeled away the black beard.

"And the scar as well, sir?"

"Ah yes. Thank you, Abbot."

Kraker put a nimble finger to his cheek and stripped off the false scar. He was beginning to look like himself again and, yet, Abbot couldn't help but notice that Kraker seemed spent. Dark circles underscored Kraker's piercing blue eyes and Abbot knew at once that those would not be so easily discarded.

"Shall I get you a drink, sir?"

Briiing! BRRIIING!

Lona jumped. This late at night, a phone call worried her. She set the novel on the kitchen table and rushed to the phone.

"Hello?"

"The Baron's been injured. Come at once to 23rd and Ryder. Someone will meet you there. Come alone."

The line went dead. Lona held the receiver to her cheek in silence. Her heart thumped in her ears. A cold sweat broke over her.

Come at once, they said. *Come alone.*

She grabbed the truck keys from the dish and her bag from the counter and headed toward the door before turning at the last second.

"Tulie, come."

Tulie fell in at Lona's heels and they both climbed into the truck. Lona drove anxiously and told herself over and over to stay calm. On the bench next to her, Tulie stared out the window, occasionally whining at the darkened city.

The further she went, the more people there were on the streets. Groups of teenagers wouldn't have worried her but these weren't kids. Men and women in groups of all sizes prowled the streets. Their clothes were marked with the symbols of their leaders. Some wore face paint and some wore masks. Black masks. Red masks. Wolf masks.

"The White Wolves?"

Lona's voice was almost a whisper. Tulie whined.

Lona Chang

The White Wolves had been all but wiped out in Captain Lightning's tenure as Arc City's hero. They were dangerous, chaotic. They seemed to strike without motive or forethought and they always left blood in their wake.

The truck rumbled onto Ryder Avenue and Lona slowed as she approached the crossing with 23rd Street. No one was there. A streetlight illuminated an empty bus stop.

Lona looked to the other side of the street.

Empty.

When she turned to look again at the bus stop, she jumped. A woman stood outside the passenger side window.

"You Lona?"

Lona heard her through the glass and nodded.

"Let me in. We need to get off the streets."

Lona hesitated. She didn't know this woman. She wore a black mask over half her face and head. A curtain of violet hair hung from under it.

"It's ok. I'm here to help."

Silver dust sparkled around the woman. Lona leaned to the side to unlock the door as two huge men emerged from the shadowed alley. They wore spiked knuckles on their fists and assault rifles on their broad backs. Black streaks of paint cut diagonally across their faces.

The woman must have read Lona's face. Her demeanor turned urgent.

"Get down!"

Lona pulled Tulie to the floorboards as the woman in black, with a flick of her wrist, unleashed an extendable staff. Silver and white, it gleamed and pulsed with a strange, violet light.

From the floorboard, Lona heard a high-pitched clicking noise.

kik-kik-kik kik-kik-kik kik-kik

She heard the men laughing and she heard their boots on the sidewalk as they approached. Then, she covered her ears, as a shrill howl penetrated her eardrums. Tulie whined and buried her face in Lona's shoulder.

Here is what Lona did not see:

One man laughed. He bumped the other man's shoulder. The other man laughed, too.

The woman, who was at least a foot and a half shorter than either man, smirked at them.

They approached her, fists raised, no need for guns yet. An easy fight.

The woman crouched into a lower stance, extended her staff. It pulsed.

The bigger man took a half-step back.

The woman's smirk grew.

The air was filled with a high clicking sound and then, as the woman opened her mouth, a higher, piercing cry. The cry was inhuman. The taller man fell instantly to the ground. Blood seeped through fingers held over his ears. The second man was still up. The woman swung her staff into his gut. When he doubled over, she thrashed it over his back. He reached around for his gun and she, with steel-toed boots, kicked him in the side of the head. He lay still.

She quickly cuffed both men and searched the bigger one's clothes. She pulled a wad of money from his front pants pocket and stuffed it into the inner compartment of her leather jacket. From a pouch on her belt, she withdrew a quarter-sized device, peeled off the backing, and stuck it to the back of one man's neck. Then, she tapped at Lona's window.

"Ok, let's go."

Lona unlocked the passenger door and the woman shook her staff, retracting it in an instant. The woman tossed her cape around her and climbed into the truck. She held out her hands for Tulie to sniff and, after a moment, Tulie licked her fingertips. Soon, the woman was scratching her behind the ears.

"Is the Baron ok? Where is he? Who are you?"

"Take a left onto George Street."

Lona put the truck in gear and they pulled away. Several of the streetlights were out.

"The Baron's going to be alright. Something to do with his shoulder. My name is Opal. He's being treated at the Sheet Clinic."

"The Sheet Clinic?"

The woman didn't answer. Lona took a left onto George Street. After a couple of blocks, they rolled into the warehouse district. Long ago, this part of the city was the bustling center of production. In the last fifty years, though, all the industrialists had moved out of town and away from the super-battles Arc City had been prone to. Now the district was home to art studios, cheap loft apartments, and grungy nightclubs.

The truck headlights beamed onto the red brick wall of one of the warehouses. Several of the lower windows were broken but, higher up, there were lights on and the sound of a violin came from within. Lona gasped when an image on the side of the building came into view.

"What's that?"

Opal shrugged.

"Pull up to 313 and go around to the back."

Lona did as she was directed. The blue truck rumbled around behind the building and pulled up to a heavy-duty garage door. She felt the tires bump over pressure plates and a monitor to their right suddenly flashed on. Lona found herself looking alternately into a camera lense and at the monitor where a woman in goggles and long, black and pink dreadlocks looked back at her.

"State your business."

Opal leaned across Lona's lap and spoke toward the camera.

"She's with me, Dispatch. She's here for the Baron."

"Gotcha."

The woman gave them a curt nod and the screen flashed off as the garage door rattled open. Lona pulled inside and found a lit garage. It was half-filled with motorcycles, dark cars with tinted windows, a couple of retrofitted military vehicles, and, in the corner, a bent propellor. A mechanic in blue coveralls was working under one of the cars. His tools clanged against the concrete floor. Lona parked beside a low, streamlined bike and turned off the engine.

Opal jumped out of the truck and met Lona and Tulie next to the tailgate.

"This is the Sheet Clinic."

As she spoke, another door opened and bright light flooded out. A man emerged and, with the light behind him, it was a few seconds before Lona recognized him.

"It's you! You were in the garage that night! I—I didn't get to thank you."

A bright smile flashed from inside the man's dark, hooded sweatshirt—decorated with white dots that made up the Hypatia constellation—and the man put his hand out to her.

"I'm Stargazer. Welcome to the Sheet Clinic."

Tulie walked ahead of Lona and sniffed at Stargazer's hand. He squatted to meet her and roughed the fur on her neck.

"Who's this?"

Tulie licked at his hands.

"Tulie. I know you said to come alone but..."

He stood and waved off her remark.

"Arc City after dark? I don't blame you. I just didn't want any of your Guild friends showing up."

Lona gaped at him.

"Come on, I'll take you to the Baron."

Stargazer led her past a reception office where the woman with dreadlocks sat blowing pink bubbles as she made notes in a big, black binder. They passed an open exam room where a man with a domino mask and blue and gray body armor lay on a table with his femur sticking out of his leg. He flipped through the pages of a comic book.

Stargazer peeked in and yelled back over his shoulder to the woman in reception.

"Stonesthrow's had enough pain meds. He needs to get into Op."

Another exam room was mostly shut and a woman inside yelped. Her voice was followed by a flash of orange light that shimmered through the cracked doorway. Lona gave Stargazer a questioning look.

"Optica. She took two in the hip tonight but refused pain treatment. She wants to get back on the street before dawn."

Finally, they came to the last room on the right and there, on a hospital bed, lay Awesome Jones. An IV ran to into his arm and his left shoulder was wrapped in metallic, green bandages. At first, she thought he was sleeping but when he heard their footsteps, he looked up at Lona.

She ran to him.

"Oh! Are you alright? What happened?"

She brushed back his hair and kissed him. A long cut, covered in salve, streaked across his cheek. He had other bandages, of varying colors, on his neck and arm. He was still wearing his mask but his uniform jacket and shirt hung over the chair next to the bed and his cane was propped against the wall. Tulie nosed up to his hand and put her muzzle in his palm.

"I'm ok. I'm ok. Don't worry. I'm alright."

"What happened?"

Stargazer, who was leaning in the doorway, smiling at them, started into the hallway.

"I'll leave you alone. Let me know if you need anything; I'll be back after a while."

Lona sat on the edge of the bed and held Awesome's uninjured hand in her own. Stargazer closed the door behind him.

"What happened, Jones?"

"I dislocated my shoulder."

Then he sighed and told her how he'd been on his way home when he spotted a gang of White Wolves breaking into one of the houses in Old Town's Victoria District.

"Hardly anyone lives there now, Lona. It's crazy. It's like a ghost town."

They'd read about the mass exodus from Arc City. Only about two weeks after Captain Lightning died, all the old (and a lot of the new) money families sold off their properties and moved elsewhere. Their elegant homes were often left adorned with forgotten items—crystal chandeliers, the mounted heads of lions, stags, and bears, and ivory mantle pieces—which were carried off by whomever could get there first. Those of Arc City's most affluent who had stayed behind had beefed up their own private security forces and firefights between the groups were now a common occurrence.

"They were plundering one of those old mansions. I went around back, hoping to take them by surprise. I didn't realize the owner was still there. She was hiding in the pantry and panicked when she saw me. She started talking to me—begging for help—but too loudly. The Wolves came running. I ended up between the old lady and those Wolves and, trying to get her out, I got pretty banged up. I carried her out of the neighborhood but my shoulder was completely shot. Luckily, Stargazer showed up and the police weren't far behind. I handed the woman off to them then went back with Stargazer to round up any of the Wolves who might still be in the house. That's when I got cut up. They all had knives and they all knew how to use them. We cuffed seven and Stargazer put a beacon on them for the police."

"A beacon?"

He nodded and readjusted his position in the bed so Lona could have more room. She settled in closer to him.

"Stargazer said the Sheets have been working with the cops—against Guild sanctions. Arc City's police force has been overwhelmed since Captain Lightning died. They need help. So, when the Sheets subdue someone, they put a beacon on the guy and the cops get the beacon's signal and come get them."

"And the Sheets are called that because..."

But as soon as Lona started her question, the answer dawned on her and she finished her own sentence.

"They're called Sheets because a sheet is what a little kid uses when he pretends to be a Cape."

She laughed to herself. The Sheets. It seemed to fit.

"Apparently the Guild heroes called them that a long time ago and they liked it. So, it stuck for them."

"But not for the Guild?"

Awesome smiled. Lona understood. The Guild was exclusionary—and maybe for good reason—but they wouldn't want their clever name turned around on them.

> "No, and I guess it wasn't such a big problem for them until after Captain Lightning died. Stargazer said there were fewer than ten Sheets in Arc City before. Then, when everything went downhill, a bunch of others started showing up from all over the world to help out. Sea City. New York. New Kyoto. Paris."

> "All because of An—Captain Lightning?"

Lona realized they had been using Andy's Cape name the entire time and wondered if Awesome thought they were being observed. She wondered if these unregistered heroes could be trusted. In that moment, Lona realized she had a hard time trusting anyone lately. They didn't trust the Guild anymore. She hadn't told Roy about Andy's last words or his glove. She hadn't told Neima where she'd heard the word, *Grayston*. She felt Julia was hiding something from her. She missed Ben. She missed Andy. She yearned for those simple nights in the cabin. At least then they felt certain who they could share their secrets with. Now, everyone Lona truly trusted was in this room.

> "They sent a woman to meet me, Jones. To bring me here. I think it was the same Cape you saw before Captain Lightning died."

> "Oh, yeah?"

> "Her name is Opal. And, Jones, she has this scream. It's just—"

> "What?"

> "It's just like the Echo's."

Before Awesome could respond, a knock came at the door and Stargazer entered with Opal and a woman in blue scrubs.

"This is Christina."

Christina greeted Lona and checked the IV and then removed the bandage from Awesome's shoulder. The flesh there was swollen and covered in blue gel. She pulled a device on a cart from the corner of the room and waved a bulky wand over the wound. After a few seconds, she put it back. Then, carefully, she replaced the bandage.

"Looks good, Baron. You'll be able to check out in the morning. You're healing up pretty quick. Still, you took a good beating. You should get some rest tonight."

"Can we stay with him?"

"Of course."

Christina shut the door as she left the room. Stargazer and Opal remained behind.

"Thank you for bringing him here."

Lona sat up higher on the bed next to Awesome. She was exhausted but alert. Who were these people, really? What did they want?

Stargazer pulled his hood back but his eyes were still masked. He had deep brown skin and a handsome face and, it occurred to Lona now, that he was smaller than she'd originally thought. He couldn't have been much taller than her. He leaned forward and flashed an easy smile at Awesome before speaking. Opal stood behind his left shoulder.

"We've been watching you for a while, Baron. We know, from our sources within the Guild that you were excommunicated. You're not the first Cape turned Sheet."

"I wasn't really ever a Cape."

"We know. But you shoulda been."

"What else do you know?"

"We know the Guild wants you brought in over any of the other Sheets. We know you and Photon have some kind of relationship outside the masks. We know you must've been related to the first Baron because I can't think of another damn reason anyone would do something as crazy as taking up his name."

Awesome let out a silent breath of a laugh.

"We don't know—but we think—that you killed the Echo."

Tulie, who had been exceptionally quiet during this exchange, now shifted closer to her owners. In the months that she had been with them, she had learned the word *echo* and she knew that tension always accompanied the utterance of those syllables. That same tension now filled the room. Her hackles raised as she felt Awesome's body go rigid. From the other side of the bed, she could smell Lona's uneasiness. When she looked to Awesome and Lona, however, she found they did not show their anxiety. She looked back at the strange new man and woman and tilted her head. Tulie could hear a high-pitched clicking coming from the woman's mouth—a sound humans didn't usually make.

"We think that's why you lost your Cape."

Awesome's fist tightened around the blanket that lay over him.

"What does it matter to you?"

Opal shifted where she stood and then cleared her throat.

"The Echo murdered my mother."

Lona studied Opal, the woman who had escorted her here. Pale, blonde hair poked out from beneath purple strands. Now, in the light, Lona could see the oil-slick streaks on the white surface of her eyes. Lona remembered the grim history lesson she and Awesome had been given in the cabin.

"The Banshee."

Opal nodded.

"Yeah, the Banshee."

"Your scream. When I heard it—"

"Yeah. She was serving in Sea City. I was just a baby. I was staying with my grandmother back in Ireland. The Guild didn't even know about me. You know how they are. She didn't want me ending up at Hartwell."

"You know about Hartwell?"

"Of course. Anyway, my mother was a new Cape in a new city and she was murdered by that monster. I never knew her. He did, though, and he took my mother's scream and—"

Awesome broke in, his voice thick, heavy.

"And used it to kill the Baron and my mother."

"So it's true. You are the Baron's son."

Awesome nodded.

"And you did kill the Echo."

Again, he answered a silent affirmative. He had never met another victim of the Echo. But, when Opal spoke, he recognized something familiar in her. Her mother had been a tool to the Echo. The means to an end. He wondered about Opal's life in the years between her mother's death and now. What path had she walked to get here?

Opal breathed hard, through her nose.

"I'm glad it's done. And it was your right. I only wish I'd been there."

Lona watched Opal's gloved fingers tighten around the back of

Stargazer's chair as she spoke. Her skin was white; her naked lips pale and tight.

Stargazer sighed and leaned forward again.

"I have a couple of questions, if you don't mind. First—your uniform. When I saw you in the papers, I thought maybe you inherited it. It's so much like his. But—seeing it in person. It's brand new, isn't it? I've never seen anything like it."

"I don't know anything about it, actually."

"You don't know where it came from?"

"No."

"It wasn't from one of your Guild friends?"

"I don't think so. Captain Lightning checked it out when I got it. He said it didn't look like their tech. I hoped you might have information."

"I could take a piece of it to analyze but, just looking at it, I can tell you I have no idea where that thing came from. Most of us scavenge our gear from Capes or the guys we bust, we buy it off the The Underground, or else we make our own."

Lona looked at Stargazer's hooded sweatshirt and suspected there was more to the article than simple cotton and sewn-on stars.

"There's something else."

Stargazer pulled a silver disc, no larger than a dime, from within his pocket and flipped it to Awesome, who snatched it out of the air. Awesome turned it over in his palm. It was plain with the exception of a pin-prick, blue dot on the back.

"It's a tracking device. We pulled it off your truck."

"Who—"

"It's Guild tech. Your friends have been tracking you."

Lona broke into a cold sweat. Her heart raced.

"But that means they've tracked me here."

Shaking her head, Opal dismissed Lona's concern.

"As soon as I approached the car, it was disarmed. The Sheets carry disrupters. Most of us don't have the protection of the Guild or the luxury of living a single life"

Stargazer picked up where Opal left off.

"Most of us have jobs, families. We can't afford to let anyone track our whereabouts. You need to be more careful. We'll give you a couple of the disruptors we use."

"Scavenged tech?"

"My own."

"What do we owe you?"

Stargazer laughed. It was a pleasant, light thing to hear after an evening of such serious conversation.

"Nothing, man. Don't worry about it."

Awesome and Lona traded looks but Stargazer waved them off.

"Look, when Captain Lightning died, it was a wake-up call. One man had been standing between Arc City and everyone and everything that was trying to eat it alive. Photon isn't up to the task—not yet, anyway. You know it, I know it, and I'll bet he knows it. This place is a touchstone for more superheroes than any other city on the planet because the Guild is here and they're *still* spread too thin. Whatever the Guild's been doing—however they've been training their recruits, their exclusionary attitude, the way they want their Capes to break ties with their families, their longtime avoidance of the New

Sciences—it's all lead up to a world with a serious imbalance. In Arc City, these thugs and their bosses outnumber us five to one. They're taking advantage of a bad situation and the Guild keeps flooding the papers and comics with what a great job Photon is doing while Arc City falls apart."

Instinctively, Awesome wanted to argue. But, everything Stargazer said about the Guild was true. Still, Andy had been part of the Guild. His parents. Neima and Ben. Julia and Roy.

"The people who work in the Guild aren't bad."

"I know. I'm not interested in taking a war to the Guild or The Capes or The Squires—even if it does seems like they're about to start one with us. All I want to do is help Arc City—my city. I grew up here. Captain Lightning saved my life. My whole building would've come down when I was a kid if he hadn't been there. We needed him. This city needed him."

Awesome felt Andy's loss more keenly now than he had in weeks. His heart ached for his friend. He wished so much that he could just hear Andy's voice again, listen to his reassurances, his easy laugh.

"I know."

"And now it needs you. The Baron was the first true hero of Arc City. You need to be that hero now. And we want to help you."

"What? How?"

"You're a good fighter but you've got a lot of gaps in your training."

Thinking of his training in the woods, Awesome was reminded of Ben and realized Stargazer was right. He hadn't finished his training. He'd barely started. He was deep in thought, remembering those days in the forest, when Opal spoke.

"You're too slow. I don't know how you're getting to the action but you aren't getting there quick enough."

Stargazer continued,

"And you aren't picking your targets properly. When there's this much going on, you need to be more selective."

Now, he and Opal were speaking in turns,

"And your cane is a problem."

"I'm guessing it was your dad's but you need to be able to fight at a moment's notice."

"You can't just carry that thing around with you. You're going to end up outnumbered and un-armed."

Awesome crossed his arms in front of this chest.

"So what are you offering? What do you want?"

Stargazer shook his head and flashed his effortless smile.

"Look, man, all we *want* is to protect the people of Arc City. You're good but you could be a lot better—more efficient. I can help you."

"How?"

"Come out with me. You should be healed up in a couple days. I'll teach you how to get around the city quicker and we'll take it from there."

Awesome and Lona exchanged looks but, ultimately, they agreed. Stargazer wished them a good night and left the room. Opal stayed behind. She remained standing but moved closer to the bed. Now, Lona could better see the woman's face. The shimmery streaks across her eyes refracted the blue-tinted hospital lights.

"I'm glad to meet you, Baron. My grandmother spoke highly

of your father."

"Your grandmother."

"My grandmother was the Fae."

Lona studied Opal's uniform. It looked to be composed of high-grade elements. Her violet cape seemed almost brand new. But, it was still mis-matched. This woman clearly had the talent, ambition, and training to be a Cape. So, why was she, at three o'clock in the morning, sitting in an underground clinic in the Warehouse District?

"Opal, why are you a Sheet? I mean, you come from Guild lineage. Why aren't you working with them?"

Lona hoped the question wasn't too forward but, with no hesitation, a wry smile broke through Opal's serious demeanor. She shifted where she stood but still did not take a seat.

"Because I'm blind."

She waved a gloved hand in front of her eyes.

"These babies aren't just for show. I can't see a thing."

"But, the way you fight—"

"Echolocation."

Earlier, Lona had heard high clicks outside the truck when those men cornered Opal. Now she remembered them.

"Those clicks—"

"Whatever it is that makes my sonic scream possible—it also enables me to sense my environment. I'm constantly sending out calls."

"Constantly?"

"Yeah. Constantly—like right now. No, you can't hear them, don't bother messing with your ears. Most of them are way above your range of hearing. My ears are just different. The same as my mother and grandmother. We think that's why the sonic scream doesn't affect us."

"Oh."

"That's why I'm not in the Guild. I probably could've gotten in if I'd really wanted to—if I'd played the parent card—no offense, Baron. But I'm not interested in abiding by Guild rules. I make my own choices—where I live, who I fight. I have a life. I have a kid."

"A kid?"

"Yeah. Anyway, I need to get going. I have another patrol to finish before I head home. I just—I wanted to say that it is good to meet you. I'm glad you're here. So is Stargazer. Get some rest. I'll see you around."

She left them alone. Wordlessly, Lona scooted closer to Awesome until she lay in the crook of his undamaged arm. He patted the bed and Tulie jumped up to lay at their feet. Soon, only Awesome was awake. He lay there for several hours, his eyes sometimes closed, sometimes open, but always he was thinking. He thought about his future as a hero and a husband. As a former Cape, former Guild-recruit, former son. He wanted to do what was best for Arc City, he wanted, as always, to get better.

He would have to practice.

SOME MONTHS AGO:

"Is he awake?"

"In a way."

Between the man and the woman, who spoke in hushed tones, lay a third subject. To this subject, the voices of the man and woman seemed very far away. The subject listened for some time, only making out various words: medical, opinion, decision, dangerous, trust.

"Yes."

The older man was talking.

"I believe so."

The voices seemed closer now. The subject opened his eyes but the images that came through were blurry—disorganized. The subject felt a remote sense of unease.

"You've replaced them."

"Both of them, yes. The entire visual cortex was damaged. Though, I confess, I would have replaced them anyway."

The woman made a noise.

"She will approve."

"Excellent."

"When will it be ready?"

"Very soon now, I should think."

"Have you tested it?"

"I need another subject."

The woman made the noise again. Her heels tapped as she shifted from foot to foot.

"You will have it."

Her heels tapped again as she left the room and shut the heavy door behind her.

THE PHONE WAS ringing when Lona unlocked their front door. Awesome's arm was still in a sling and Tulie nosed into the door and barked at the phone. Lona rushed to it and jerked it off the cradle just when she thought it might stop.

"Hello?"

She let her bag slide off her shoulder and turned to see Awesome filling Tulie's water and food bowls.

"Hello?"

"Lona? Are you there? We've been calling all night."

"Mama! I'm so sorry. Awesome was hurt and we had to see a doctor. What's wrong? You sound upset."

"The store was robbed last night."

"What? Are you ok?"

"Yes. It was those Wolf people. They didn't get into the apartment. They broke through the store windows, took a lot of your Bàba's favorite paperweights and of course that jade tiara I loved so well. But they were gone as quick as they came. Can you come over?"

"Of course. We'll be right there."

Awesome had gone off to the bathroom to wash up and change and when he got to the bedroom Lona was pulling a fresh t-shirt over her head. She explained what was going on and, about an hour later, they pulled up in front of Chang's Antiques Emporium.

Through the broken window, Lona spied Mrs. Chang sweeping up glass while Mr. Chang packed an ancient cuckoo clock into a wooden crate. The shop seemed almost empty. Red tape was strung up across the front of the building.

Furious at the sight of the Changs' demolished storefront, Lona stormed out of the truck and across the street with Awesome following close at her heels. When she got nearer, Lona could hear her mama humming a song from Lona's childhood but, in her haste, she interrupted the tune,

> "What's going on? Why hasn't anyone replaced the window yet?"

Mrs. Chang stopped sweeping and looked up at her adoptive daughter. She smiled but it was clear that exhaustion and the remnants of fear lay heavy on her still. She knelt and collected the dustpan and the glass tinkled as she let it fall into the waste basket.

> "They said they would. Some men and women in suits came early this morning but we are only the latest in a long list of victims. They can't do it all at once."

Lona shook her head in dismay and turned to Mr. Chang.

> "And what's this? Are you packing up the shop until they replace the windows?"

Mr. Chang sighed and put down an old glockenspiel he'd been wrapping in brown paper.

> "No, my dear. We are packing up for good. Your mama and I are leaving Arc City."

Lona Chang

Lona's eyes widened at his words but she didn't speak. She couldn't fathom an Arc City without the Changs. They loved it here. They had lived in this city for several decades. They had raised her father here and her after him. Now they would leave?

Mr. Chang bid them go upstairs and have some tea. Awesome offered to watch the storefront while they were busy and Lona followed Mr. and Mrs. Chang up the narrow staircase to the little apartment in which she had grown up.

Here, it was a very different scene. The Changs' parlor was pristine. Refinished hardwood shined beneath their feet. Lovely, plush chairs were situated just so upon a floral-patterned Persian rug.

Mr. Chang begged her to sit but Lona followed Mrs. Chang into the kitchen instead where Mrs. Chang stood at the kettle with her back to Lona.

"What does he mean you're leaving? You've been in Arc City forever, Mama!"

She was more forceful than she meant to be and realized she sounded like a petulant teenager. She let out a long, heavy sigh. It felt as though her entire life was being broken and boarded up. She told herself to stop mentally collecting images of the people she had lately lost—or felt she had lost—that it wasn't doing any good.

"I'm sorry, Mama. I'm sorry. I didn't mean to yell."

Mrs. Chang turned.

"Lona, darling. I'm sorry as well. We just can't do this anymore. The shop is a liability here now. It's a target. Your bàba and I are too old. We just need to move away from Arc City. It's time we retire, Lona. Maybe travel."

Lona knew the Changs had used very little of the money her father had left them. They ought to use it now, she thought. They ought to see the world. Her bàba had always wanted to see Australia, she knew.

"Oh, Mama. But, I'll miss you."

Tears filled Lona's eyes and streamed down her face. She sniffed as she felt her nose redden and drip. The old woman opened her arms to her daughter and Lona walked into them. Standing there, she sobbed as the tea kettle whistled and Mr. Chang came in, took it off the stove, and then pulled Lona into his arms.

Lona buried her face in his shoulder and smelled his familiar smell. Shaving soap and furniture polish. His stiff, cotton shirt soaked up her tears until her face was finally dry. Mrs. Chang escorted her into the parlor and made her drink two cups of almond blossom tea.

"Or else you'll get a headache from your cry."

Mr. Chang told her about their tentative plans to visit Paris, Sydney, Thames Town, Prague and Xin Shanghai. They hoped to spend time in the country, visiting the towns that had produced so many of their beloved antiques.

"You'll be careful."

"Yes, of course. Of course. But, Lona, we're more worried about you. Wouldn't you and Awesome like to accompany us? I know you've always wanted to travel."

For a few moments, it was tempting. This was not the same Arc City Lona had grown up in. As a girl, she had walked through this neighborhood to go to school. She had stayed out late to see movies and go rollerskating and never worried about walking home by herself. She had never seriously worried about her safety or that of the Changs'. Now, they were leaving and she was staying and her fiancé was a superhero with no support. Then, she remembered where she had been the night before. He did have support now. The Sheets would help them. She hoped.

"We'll be alright."

Lona Chang

Mrs. Chang leaned forward and put a cool hand on Lona's knee. Her dark eyes were misty.

"If the city becomes too dangerous, please promise me that you will also leave. Come along, Lona, we worry about you enough already. Please promise me."

Finally, Lona nodded.

"I promise, Mama."

"Good. Now, I have a few things for you. I kept a box of Humphrey's things, just the odd items from his old rolltop, when we learned of his fate but, over the years, it was moved from place to place in the apartment and I forgot all about it. Luckily, I found it this morning in the back of the linen closet as I was packing things away."

A couple of hours later, after Mrs. Chang had ordered delivery Thai food and they all sat in the shop to eat, discussing some of Mr. Chang's favorite pieces, and after a few Suits came by with a construction crew to install new shop windows, Awesome and Lona found themselves back in the kitchen of their little house, staring into the box Mrs. Chang had given Lona.

A book of poetry—in Greek. Old photographs.

The box also contained a few odd objects. A compass. A miniature, leather bound notebook—still empty. A scrimshaw folding knife. A skeleton key strung on a red ribbon. An old passport completely full of stamps. An envelope of receipts from the purchase of dinners, films, operas, art supplies, a baby cradle. Plane, train, and ship ticket stubs. A crocodile and silver flask with engraving that said, *To Humphrey with Love, B.B.*

Awesome and Lona studied the items in awe.

"When I was little, I used to read his old books—or try to—

and picture the places he had gone. I wanted to believe he might still come back and I imagined him alive, on adventures in exotic places."

Lona shuffled through the pictures. She ran her finger over the faces of her parents. She could see her reflection there. A mix of their features. A blend familiar and yet strange. She went through the passport and studied each of the beautiful stamps. She opened the empty flask and looked inside to find it clean and dry.

But, it was the skeleton key, among everything else, that seemed to shimmer when she touched it. Little gold sparks erupted from its surface. Instinctively, Lona slid the ribbon over her head and around her neck and the key came to rest against her chest.

After a while, they pressed the lid back onto the box and Lona set it on the kitchen shelf next to her stack of Kraker novels and her father's now-neglected journal.

"Let's go for a walk."

At that, Tulie jumped up and ran to the door, wagging her tail.

"ONE!"

Lona, a southpaw, jabbed with her left hand. In the last few weeks, she had realized that, even though it was customary to keep one's dominant hand back, she was more comfortable leading with it.

"One. Two!"

Left jab, right cross.

"One. Two. Three. Two."

Jab. Cross. Hook. Cross.

She panted and sweated as she twisted and threw, her body adapting to the sequence of movement.

"Keep your hands up. Guard."

Raising her gloved hands back to her face, she took a hard breath then continued following his sequence. Her hands slammed into the pads. Her arms, chest, and face were hot, red, and dripping with sweat. A timer jangled on the patio table and Tulie snapped at it.

"Alright, now you're warmed up. Let's get something to drink and then we'll work on your defensive throws."

The morning sun was warm on their skin. Curls fought to escape the bun Lona had forced them into and she brushed them back with shaking hands.

"Am I ok?"

"Yeah. That'll go away. Your body's just adapting."

They each drank from tall glasses of lemony water as Awesome surveyed the patio. All the pots and the pottery wheel had been pushed against the wall to give them more room to move. Staring at his wheel, Awesome realized he hadn't used it since he made Andy's mug. He sighed. Looked back at Lona. The muscles in her arms, shoulders, and legs were more pronounced now. Taut ropes seemed to move under her skin as she threw punch after punch during their practice and Awesome was impressed by her endurance and determination.

She clanked her water glass back down on the table and wiped her mouth with the back of her hand.

"Alright, let's go."

He had been teaching her to use her opponent's own strength and momentum against them and now he moved toward her and prepared to be thrown. Lona grabbed his arms, turned, thrust her hip into him, swept her inside leg around his outside leg, turned her head and body away and he felt himself fly, head over heels. His breath rushed out of his lungs as he smacked into the patio floor.

"Good!"

He looked up, into the sun, and saw Lona there. The sun seemed to set her hair on fire. In this light, she always seemed to shimmer. He grinned up at her as she offered him her hand but, out of his peripheral vision, he saw a shadow pass.

Awesome snapped to his feet, stood between Lona and the shadow, and took a fighting stance. Tulie shot out from under the table and took up beside him, growling in the direction of the roof. Lona shielded her eyes in the sun and looked, over Awesome's shoulder, toward their roof.

"It's alright, man. It's me."

The form came into focus. Noiselessly, Stargazer hopped down from their roof, onto their patio wall, where he perched like a cat about to pounce.

"I just came to pick up the Baron for training but it looks like you're already putting him through the ringer."

"So you know where we live?"

"Of course. I said we've been watching you," he laughed, "well, Opal's been listening. You know."

He laughed again at his own joke and it occurred to Lona that, however talented and intelligent Stargazer was, he absolutely knew it. Lona regarded Awesome worriedly.

"Don't worry. I promise I'll bring him home safe."

She crossed her arms in front of her chest.

"I'll hold you to that."

AWESOME STOOD WITH Stargazer in the second floor of the Sheet Clinic. It was mostly an empty warehouse space but Stargazer had added a few large, wooden boxes, an old pommel horse, and what looked like a few cast-offs from construction sites—a huge concrete tube, a few wooden pallets, propped against the walls. A punching bag hung in one corner next to a shelf full of mis-matched weights.

"Who else trains here?"

"A lot of us come in here. We work with each other or we just let off some steam. Opal is in here a lot. Night Terror and Panthera train here. But, for the most part, if you're a Sheet, you get a lot of training in the field. Especially now, man. It's brutal. Even the veterans piling in from other cities are fighting a hard fight. That's why we need you, Baron."

Awesome raked the back of his hair with his fingers.

"I'll do my best."

Stargazer explained that Awesome would need to learn to move across the city like a cat.

"I can show you the basics but you'll have to adapt it to your own way—the way that feels best for you—for your body, you know?"

"Yeah. I just need to be able to practice. I need do the same thing over and over."

"Yeah, everyone does. Practice makes perfect, right?"

"Yeah, but, that's how my ability works. I practice and then I get a lot better."

"Like 'super better'?"

"Yeah."

"Oh man, you should not have told me that."

Awesome thought Ben's training regiment was intense but Stargazer gave the Red Fox a run for his money. Awesome worked on jumps, landings, and rolling for ten hours. Awesome began to feel confident about learning to move. His body—though sore—was beginning to feel agile and fluid. Then, Stargazer took him out to the streets and they climbed up the fire escape of one of the old warehouses. That's when Awesome suddenly had a problem.

"So now you're just going to take what you've already learned in our building, and apply it to rooftops."

"Rooftops?"

"Yeah. Whoa, you ok?"

Awesome was not ok.

"Yeah. I'm fine. I'm fine."

Stargazer smiled and then took off running. At the edge of the roof, he leapt into the air and crossed the seven or so feet of empty space before effortlessly landing on the next roof. He then motioned for Awesome to follow.

Pale and sweating, Awesome nodded and started to run. But, as soon as he neared the edge of the roof, he let up.

Stargazer took another running jump and leapt back, grabbing at the higher roof and pulling himself up with ease.

"What's going on, man? You look sick."

"Yeah, uh, listen—"

"You're afraid of heights."

Awesome was ashamed and afraid that Stargazer would mock him but his new friend's voice was all sympathy and understanding.

"Why didn't you say something?"

"I haven't been on a rooftop in years. I was hoping that, with the training, and with everything I've been through, by the time I got up here, I would've gotten over it."

Stargazer shook his head.

"Oh, man."

"Anything over about two stories and I get vertigo."

Awesome plopped down on the cement and buried his face in his hands.

"Has it always been this way?"

"No. I loved climbing when I was a kid. But one afternoon, I went outside and got up onto the roof and—I idolized Captain Lightning, you know? Anyway, I tried to fly. I broke my arm in three places and after that, I just couldn't do it anymore."

"Alright. It's ok."

Awesome shook his head.

"No, really. It'll be alright. You get better a little at a time, right? So we'll just do that. You're going to have to get around this city faster. It's not a choice. Being able to use Arc City's rooftops will make you faster. So, you're just going to have to practice. Ok? We'll start small and work our way up."

THE MUSEUM FLYER poked out of Lona's bag as she set it on Julia's coffee table.

"How are you feeling?"

Neima smiled but her face was more care-worn than Lona would've liked.

"How's Awesome?"

"Good. He's working."

"Good."

A silence fell over them. Lona was unsure what she could or should say to Neima about the Sheets. She wanted to tell her everything, to tell her about the clinic, and Opal and Stargazer. She wanted to tell her that Jones had spent the last several days trying to work through a debilitating fear of heights. She glanced at the corner of the flyer and a knot of guilt grew in her stomach. She wanted so much to explain to Neima everything Andy had said, how she had kept his glove, and why she was going to the museum as soon as she left. Instead, she listened to the traffic rush by outside. A warm breeze blew in from the street and smelled like the bagel shop across the way.

"The Changs are leaving Arc City."

The words tumbled out of her mouth and she watched as Neima's already compassionate expression grew more so.

"I'm so sorry. I know you'll miss them."

"I will. But it's what's best for them right now, I think."

Neima nodded but she seemed distant now, as though her mind had gone running off on another trail.

"They gave me an old box of my father's things."

"Oh? Anything curious? Were you able to divine anything from it?"

The ribbon slid softly against her neck as Lona pulled the key out from under her blouse. She held it up in the light and Neima cocked her head to the side, studying it.

"It's certainly suggests potential. Your father really had a knack for secrets, it seems. I can feel the significance of this piece but—I can't see what it leads to—what it unlocks. I'm sure you'll find it."

"I hope so."

Lona dropped it back against her chest. She had grown used to its weight.

"Does the knowledge of your father's ability change anything for you?"

"It does. I mean, it does and it doesn't. I never really knew either of my parents so they've always seemed like mysterious—almost mythological—people to me. Learning about my mother, about her life as an artist, her friendship with Awesome's mother, I was so grateful. But, it almost feels like all that history just fell into my lap. Like an unexpected treasure. This stuff, everything that has to do with my father, it feels like I'm chasing something. It's as if I'm trying to find the treasure but I only have half the map and a few muddled clues."

"Your father was a detective. And now you're one too, Lona. You can do this.And whatever else you put your mind to."

At this moment, Neima paused and a knowing look came over her face and Lona wondered whether Neima's abilities had allowed her to see Lona's deeper knowledge of Andy's death and her determination to understand what had happened to him. But now Neima continued,

"I think Humphrey must have known that, even when you were a little girl. He must have seen that potential in you. And this is just his way of bringing it out."

"Oh Neima, it's so good to see you. I've missed you."

Neima leaned forward on the sofa and patted Lona's shoulder.

"I've missed you too, my girl. I'm sorry I've been so distant. I know you needed me."

"I did—and still do—but I want you to be healthy more than anything else, Neima. You're my mentor and you mean so much to me. I can't believe I'll never not need you."

Neima let out a short breath of laughter and she smiled.

"Can you stay much longer?"

"I need to be going in a few minutes. I'm just going to go down to the museum."

"Ah. Well, I have some soup going in the kitchen. I'll just check on it."

The way Neima moved hadn't changed. She rose from the sofa with weightless grace and her steps across the wood floor were soundless. She had an ethereal yet somehow earthy quality that Lona thought was almost out of place in the grit and noise of the city.

Lona listened as Neima opened a drawer in the kitchen and went through the silverware. Then, from the other side of the apartment, came another noise. Something had crashed against the floor.

With newfound instinct, Lona jumped to her feet. Alert, her heart thumping, she padded down the hall toward the apartment's two bedrooms. She stopped outside the door to Julia's bedroom. Green dust seeped out from under the door and shimmered in Lona's field of vision. She took a deep, silent breath but her mouth snapped shut as she heard footsteps creaking beyond the door then, the scrape of glass across the floor.

WOOSH-SLAM!

Lona threw the door open and dropped into a low stance, ready to take on whatever was there.

Julia screamed and dropped the pieces of glass she'd been picking off the floor. In her surprise, Lona also shrieked and Neima came bounding down the hall.

"What's happened?"

Baffled, Lona turned.

"I—I'm so sorry. I thought Julia was at work. I thought someone was breaking in."

She looked from Neima to Julia and found that they were staring at one another in surprise or dismay. Julia shook her head and stared down at the glass as Neima spoke.

"Julia wasn't feeling well today. She was going to stay home. I thought she was still asleep in bed."

"Yes. But, I couldn't sleep. So, I, uh, decided to go into work. I was just putting some lotion on when I knocked the perfume bottle into the floor. I didn't mean to scare you Lona, I didn't even know you were here."

Lona was already on her hands and knees, though, picking pale green glass out of a lavender scented pool.

"No, it's not your fault Julia. I've just been a little on edge lately. I shouldn't have gone through your house like some kind of…"

"Cape?"

Julia laughed and crossed her arms over the long, drapey shirt she was wearing. She grabbed a little metal wastebasket and helped Lona while Neima found them a towel. When they had collected all the glass and cleaned up the perfume, Julia sat back on the bed with a groan.

"We aren't normal people, are we?"

"Is anyone in Arc City normal anymore?"

They both laughed.

"I'm heading down to the museum, actually. I can walk you down."

Julia shook her head.

"That's ok. It'll take me a little while to finish getting ready."

"Alright. Maybe I'll see you there."

THE MUSEUM'S LECTURE hall was fairly small but, given the lecture's low attendance, it was more than serviceable. Lona took a seat in the back and pulled out the little notebook she had found in the box of her father's things.

After a few minutes waiting in silence, Charlie Moss, Professor of Thermodynamics and the Physics of Superhumans, from Arc City University, took the stage. He had made a career studying Capes and he had at least a hundred copies of "First in Flight: What We Can Learn From Extranormals" stacked into a pyramid on the table next to the lectern.

Moss, Lona thought, was probably in his fifties with gray in his hair and brown eyes behind wire-frame glasses. Taking a loaded, metal chalk holder from his vest pocket, he immediately began drawing diagrams on the blackboard behind him and a few people in the room took notes while others merely listened. He went into numbers so abstract that Lona realized, halfway through, she was frowning at the board and completely lost. At the end of the hour, the lecture broke up and a few people went up to the front to purchase his book or have him sign the copy they'd brought with them.

Lona waited until they were nearly all gone before she stepped up to the front of the room. By then, Professor Moss was packing the unsold books into a cardboard box. She grabbed one from the disheveled pile.

"Dr. Moss, I have a question."

"Oh, the book?"

He took a pen from the same vest pocket the chalk holder had come from and held his hand out for the book. She gave it to him and, as he was signing his name in blue ink, she fingered the flyer that had dripped dust only this morning. She hoped she was right. Her heart thumped.

"I wondered if you might look at something for me."

Moss handed the book back to her and she took it with one hand as she opened her little notebook and took out the small plastic baggie in which she had placed a cutting from Andy's damaged glove. She looked at the tiny, perfectly circular holes dotting the silver material as she placed it into Moss' palm.

Pushing his glasses higher on his nose, he held the material close to his face and then up to the light.

"Interesting."

"Do you know what might have caused that type of damage?"

"Hmm."

He retrieved a compact magnifying glass from his inside, jacket pocket and opened it up over the material.

"Professor?"

"You know, I've never seen this but—these holes—did they go straight through? Clean?"

"Yes."

Nodding in a meaningful way, he handed her the magnifying glass and she peered through it. Now, she saw the tiniest silver rim around the hole. It looked almost like mercury.

Lona Chang

"Do you know of any current superhuman who has the ability to do this, Professor?"

Taking the glass back, he snapped it shut and shook his head.

"I don't. But—I confess I don't keep a mental catalogue of every extranormal person. The few people that have allowed me to sample their blood have given me a lifetime of research but everyone is unique. Nearly all of my work is based on flight—I'm really not sure what this is—though, I must say, it does seem familiar."

Lona took the material back, slid it between the pages of her notebook and heaved a deep sigh.

"Twenty-four dollars, please. I'm sorry I couldn't be of more help. I do hope you find what you're looking for Miss—"

"Gold."

The name fell out of her mouth before she had time to think and, she had already turned to leave but, instead, went back to him, opening her notebook as she approached. She took the pen from behind her ear and wrote her number on a blank page, which she then tore out.

"Listen, if you think of anything—anything at all—would you mind calling me?"

He took the paper, folded it and slid it into his jacket pocket.

"If you like. Though, I'm afraid I'm leaving Arc City soon. I've accepted a research position in Edinburgh."

"Oh, congratulations."

"Thanks very much. Still, I'll keep your problem in mind, Miss Gold."

Lona nodded and wondered whether anything would actually come of the little slip of paper in Professor Moss' pocket. Whether he would ever think of "her problem" again. Still, she thanked him and tucked her notebook into her backpack and left.

WHEN AWESOME GOT home THAT NIGHT, exhausted and frustrated after his day training with Stargazer—jumping from box to box inside the Sheet Clinic training room—he found Lona sitting at the kitchen table with a mug of tea and her father's journal laying open and face down on the chair next to her. Instead, she was completely focused on the cover story of the newspaper.

Awesome sat at the table and read through the story. Photon was seen, with a group of men in black, pursuing a known super-powered criminal—Shadow Slider. He fought but was quickly taken into custody by Photon with the help of his men in black and Arc City's police force. Awesome read the hyperbolic write-up twice before setting the paper down and looking back at Lona.

"Not really satisfying, is it?"

She shook her head. He asked if she was hungry. When she nodded, he got up and took two plates from the cabinet before proceeding to make late-night grilled cheese sandwiches.

"It doesn't line up."

He buttered bread while Lona took out the block of cheese and a knife and continued her thought.

"I mean, Shadow Slider. When's the last time he was even active?"

Awesome thought back.

"Ten… fifteen years ago? At least."

"Exactly. He was basically retired. Why come out now?"

"They said he had a grudge against Captain Lightning but, aside from the fact that he just happened to be based in Arc City, I don't remember him having any particular predisposition for feuding with Andy."

"Right. I mean, even back in those days, Andy had more fights with Krysis than anyone else. And Krysis was extradited back to Russia like ten years ago."

The burner clicked until it caught fire and Awesome put the skillet onto the flame.

"And his powers... he could supposedly travel through shadows, right? And wasn't there something else?"

"Some kind of projectile from his hands, I think."

The room was quiet as they both weighed what they knew about this apparently-not-retired villain against what they had seen the night their best friend died. Lona, with a grimace, remembered the holes that had sliced through Andy's body. The way he shook and shivered. The way his body seemed to be trending toward entropy. Then, Lona explained her trip to the museum and what she had learned, and not learned, from Moss. Awesome frowned and slid the sandwiches onto the plates before cutting them in half with the spatula.

"We'll get there, Lona. We'll figure this out. You'll figure this out."

"I hope so, Jones."

THE AIR WAS moist but the heavy, gray clouds above refused to open up. Awesome and Stargazer stood together on the roof of the Tyson Building, looking out over the river. It rolled by in lazy, gray-blue waves. A ferry rode along, carrying commuters back to the suburbs that began a few miles from the opposite bank. Awesome watched it, thinking of Pop. His grandfather had worked in the city for years and took the ferry there and back again every day.

"Thinking about moving to the burbs, man?"

Awesome laughed.

"I grew up there. After my parents died, I lived with my grandparents."

"They still around?"

"My Pop is. What about you? Did you grow up here?"

"Yeah. The Marshes."

"Oh."

"Yeah."

Everyone knew The Marshes was the most dangerous neighborhood in Arc City—or it had been. Nearly every year, when the river swelled, The Marshes flooded and the tenement buildings that housed its residents were filled with water halfway up the first floor. Eventually, the city demolished the entire area and re-developed the land, putting in a sprawling public park at the foot of a new skyscraper. But, as far as Awesome knew, it was still called The Marshes.

"But we got out. My whole family got out—eventually."

Thunder sounded in the distance, a long, rolling rumble that gradually made its way across the land. They turned from the river to the city as if they might follow the sound with their eyes. Still, there was no rain.

"Listen, Baron, I've been hearing some rumors. That guy you helped bring down a couple months ago—Ironhide? He hasn't been transported to Claymore. Or Lobos. And, the thing is, about three weeks ago me and Nebula brought down Wildfire. We watched and waited while the police and the Suits came for pick-up. You remember this guy? He was a first-class ass. He broke out of Lobos a few years ago. He has that weird green fire that comes out of his hands."

"Oh yeah. He's the one that torched all those Under Arc guys when they broke a deal with him, right?"

"That's him. So he's a multiple offender, a deadly threat, and he's broken out of at least one Guild facility. That means he ought to be dealt with by a Guild Tribunal—just like Ironhide—and then sent to Claymore where he'd probably live out the rest of his life."

"But he hasn't shown up?"

"No."

"And he's not at Lobos?"

"Not as far as my sources can tell."

"So where was he taken?"

Stargazer shook his head and slid his hands into his pockets.

"I don't know, man. But it really doesn't sit right with me."

A *skid, slide, tap tap,* came up behind them and they both turned to find Opal coming toward them. Her uniform was covered in dirt and blood and her violet cape whipped around in the breeze.

"You telling him about the prison thing?"

"Yeah."

She directed her attention to Awesome.

"What do you think? Weird, right? I was talking to Nebula last night and he agreed."

"Nebula?"

"He used to be the Mist. Your Guild pals kicked him to the curb."

The Mist. The name sounded familiar and then Awesome remembered why. When he was staying at the Guild Hall, Roy had told him about how the Mist's nemesis found out about the hero's girlfriend and brutally murdered her.

"I've heard—"

Opal put her hands on her hips and smirked at him.

"Was it the dishwasher or the fridge?"

"What?"

"They've been passing around horror stories about what can happen to your families at the Guild for *literally* hundreds of years. The Mist's girlfriend didn't get murdered. She works in our reception office. The chick with dreads—Dispatch. And, she's his wife now."

"So what happened?"

"Well, Rat Fink *did* find out about the Mist's girlfriend. And he *did* capture her, threaten her, and he *did* hold a gun to her head when the Mist caught up with him. And that was enough for the Mist—Nebula now. You know how his power works, right? Anyway, he took out Rat Fink right then and there. Went in the next morning and handed in his Cape."

"But he didn't leave Arc City?"

"No way. That guy was born and raised here. So was Dispatch. So they weren't going anywhere. They've been Sheets for like ten years."

"So—if she's a Sheet, she has some kind of ability, right? And, if they've been around for ten years, if they've been serving in Arc City all this time, why doesn't anyone know about them. About any of you—us—I mean."

"Well, Dispatch is fantastic, first of all. She might not have magic powers but, just because she's a regular person, that doesn't mean she can't serve. And anyway, she was a fighter pilot before she became a Sheet."

Stargazer stepped up to answer Awesome's other question.

"As far as the mystery of us goes, you never hear about us because the Guild runs the papers, the comics, and the news. Not technically, right? But, unofficially, they control the flow of information. With the exception of you, Sheets don't get coverage and that's fine with us."

"But I get coverage because…" it dawned on him even as he said the words, "because I'm the Baron."

Opal laughed.

"Right. But your coverage pretty much disappeared after Lightning died, right? It was all about Photon after that."

"Yeah."

Awesome thought about Andy and wondered if he had stayed Pythia's hand when it came to keeping him out of the news. And, if that was so, what else might Andy have kept the Guild from doing where he was concerned.

"The Guild can't have people in the streets begging for a hero they can't control, man. But you're the Baron. Arc City wants you and they need you. The Baron is still a powerful image for these people."

Thunder rumbled again and, this time, the clouds broke apart and drops of rain came at them sideways. Stargazer slapped his palms together and blue sparks flew off and sizzled in the newly formed rooftop puddles. He smiled at Awesome.

"Let's go, Baron. Time to see you how do in the rain."

He turned north and ran the length of the building before leaping down to the next roof. Opal laughed as he went. Awesome gulped. He would have to take the fire escape until at least the second floor.

"Just stay focused, Baron. Stargazer will get you there. I've got to follow up on something else but I'll see you around. There's some chatter about the White Wolves hitting another string of stores last night."

He nodded and watched as she went the opposite way.

Finally, he took off after Stargazer, the rain slapping him as he ran. He could run faster, jump higher, and land harder but so far it hadn't mattered. Whenever Awesome came to the edge, he couldn't take the leap.

THE GRANITE ARCHWAYS overhead seemed to shake with the rumble of thunder and Lona listened as rain finally tapped against the windows of the library. She wondered about Awesome and whether he was spending the day on Arc City's rooftops. She hoped he was alright.

"How's it going?"

Pulling a strand of brown hair behind her ear, Jolie looked over Lona's shoulder at a book that detailed the history of Arc City. Lona had a list of the Grayston possibilities.

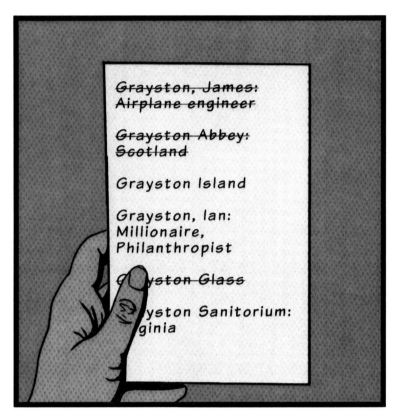

Lona leaned back and stretched her arms over her head. The day had been warm and muggy and Lona wondered what the summer would hold. Their life felt so off-kilter. So unpredictable.

She reached out and snapped the book shut then walked around the table to the window. The third floor of the library provided a lovely view of Arc City's Old Town. Gray and brown stone architecture swept up and down in diagonal lines and contrasted sharply with the buildings' perfect, half-circle arches. Cylindrical towers reached for the sky and Lona was reminded of the wonder she'd felt as a girl in Old Town. She started speaking, almost to herself.

> "When I was little, my parents would take me on walks through this part of town, down to the Terrace Gardens Park. I grew up

over on Chestnut. I loved this part of town. I used to imagine that princes and princesses lived here—wizards. I remember looking up at the towers, through the trees—they were pink, apple blossoms—and I remember looking through those flowers and imagining the elegant things going on behind the stone walls."

Now, rain battered the gray stone and sloshed into the street where papers blew about the road. She didn't see any families—any children. The trees wore wet, green leaves; their pink blossoms had already fallen and Lona had missed it.

"It's hard to imagine it now."

Jolie leaned against the wall next to the window. She looked out as well and her breath fogged the glass.

"It'll get better. Didn't you see the paper? They caught Captain Lightning's killer."

Lona frowned at the rain as Jolie continued.

"And…the Baron's back. At least, there are rumors that he's back. Just when we need him."

The rain was still pounding when Lona left the library. She raised Awesome's black umbrella over her head and whisked down the slick stairs. As she approached the street, a car splashed by, sending a wave of rainwater onto the sidewalk. Lona took a step back and turned away just in time to avoid the spray and, in doing so, her gaze turned to the statue of Henry Richardson, the library's founder.

Plastered upon his pedestal was a poster like the one she had seen in the warehouse district.

The poster was peeling away from the pedestal and, as Lona stared at it, she saw gold dust dripping like molten metal from behind it. She squinted and pulled at the poster until it fell, waterlogged, into her hands. Beneath it was a plaque, which said,

> Henry Richardson, founder of five free, public libraries in and around Arc City. This monument is erected in honor of his friend and mentor, Ian Grayston, who gave his time and resources to helping those less fortunate—it is Mr. Richardson's

hope that this building will stand with those of Mr. Grayston's as one of Arc City's greatest, and most beautiful public works.

"Buildings?"

The word seemed to glow. She put the pieces together. Grayston was a philanthropist. He must have donated buildings to Arc City.

She checked her watch then ran around the corner and jumped in the truck. In a few minutes, she arrived in front of the Arc City Courthouse. She was reminded of the last time she stood at the base of these stone steps and glanced across the street to the bank. She remembered the steely-haired woman—the Alchemist— and her wry smile as she held her wrists forward so Andy could snap the cuffs on. Sighing, Lona turned and jogged up the steps and into the courthouse.

She click-clacked down the hallway—no longer marble. The flooring had been replaced with cool cement. Lona stopped for a moment to view the space where the mural had been. Now, only pieces of it remained. A corner of the Baron's top hat. A sliver of Silver Siren's glossy hair. The blue boot toe of The Arc City Avenger. The pieces of painted plaster had been swept away and not replaced and Lona bit her bottom lip as she examined the pockmarked wall.

Finally, after turning a few corners and wandering down a couple hallways, Lona found her way into the public records office. An older man stood behind the counter, hunched over a newspaper. Photon's face was plastered on the discarded front page and the man was doing the crossword puzzle. As Lona approached, he set down his pen.

"What can I help you with, ma'am?"

Smiling at the man, Lona took out her little notebook, opening it to the front-most, blank page.

"I'm looking for information about a building—or buildings—

commissioned by a philanthropist. I'm not sure how long ago. His name was Ian Grayston."

"Well, that's just shameful."

Color rushed to Lona's cheeks.

"I'm sorry?"

"Don't they teach that stuff in school anymore? How old are you anyway? Don't look much older than my granddaughter. Time was, you wouldn't have to wander into a courthouse to find this stuff out. You'd just know it."

"Oh. Well, I only just found out about him. I was at the library in Old Town and saw the plaque. I was just curious."

"You know what they say about curiosity, don't you?"

Lona glanced down at the paper and then back up at the man.

"That it makes people good at crosswords?"

Laughing, the man finally cracked.

"Alright, you work on nine down and I'll go get the addresses."

"How many are there?"

"There used to be thirteen—just in Arc City—now it's only the four."

The man walked away as Lona read the clue. She looked over the adjoining words before picking up his pen.

"What happened to the others?"

He shouted his answer from the back room where he was opening and closing filing cabinets. The sound of the paper slipping in and out of folders and then in and out of drawers reminded her of Akai Printing Company and of Awesome Jones.

"What do you think? This is Arc City and those buildings were a hundred years old. It was only a matter of time before they came down in one of those super fights. I've worked in this courthouse thirty-three years and it's almost come down twice in that time."

He sighed and pottered back into the front room with a sheet of paper and pencil.

"Here they are. Names and addresses. This one here's pretty far out. And this one's not a library anymore. It's a fancy restaurant no one can afford. The architecture's still standing though—such as it is."

Lona took the paper and slid it into her notebook.

"Thank you. I really appreciate it."

"Did you figure out nine down?"

"Yep."

She turned and walked away as he read the clue once more, "sticky-footed eye, 7" and then at her neat handwriting, "gumshoe."

THE RAIN WAS still pouring the next morning.

Steam rose from the ham and potato fritata, cut into slices and plated with fresh cherry tomatoes. Lona poured two cups of coffee as Awesome refilled Tulie's food and water bowls. The rain had beat like a thousand drums against their roof and windows all night and seemed even more tenacious as the morning wore on. Inside, things were quiet.

"Are you going to go looking for these today?"

Lona nodded into her coffee steam and held the cup close to her mouth.

"I'll go with you."

"You don't have to. You need to train. I can just take Tulie."

Tulie wagged her tail at the mention of her name though, whenever she heard the peal of thunder, she whined. She'd been doing this since the night Andy died.

"Lona, whatever Andy was into—it was dangerous. Whoever or whatever Grayston is—they killed him over it. Please just let me come with you."

Lona nodded and it occurred to her then that they hadn't spent a whole day together in a few weeks. She liked the idea of driving around in the rain with Awesome.

"Alright. I'll pack a lunch."

The truck rumbled to life in their driveway and Awesome flicked on the windshield wipers. Lona sat on the passenger side, her legs curled up on the bench seat, and looked at the list.

"I can't imagine what Andy had to do with this restaurant but it's the closest one so we might as well check it out first."

Awesome put the truck in gear and, about fifteen minutes later, they were rolling to a stop in front of what had once been the Grayston Public Museum. The granite, single story building was domed and featured tall, arched windows. A spindly, modern sign, which read, *Paradiso*, hung from the stone portico. Awesome and Lona got out of the truck and walked up to the restaurant door. As they did, a man came out with a heavy lock and chain.

"Sorry, folks. You just missed us. We closed down last night."

"For good?"

"So it seems."

"Why?"

"It's been too slow. This is a four star establishment and the four star clientele don't live here anymore."

"I'm so sorry, how long were you in business?"

"Five excellent years. Oh well, I've got an offer to open a new place in Sea City."

"I hope it works out."

"Thanks very much, miss."

He snapped the lock in place and jiggled the door then put up his umbrella and tromped down the stairs. Awesome and Lona peered into the restaurant and saw only bare tables with their chairs stacked on top. They returned to the truck and crossed the restaurant off the list.

Half an hour later, they came to the next building, which appeared much the same as the restaurant. Rain pounded the stone and Lona watched from the truck window as a few people came and went from the Arc City Free Clinic. They went inside only to find a harried nurse in scrubs tending to new patients while another escorted people into exam rooms. They turned to leave as one of the nurses stopped to address Lona.

"Can I help you?"

"I'm, uh, looking for my uncle. I think he was admitted here this morning. Herbert Gold?"

Lona watched as the nurse ran down the list of names, came to the end, flipped back to the front, and then ran over them again.

"I'm sorry. It doesn't look like we've taken anyone by that name. Are you sure he was here and not The Marshes Clinic or New Haven?"

"Oh, you know, you're probably right. It's probably The Marshes. I just assumed he was here."

"I can call them for you, if you want."

But, Lona was already turning for the door.

"Thanks, I'll just head down there."

When they were back in the truck, Lona made a note beside the clinic's address. Awesome ran a hand through his wet hair and smiled at her.

"Your uncle?"

"Yeah. Kraker always has an elderly uncle in trouble."

"Herbert Gold?"

"Yeah. Uncle Herbert's always got something going on."

She grinned at him and they shared a laugh together. And, in their laughter, they both realized that it seemed a long-lost sound to them. Lona leaned toward Awesome and kissed him.

"Thanks for coming with me."

"Thanks for letting me."

He put the truck in gear as she read the next address to him.

"This one's out of city limits but I figure we should get to it first and then we'll probably be making our way back as the city traffic is dying down."

"You got it."

As they drove, Awesome told Lona about his training with Stargazer. About his inability to make the jumps and his frustration.

"But it's always like this. I mean, when you were working with Ben, it took a long time before your strength clicked into place. I know it's hard but I think you just have to be patient and keep practicing."

They drove southeast, along the river. Lona watched out the window as she ate grapes from a plastic container, occasionally handing one or two to Awesome. The river, now gray-brown with runoff, was surging against the banks. Eventually, they crossed it via the high, green suspension bridge everyone in town called Green Gate. Lona had always thought of it as the way into Arc City. Now she wondered whether it was considered the way out.

A few minutes later, they were driving through rolling, green countryside. On all other sides, Arc City was surrounded by suburbs or factories but, for some reason, the southeast side was home only to a lake, rolling hills, and a few old farm houses.

Lona took their map out of the glove box and ran a finger down the line that marked their current route.

"It's the next right but it looks like about fifteen miles."

Several minutes later, they turned down a gravel, treelined road and went on for what seemed an eternity.

"Are you sure this is the right road?"

"Well, I think so."

She breathed deep and focused on the address and then on the map. She willed the dust to appear but just as she thought she might have felt something, she realized Awesome was speaking.

"What?"

"There it is. I mean, that must be it, right?"

Behind an old, chain-link fence, and across a long, green field, Lona could see the sprawling structure. Just like the two they had visited that morning, this one was built of solid rock. But, instead of a Romanesque style, this one, situated in a meadow and sporting both a tower and a turret as well as a tall, stone archway before the entrance, looked more like an old castle than a modern, mini-pantheon. But, if it was a castle, it seemed dilapidated and disused.

"This is the oldest one Grayston built."

"What was it?"

"It was some kind of public building for the people out here in the country."

"What people? There's no one out here."

Peering through the truck windshield, Lona stared at the old building, the overgrown meadow. There were shingles absent from the roof and missing stones from the exterior.

"I don't know. It looks like this place has been closed up for a long time."

Thunder cracked overhead and released a new torrent of rain. It crashed onto the truck's metal roof.

"I'm worried this road is going to wash out. Let's go."

They backed slowly down the drive and Lona watched as the Grayston building disappeared behind the trees. With only the sound of the rain to fill their ears, they rolled down the highway, back toward the city. They met the river again and, after a while, came to a pull-off on the side of the road. They stopped and parked. A man in a rain slicker was packing up his folding chair and tackle box, his fishing plans apparently canceled. His dog, a soaked golden retriever, slunk back to an old station wagon alongside his owner. Awesome watched them while Lona took their sandwiches and chips and cans of soda out of the lunch basket.

"I've been here before. Pop used to come here to fish. Sometimes, in the summer, I'd come with him."

"Did he have friends out here?"

"A few other fishermen. Even then, though, not too many folks lived here. Some farmers, I think. But he came here for the quiet. He used to say it was the closest place to the city to get a little peace. I think he and my grandmother used to come out here on picnics before they got married."

He took a bite of his sandwich then looked down thoughtfully at the delicate silver ring on Lona's finger and sighed.

"I wish it had worked out that day."

"It'll work out. It'll be perfect."

But they were both unnerved by how much their lives had changed since the day they had tried to get married. They both thought of Andy and missed him and wished he could be there.

Eventually, they pulled out of the little parking lot and, as the rain cleared up, they drove back to the city. The final building was in Willow Heights, the southernmost neighborhood in Arc City, and it would be on their way home. The truck rolled on the road, wavelike, up and down through the hills, until they came to the address.

Kitschy new restaurants and thrift stores were nestled next to butcher shops and old bars and, at the top of the hill, was the Grayston building.

"What is it?"

"I don't know."

They parked across the street and walked up to its entryway. This building was slightly smaller than the others but it was still clearly in line with the Grayston style of architecture. An old bronze sign stood in the building's barely tended yard and said, "Willow Heights Community Center."

But, as Lona approached, she found another sign hung on the door, which read, "Closed For Renovations." The sign was rather weathered and faded. Lona walked over to the windows and tried to look inside but long, white curtains hung there and completely obstructed her view. She stood in the wet grass with her arms crossed for a while, thinking, again trying to focus, trying to will her ability to surface. Then, she found that she was whispering to herself.

"Come on, dad. Show me how to see the secrets."

She closed her eyes and breathed but, as she began to settle in, she heard a lovely, lilting music. She opened her eyes and turned to the sound. A woman, her hair wrapped in a bright, saffron scarf, was pushing a stroller and singing an old, familiar tune. Lona caught a couple of the words, *little shepherdess, your flock tended long…*

Lona blinked as tiny sparkles of dust tumbled out of the woman's lips and flickered into nothingness.Lona called out to her, interrupting the song.

"Excuse me, miss. Do you live around here?"

The woman stopped and sized up Lona. It was daylight yet, but Lona realized that Arc City wasn't really the kind of place where one just went around taking to strangers—or neighbors—anymore. She changed tack and took Awesome by the arm and smiled as she approached the woman in as genial a fashion as she could muster.

"My fiancé and I have been looking for a pretty place for the wedding and I heard about this old building. I was just wondering when it might be open again."

The woman's mouth broke into a relieved smile and she stood and pushed the stroller back and forth as she spoke.

"I really couldn't say. I'm sorry."

"Do you know how long it's been closed?"

"Well, I moved here about five years ago and it's been closed the whole time."

Lona sighed and stared down at the chippy sidewalk. The baby cooed and hiccupped and the mother knelt into the stroller and hummed a bit more of the song before rising up and speaking again.

"Actually, I remember asking about it myself, when I first got here. Miss Solarte said they'd already been closed for some years. Something about a leak."

Lona thanked the woman and listened to her gentle voice trail away as she glared at the building with her arms crossed.

"Must be some leak."

Finally, they trudged back to the truck and started it up. Lona let her head fall back against the passenger seat and wondered whether they'd actually made any headway or if she and Awesome had just spent the entire day chasing nothing. She resolved to take some time to think and let it all sink in.

"Let's go home and get something warm to drink."

"You sure?"

"Yeah, we're not going to figure this out in one day."

They drove back to their neighborhood as a cool, gray fog rolled into the hills and settled over Arc City.

THE HEAT FROM the oven reddened Lona's cheeks as she wrapped her mitted hands around the handle of her cast iron skillet and pulled a steaming apple cobbler from within. She was just putting it on the counter as a knock came at the door and she listened as Awesome moved through the house to greet whoever it might be.

"Oh, Roy. What's going on?"

Roy followed Awesome into the kitchen and Lona turned to smile at him. He was wearing street clothes this time but, instead of his old, ragged t-shirt and jeans, Roy was wearing a button up shirt, with the sleeves rolled up to his elbows, and dark gray trousers. Lona couldn't help but squint at him when he walked in but she managed to recover.

"Hey, Lona. Good to see you. I said I'd come by more, right?"

Lona nodded and pulled her oven mitts off.

"You're just in time, Roy. I made apple cobbler and there's quite enough."

Roy waved his hand at her in a very grown up fashion.

"Oh, I couldn't. I ate too much at the Hall, I think. Anyway, I came by to extend an invitation to you."

"Oh?"

"Yeah," And, for a moment, Roy beamed with excitement, "Pythia wants to see you."

"When?"

"At once."

"What, now?"

"Yes."

"Why?"

"I don't know, but Sharmila made it sound urgent."

Lona crossed her arms in front of her chest and she felt her face heat up again.

"Are they arresting him?"

"No."

"But—"

"Roy, I don't think—"

"Look, Awesome, I'm pretty sure Pythia wants to bring you back into the fold."

Awesome and Lona exchanged a suspicious glance but, in the end, they acquiesced. It wasn't like the Guild to do things in an underhanded fashion. If they were going to arrest Awesome, they would do it in an official capacity, not by tricking him into paying them a visit.

Lona double checked the oven and covered the fresh cobbler with a dishtowel before following Roy out to the Guild-issued black sedan.

They pulled away and Awesome was reminded of the night he, Lona and Sharmila rode to the cabin in a car driven by the Supersonic

Sleuth. It seemed like a lifetime ago. Now, as before, they made awkward conversation. How were they? How was he? How was life at the Guild Hall? Did they find that they enjoyed dog ownership as much as they'd hoped?

It wasn't until he asked about Julia that some real sense of emotion broke through Roy's veneer. Lona explained that she was still recovering and asked why he didn't go see her himself.

"I can't. I mean, you know we can't... have that kind of relationship."

Lona sighed and watched as Roy absentmindedly raked his fingers through his dark hair. Though it had been slicked back, some of it now escaped whatever product had been securing it, and a few strands fell onto his forehead. He stared out the window.

"Are you off for the night?"

He seemed to snap back to reality and sat up straighter.

"No. I'm going on call in an hour. A couple other Agents are in Arc City right now and they took care of things for me this afternoon. Pisces came in for some new gear and Supersonic Sleuth had to get his mask replaced—again."

They drove through Old Town and Lona watched the old, stone buildings pass by. Newly washed with rain, they were cleaner now, but still stood like cemetery statues, watching over Arc City's citizenry.

Sharmila greeted them briskly in the foyer of the Guild Hall and pinned visitor badges to Lona and Awesome's shirts. As they entered the elevator, Awesome remembered the nervous excitement he had felt the first time he stood in this builting. Anxiety still crept in on him now, but it was accompanied by the same ready vigilance he had when he went on patrol in Arc City's most dangerous neighborhoods.

Roy hit the button for the twelfth floor and Awesome actually managed a smile.

"Finally said goodbye to the tenth floor?"

A surprised burst of laughter escaped Roy's mouth and he grinned back at Awesome.

"Oh yeah. Floor twelve is where it's at."

They shared a chuckle until the elevator glided to a stop at the sixth floor. Sharmila strode out and held the door for Awesome and Lona as they said goodbye to Roy.

"Be careful out there, Roy."

Their old friend nodded back to them.

"You too, Awesome. Night, Lona."

"Goodnight, Roy. Come by again. For more than just a pickup. Ok?"

"Ok."

The elevator doors slid to a close and Awesome took Lona's hand as they followed Sharmila into the command center. The three-leveled room was bustling and full of suited workers who buzzed about, making notes, phone calls, orders, and no conversation. Awesome glanced at the monitors and saw the same views of Arc City he had seen before.

Old Town, The Marshes, New Haven, The Towers, Haywood. On and on. But, Awesome noticed several monitors in the Arc City section were also blacked out. He viewed a bank of other monitors and saw glimpses of Cape Town, London, New Kyoto, and Paris as they climbed the stairs to Pythia's office.

PYTHIA SEEMED COMPLETELY unchanged. Her pale blue eyes were in stunning contrast with her smooth, earthy brown skin. Tapping her long, emerald green nails against the hardwood of her desk, she watched Awesome and Lona quietly enter the room.

Neither Awesome nor Lona had seen Pythia since they had been sent away in the dead of night to take refuge in the cabin. When Awesome was dismissed from the Guild, it had been Sharmila who met him in a nondescript meeting room on the fifth floor and had him sign the paperwork that meant he was officially and immediately excommunicated from their organization. Sharmila remained in the office now. She stood in the corner behind Awesome's left shoulder.

Pythia leaned back in her plush chair and pursed her lips, readying her words. Finally, she spoke.

"Awesome Jones."

"Yes, ma'am."

"And Lona Chang. Or, should I say, Lona Langdon?"

"Chang is fine, thank you."

"Or would you prefer Jones? I hear a wedding is in order."

It unnerved Lona to hear the personal, technical details of her life said in this room, by this woman, who uttered the syllables of Lona's past and future names with a casual, almost uninterested air. She felt her teeth set. What were they in for?

"Yes, ma'am. As soon we can find the time."

"Ah yes. The time."

Was time even a consideration for this woman, Awesome wondered. She seemed to exist outside of time, outside of reality. She observed him the way a human might observe a dandelion. She saw him. She even spoke to him. And yet, he wondered whether she truly acknowledged his worth.

"I'm sure you've had no time to spare with all of your *activities*. Your assistance in the capture of the Alchemist was, according to the late Mr. Archer, nothing short of excellent. Still—what you are doing now, on your own—"

Awesome cleared his throat.

"It's not a crime to help people."

"No, Mr. Jones, it is not. And yet, it *is* dangerous."

A strange feeling crept over Lona. It seemed that an iridescent dust glimmered just at her periphery. Her breath was short. Suddenly, the image of Andy, lying dead in Awesome's arms, snapped into her mind's eye. Her heart raced and Pythia went on in her eerily beautiful voice.

"Mr. Archer would have attested to that—the danger."

Lona let her hand fall between their seats and Awesome took it and gave it a squeeze.

"What's this all about? Why have you brought us here?"

Swirling, spinning, suddenly rushing, the dust exploded in Lona's vision as the memory of Andy's voice rang in her ears. In an instinctive panic, she shut it out. The sight of Andy, the words he had spoken, and everything she had considered since then, was closed. She imagined reaching for the knob of an old door and then she imagined heaving it shut.

something else. something else. think of something else.

Lona thought of the apple cobbler. She thought of the smell that had wafted through the house. She thought of slicing the apples, the sound of blade through apple flesh and onto the board, the sound of the bottle of cinnamon as she twisted off the cap—metal against glass. She thought of the heat that rose onto her face and permeated her mitts. She looked up now.

Pythia had stopped drumming her nails and was stretching out her fingers, laying them flat against the cool wood.

"Mr. Jones, I thought very highly of your parents. Their passing left a gap, which Mr. Archer luckily filled. And his unfortunate passing has left a new gap. Your friend, Roy, is doing his best, I believe. But it may not be enough."

"He brought in Andy's killer though, right?"

Pythia hesitated then and squinted at him through long lashes. She knitted her fingers together.

"Yes."

"What will happen to him?"

"To whom?"

"To Shadow Slider. What will happen to Andy's killer?"

Her gaze drifted from Awesome to Lona. Perhaps studying two similar but distinct dandelion specimens.

"He will be sent to Claymore."

"After a trial?"

"Yes, of course. A trial by his peers."

"His peers."

"Us, Mr. Jones. His elite peers."

"In a tribunal?"

"Of sorts."

Now Awesome studied Pythia. Still, her skin was smooth and not at all careworn. Still, she seemed ageless. Both smooth as silk and hard as steel, Pythia seemed not to follow the rules of the world in which Awesome lived.

And yet, beneath her stillness, beneath the ethereal calm, Awesome could sense that she was unnerved. But why should she be unnerved?

"I ask again, why have you called us here?"

"It is my opinion that you were dismissed in haste. I am offering you a return to the Guild. You *and* your betrothed. I understand you are both in possession of unique abilities and could be of service to the Guild. You, Mr. Jones, would receive full Agent status and Ms. Chang would no doubt be of use within one of our operations departments."

"You want us to come and work for you?"

Lona became keenly aware of the tension in Awesome's hand. She watched as Pythia leaned forward and pursed her lips again.

"We want you to be a part of this organization. As your parents were before you. We will accept your relationship as we accepted theirs."

"And the Echo?"

"We are willing to overlook his death as a matter of self-defense."

The dust shook and spun, erratic as if it were whipped by the wind. The door in Lona's mind shuddered. She thought of the Echo. Of his massive body lying breathless and bloodless upon the wet earth. She felt sick. She tugged at Awesome's hand.

"We'll think about it."

"You will—what?"

"We'll consider your offer. Now, we must leave. I'm afraid we have to get back to our *activities*."

IT WAS AFTER dark when the Guild car rolled to a halt in front of their little house. Awesome stared at his house from the street. The lights inside were off, with the exception of a small light in the kitchen, which Lona always left on. The light, emitted by a little bulb over the stove, created a gentle, amber glow in the kitchen window. It was beautiful, Awesome thought. A place of peace in the chaos of Arc City.

He and Lona had remained silent on their way out of the Guild Hall and had only spent their words on polite conversation with the Guild driver up front. Their fingers were woven together in the backseat and no mention of Pythia's offer was made. Awesome had suspicions when it came to Pythia's motives and he was sure Lona must feel the same. He couldn't wait to get inside—to the privacy and comfort of their little kitchen—so they could speak freely.

The Guild sedan rolled away and, hand-in-hand, Lona and Awesome walked up the path toward the house, both focusing on the peaceful glow from their kitchen. Then, just as they approached the front door, a shadow passed behind their sheer, kitchen curtains. Lona started. They both dropped back, off the path, and looked at each other.

Awesome gave Lona a look as if to say, "Who could it be?"

Lona answered with an anxious shrug.

From within, they heard the shuffling of glass. Was someone going through their cabinets? Had someone broken in?

Awesome motioned for her to stay there as he bounded around the side of the house, over their patio fence, and toward the sliding, glass door. The door was still open a crack and, within, he heard laughter and then Tulie's bark. He slid the door open with a woosh and found a woman with white blonde hair, pulled into a low ponytail, sitting at the table, eating a plateful of Lona's apple cobbler.

"Baron?"

And then he recognized her voice, and the white cane propped against the wall.

"Opal?"

Just then, Lona came in from the patio.

"Opal? What's going on?"

"Can we talk?"

Lona closed the door behind her and looked toward the living room when she heard a noise.

"It's just my kid. He's asleep. I hope you don't mind, I covered him up with your quilt."

Lona leaned into the living room and saw a little boy, about eight or nine years old, sound asleep on their sofa. His cheeks were red and his pale hair was plastered to his face with sweat.

"No, of course it's fine. Is everything ok? Can I get you anything?"

It was odd to see Opal in real life—just a regular person in a loose, gray t-shirt, jeans and tennis shoes. Behind her mask, her strange eyes had almost seemed to be part of her uniform but, in harmony with her fair skin and white hair, they were miraculous. She scraped the last crumbs of apple cobbler off her plate and shook her head.

"Can I have something to drink? I'm sorry, I was starving. I went over to Dave's and then I had to pick my kid up early and I needed to talk to someone but I didn't want to leave him at home and I don't ever take him to the Sheet Clinic."

Lona poured her a tall glass of milk and then poured one for herself and Awesome as well.

"Dave?"

Opal took a long drink and wiped her mouth. When she was finished she sighed.

"David Estos. He was the Shadow Slider."

"Captain Lightning—"

"Yeah. The thing is…he's been retired for over a decade. *Really* retired. His rap sheet wasn't even too awful to begin with. His ability made him a good burglar and he fell in with a pretty bad crowd—pulling riskier, more high-profile jobs. Lightning took him in and he served five years in a shadowless cell in Claymore and got out on good behavior. But, you know how it is, former super-felons can't get any work when they get out. He was broke. He had a daughter to take care of. Her mom was killed when Tower Bridge collapsed during that fight between Marvellous Man and Commander Clay a few years ago. So he was all she had. Anyway, he's been my CI for the last four years."

"He was informing?"

"Yeah. The group he'd fallen in with back in the old days would come around asking him to help them with a robbery or he'd hear stuff through the grapevine or down in The Marshes when he'd go see his old friends. Anyway, I'd visit him a few times a month and I paid him for the information and it helped keep his daughter up.

The last time I saw him was about two weeks ago. Everything seemed the same as always. His daughter had just moved into her own apartment, he'd bought her a nice new sofa, he said, and she was going to start at Arc City U in the summer to pick up some extra credits. He didn't seem any different than usual.

But then I heard about how he supposedly killed Captain Lightning. It didn't feel right but, I figured, anything's possible. Still, I went by his apartment. Everything was gone. *Everything.* The place was *clean.* Like no one had ever lived there."

"The Guild took it all?"

"I guess. But that's not the weird part. I was worried about Cassie—his daughter—because she has this condition. It's manageable but her medicine is expensive and Dave always paid for it. I wanted to make sure she was going to be alright so I went over to her apartment and *her* place was clean. I mean, there was nothing there. It's like someone came by, in the middle of the night, and took every fork and spoon and bra and shoe and *everything.*"

"And you think it was the Guild?"

Opal nodded and turned toward the living room where her son was coughing. She stood and Lona poured a glass of water and pressed it into her hand. Awesome and Lona looked at each other in silence while Opal was out of the room. They heard her offer her son the cup and listened as he wheezed and grumbled. They heard her voice, fairy-like, quietly soothing while the boy tossed and turned and then settled down.

"Get some sleep, kiddo."

Tulie had followed Opal into the living room and then stayed there, lying on the carpet, watching the sleeping boy. When Opal returned, the glass was empty and she sighed.

"Is he alright?"

"Yeah, he'll be fine. It's just a thing going around at his school. I'm going to take him down to the free clinic tomorrow but I couldn't go out on duty tonight. I'm sorry I had to bring him along."

"No, it's fine. Don't worry about it."

She nodded and sat back down.

"Anyway, yes, I think it was the Guild. I mean, they arrested Dave publicly and made a big deal about it. I guess I get why they'd clean out his whole place for evidence. But why Cassie? It just doesn't track. And you know these people better than anyone—you knew Captain Lightning better than anyone. That's why I came to you. Because, I had to know—does it make sense to you?"

Awesome shook his head. He frowned at the tile floor as he thought about it.

"They are acting strangely," he paused for a moment and cleared his throat. "Lona and I were just invited to come back."

"What? When?"

"Tonight. That's where we were when you broke into our kitchen."

"Ok, yes, I *did* technically break in. But look, I can't drive so I had to take a taxi down here and I didn't want Danny to have to sit outside in the wet. And I didn't steal anything...except this cobbler, which—by the way—is delicious."

She gave Awesome her familiar half-smile, half-smirk and, for a minute, he was reminded of Andy. Of the easy way he scoffed at the rules he didn't buy into, the way he put justice first, the way he cared more about the people of this city than anything else.

"So what did they say? Why are they letting you back in?"

Lona sat at the table across from her.

"They said they had been too hasty to dismiss him. And they said they were willing to overlook both our relationship and the Echo's death. But, it's just like all this stuff. It doesn't feel right. The whole time we were there, I felt like...I felt like someone was inside my mind, trying to look around. I shut them out but I get the feeling that at least part of our visit there was so Pythia could find out what we knew about Captain Lightning's death."

"But they supposedly have their guy."

Opal shook her head.

"Unless he's not their guy."

"Do you think they know he might be innocent?"

"Do you think they care?"

And then, another idea dawned on them, all at once. The thought of a man who had already paid his debts—a man who had been working with the Sheets and keeping his nose clean and taking care of his daughter—arrested publicly but perhaps wrongly.

"What if an innocent man is about to pay for the death of Captain Lightning?"

THAT NIGHT, OPAL and her son stayed in the living room of Awesome Jones and Lona Chang. While Opal's son slept peacefully on their sofa, Lona took an extra pillow and blanket from the linen closet and gave them to Opal who had curled up in their armchair.

Lona stood in the entryway and watched Opal's body move with her breath as she slept. Whenever Danny woke coughing, she said, "It's alright, baby. It's alright," through her dreams and he would drop off again.

Awesome and Lona quietly cleaned up in the kitchen and shared a saucer of cold cobbler. Finally, they switched off the lights and went to bed, leaving Tulie in the living room to watch over their guests.

In the morning, after Awesome left to train with Stargazer, Lona made french toast and poured coffee for Opal and honeyed tea for Danny. She sat at the table and watched the pair eat and drink.

"What's your dog's name?" the boy asked.

"Tulie."

"She slept next to me last night. She's a good dog."

Lona smiled and scratched behind Tulie's ears while the dog yawned, apparently having stayed up all night.

"I know. She's a really good dog."

He coughed into his sticky fist.

"You sure you don't mind to drive us down to the clinic?" Opal asked, as she finished her coffee.

"Absolutely. I'm going out anyway and you shouldn't have to pay for a cab."

Opal nodded and smoothed her pale hair into a low ponytail before directing her attention to Danny.

"Say thank you to Lona."

"Thank you, Lona. Can Tulie come with us?"

Lona looked down at Tulie.

"I think she's going to stay home and take a nap."

"Can I come back and play with her sometime?"

"Oh, Danny. He's desperate for a dog," Opal said, as she ran her hand over Danny's hair.

Lona shrugged as she took their dishes to the sink.

"Sure thing. Anytime you want. Just call first and I'll make extra dessert."

Danny patted his lap and Tulie instantly scooted over to him and licked at his fingers.

A while later, Lona was driving through New Haven toward the free clinic she didn't even know existed until recently, guided by a blind woman and her sick son.

"Do you guys live around here?"

Danny nodded and Lona heard a few high-pitched clicks from Opal as they turned a corner.

"We live in the Maple Leaf Towers. The turn is just up here. Tell her what the clinic looks like, Danny."

"It's a brown building with gray steps. And there's a park next to it where people walk their dogs."

Lona pulled up next to the building and Opal got out and extended her white cane. Danny followed her and coughed again before flashing a smile up at Lona.

"You sure you don't need a ride back to your house?"

Opal shook her head.

"No, we'll be alright. We're not too far from here. Tell her thank you, Danny."

"Thank you."

"You're welcome."

Lona smiled at them both and found that she was still smiling as she drove away, thinking about Opal's tendency to say thank you through her son. She rolled north and away from New Haven and made her way to Old Town, the museum, and Neima and Julia's apartment. As she turned, stopped, and turned again, she thought about the feeling she had had in Pythia's—the feeling that someone was inside her mind. She'd felt it before. In her training with Neima.

Now, Lona needed her mentor again. She needed to understand what had happened and why. She needed Neima's guidance, her thoughtful advice, her friendship.

But, when she reached the door to the familiar apartment, it was Julia who answered and she was in tears.

"What's happened? Julia, what's going on?"

Julia scraped at the wet on her cheeks with the backs of her wrists and pulled Lona into the apartment.

AshleyRose Sullivan

"I've been trying to call you. Neima's gone."

DEAR LONA,

I never meant to leave you like this. For the first time in years, my life is completely unpredictable to me. I struggle to find my intuition. My path seems buried in the folds of space and time. It's hidden to me. I know that I'm your mentor, and Julia's now as well. But I cannot help you unless I can help myself. There's only one person I can think of that might understand what's happened to me and that is my own mentor. I must find him—if he still lives. I don't know when I'll return.

You are not alone. Neither is Julia. You have each other.

Help her. I know you can.

You are wiser than you think and more powerful than you imagine.

With Love,

Neima

Lona read the letter twice. She folded it and slid it into the envelope on which her name was neatly written. Looking around the living room, she saw another envelope on the end table next to the sofa with Julia's name.

"Did you have any idea she was leaving?"

Julia shook her head.

"I got up this morning and she was gone. Lona, what am I going to do?"

Julia walked away without an answer and drifted to the balcony where she threw the door open and let the city air blast in. Lona watched as the breeze tugged at Julia's gauzy cardigan. She was beautiful, Lona thought. And strong.

Lona tried to breathe deeply but she supposed that, like Julia, the air didn't feel right without Neima. She stepped onto the balcony next to her friend. Cars whizzed by below. People hurried up and down the sidewalks.

"Julia, it's going to be ok. We can get through this."

"I needed her."

"I know. I did too."

Julia bit her bottom lip and pulled her arms around her own body. As she did so, her cardigan slipped away from her shoulder and there, upon Julia's chest, Lona saw for the first time, a ragged scar. The pale line told the story of her encounter with the Echo. A shattered mirror—Julia had said. Lona was ashamed to admit to herself then that she hadn't considered whether shattering the reflection had marred the original.

Lona searched for the right words to say but it was Julia who spoke next.

"I hope she's alright."

"Me, too. But, Neima knows what she's doing. She must."

"I hope she does."

Wondering what Neima would do now, Lona tried to put herself in her mentor's shoes. She came forward and put her hands firmly on Julia's shoulders and looked into her friend's eyes with what she hoped was reassurance.

"We can carry on. She wouldn't have left if she didn't think we would both be alright."

Julia sniffed but nodded.

"You're right."

The young women trailed back into the apartment where they spent the morning meditating together. Julia revealed that, since her encounter with the Echo, she had been having nightmares.

"They're awful. Every night, I die and then wake up. Oh no, don't look so upset. That's what happened. I died. I remember dying. I know what all of my copies are doing, all the time. I feel them. I hear them. I see through their eyes even as I see through my own. I felt my death. The shock and the blank nothingness. And, every night, I feel it again."

"Since that night?"

"Yes."

They sat cross-legged, face-to-face, and Lona put her hands out, palm up. Julia laid her own upon them. Palm to palm, the women peered into each other's eyes. Green to brown. Lona watched as dust appeared around Julia and shimmered—iridescent. The color fluctuated wildly and the specks died as quickly as they were born. But, in the few instants that they were visible to Lona, she saw several, diverging branches—all leading away from Julia and into the unknown. Then, just as quickly as they had emerged, they were gone.

She inhaled deeply and focused again. Her path was clearer as she exhaled and a stream of blue dust undulated, weaving around their bodies.

"Tell me."

Julia told Lona about the moment the Echo's knife had split the chest of her mirror image. How she, and every Julia, had seen a flash of red, had felt a searing pain, had stared into the face of death and taken his hand and let him lead her into the darkness. And yet, she was still here.

"Mostly. I'm mostly still here."

"You are here."

"I have to check sometimes. I have to make sure. Do I still exist?"

"Of course."

An uncertain nod.

"You exist, Julia. You're here with me. Feel my hands."

Now Lona realized how cold were her friend's fingers and palms.

"When you wake from these dreams, it's because you're still here. Your heart races and sweat drips out of your hair. You're alive. You feel it because you're alive. Even if you're changed. And, even though none of us went through what you did, we all were changed that night."

A wry laugh escaped Julia's mouth.

"It seems like the whole world changed that night."

"I know."

Taking Julia's hands more tightly, Lona focused again.

"When I dream of that night, and I wake up in the dark, I'm afraid that I'm still in that dream the Echo showed me. I'm afraid I'm still being influenced by the power he stole from Awesome's mother. I'm afraid I'm still just trapped inside the place I *wanted* to be—seeing what I wanted to see—and none of this is real. But then—"

"But then Arc City went to hell."

Now Lona laughed.

"Pretty much."

"Everything that's happened since that night...You know, when I left Philly, I was running away from a bad place—a bad situation. I knew when I left I could never go back. And I didn't want to. I worked all over the country. I waited tables. I worked kitchens. I was even in a magic act. But then the Guild Scouts found me and brought me here. And, from the beginning, I loved it. I was working at The Guild Hall and I met Roy and I saw Agents coming in from the field and I'd go out on the weekends and explore the old neighborhoods. It felt like nothing bad could ever happen to you in a place like Arc City. Not as long as the Guild was taking care of everything. Not as long as Andy was watching over us."

Julia took a long breath before she continued,

"But then Andy died? He just *died?* Like a regular person? When my dad died, it felt like the end of my world. I remember standing next to his coffin and I remember seeing his squadron fly missing man against the gray sky and I remember the way the flag looked in my mother's arms. That's the day I realized I could split—the day I found my ability. My dupe rode back to the house with my mother. But I stayed at my father's grave. I slept against his tombstone. I walked home at dawn and found myself asleep in my bed.

My whole life started over that day. It started over again when I came to Arc City. And again when I faced the Echo. How many times can I start over? I feel like I'm wearing thin, Lona.

"I know. I'm so sorry."

Lona tried to think what Neima might have said, what Andy might have said, what Ben might have said. They were all gone.

"You're still here, Julia. And, I'm here with you. For whatever you need. We have to go on, you know? It will get better."

Julia leaned back on her hands and nodded at Lona.

"I'd like some tea, I think."

"Ok."

Lona made tea in the cups Neima had favored and hoped that she had done well, had said the right thing. She gazed at the rising steam and wished, desperately, that she knew where Neima had gone.

Hours later, Julia seemed improved enough and said that Lona ought to go on with her day.

"Really, I'm alright."

"You'll call if you need anything?"

"Yes, of course."

"Alright. I can be here in twenty minutes, and you're welcome to come and stay with me and Jones. We'd love to have you."

"I know. I'll think about it."

They said goodbye at the door and Lona trudged down the stairs, onto the street, and, finally, into her truck. Once she was safely inside, she found herself resting her head against the steering wheel instead of starting the engine. Tears came to her eyes. Hot and angry, they coursed down her cheeks and dripped into her lap.

Her heart pounding, Lona remembered the sight of Julia screaming her name and then falling to the forest floor with a knife in her chest. Lona remembered the way her skin had gone gray and cool as a river stone. And, she remembered the reason Julia had been in the forest to begin with. To find Lona.

A hard knot formed in her throat as guilt and shame washed over her in waves. Why had the Echo come for *her*? Because of her power, her luck? She didn't feel lucky now.

She opened her eyes and surveyed the street before her. Scraps of dirty paper blew across the road. A harried-looking police officer waved traffic through a broken stoplight up ahead. The windows in the shop to her left—what had once been a tailor—were boarded up.

Leaning back against the old, leather seat, Lona closed her eyes. She took long breaths and tried to steady her heart.

It wasn't her fault the Echo had come for her. It wasn't her fault that Julia was so haunted and sick now. It wasn't her fault that Ben was gone, that Neima had left. It wasn't her fault that Awesome had been excommunicated. She said these things to herself and she tried to believe them.

"We have to go on. It'll get better. It has to."

The sound of her own voice awakened Lona's senses and she opened her eyes. The city seemed less bleak now. The tailor may have closed but the bagel shop was still open. An early summer breeze was pushing through the streets. A father and his kids were walking toward the museum. A woman carried a bouquet of orange tulips from the flower shop.

She inhaled again and the yeasty scent of the bagel shop filled her nose. She opened the door and got out of the truck.

Brass bells rang as she entered the shop and its keeper, who had been sliding a sheet of poppy seed bagels into the back case, turned toward her.

The woman adjusted her floury apron and then started to greet

Lona but, instead, leaned on the glass toward her and cocked her head to the side. After a moment, her expression changed to one of sympathy. Lona was reminded of Mrs. Chang, greeting her with tea and a fruit tart, after she struggled through her first days of middle school.

"Bad day?"

Lona nodded and put her fingertips to her cheeks. They were hot and probably red.

"Not to worry. Sit down. I'll fix you up."

The woman pulled a fresh poppy seed bagel from its shelf and cut it in half with a broad knife. She spread a generous helping of cream cheese over its surface in one, fluid motion and then laid marbely slices of smoked salmon over it. She finished it off with paper-thin slips of red onion and a few capers then set it before Lona with a cup of hot coffee.

"My father always set out bagels and lox when I visited him. Now, any time I cry, I eat it. It tastes like better days."

The flavors and scents washed over Lona. Smoke. Salt. Cream. The tastes came together separately and all at once and Lona found herself smiling at the very first bite. The woman went back to work and Lona sat alone, eating the meal and drinking the coffee and believing that it did taste like better days.

But, Lona hoped, it was better days to come.

LONA FOLDED THE paper. The sun warmed her legs, which stuck out from under the patio table canopy and she stretched out and sighed. She closed her eyes and tried to focus. The White Wolves. Awesome. Andy. Shadow Slider. The Guild. The Sheets. Images from the last few months whirled through her mind uncontrollably. Frustrated, she breathed out a huff of air and grabbed her father's journal from the bag at her side. It had been weeks since she tried to decipher the code but maybe now, with fresher eyes, she could do something with it. She flipped through the pages and let them fall open where they would.

"Come on, dad. What were you doing? What is all this?"

From the back of Lona's mind came an old memory. She sat in her father's study, drawing a pretend map onto a piece of her father's fancy paper while he worked at his desk. She stuck her tongue out as she drew, blue rivers and lakes, yellow and green lands, violet mountains. She stared up at the maps on her father's wall. A gust blew in and the long white curtain billowed. Birds chirped. Her father hummed as he worked.

BRRRRRING! BRRRRING!

Lona slammed the book shut and went inside to answer the phone.

"Hello?"

Tulie was wagging her tail against Lona's leg, her fur sticking to the beads of water that clung to Lona's skin.

"Ms. Gold?"

Lona Chang

A long moment passed before Lona recognized the voice of Professor Moss and realized that she was, at least as far as he was concerned, Ms. Gold.

"Yes. This is she."

"Ms. Gold, I was just cleaning out my office and came across a series of old papers. Honestly, it's the strangest thing. I thought I'd gotten rid of these years ago. I gave them to my Graduate Assistant to be disposed of but, lucky for us, she did not follow my direction. Actually, it's doubly lucky because I also thought I'd lost your number. I'd apparently dropped it into a box of my books and found it again as I was packing."

Lona half laughed, picturing the wreck of an office Mr. Moss must be facing as she listened to the squeal of his desk chair and the shuffling of papers.

"Yes, very lucky, Mr. Moss. I'm glad to hear from you. What have you found?"

"Those rings on your fabric—I was sure I'd seen something like it. Or, at least, that I'd read about something like it. It was many years ago, though. I was still a student and her research had just been published. She seemed like such a promising scientist, I can't fathom why she did what she did."

"I'm sorry, Mr. Moss, you've lost me. Who are you talking about?"

She listened as he heaved open a window. Then, papers shuffled again.

"You aren't looking for a super-human, Ms. Gold. This wasn't the work of someone with extra-normal abilities but an extra-normal brain. You're looking for Dr. Eleanor Woods."

The name rang a bell but it seemed distant to Lona.

"Woods?"

"I honestly had no idea what she'd been up to all these years. But, as soon as I saw her in the paper, I knew it wasn't some other Eleanor Woods. No one else could've done what she's done. You know, when I was a student, it seemed as though she was publishing a new paper every other month. Then, she just fell off the grid. A lot of lady scientists in those days ended up getting married and dropped out of the field to start a family but she didn't really seem the type. If you get my meaning."

She didn't. He continued.

"I met her at a conference once, when I was a student. She was doing research here at the university. Completely brilliant. Such a shame. Anyway, it'll be hard to get in there now."

"Get in where?"

"Onyx Island. I'm sorry, I must not have said, Dr. Woods was the Alchemist."

And then, all at once, Lona remembered she had read the name—the history—in the newspaper when the Alchemist was arrested. Eleanor Woods, exceptional scientist, left the field for a life of crime and had been arrested by Captain Lightning with help from Photon and the Baron. And, as it happened, Lona.

"Onyx Island."

She repeated the words in such a far off, hollow way that Professor Moss didn't understand what she'd said.

"I was just wondering how I might get in to talk to her."

"Ah, well, I'm afraid I can't help you there. I visited Claymore and Onyx Island a few times but it's a long process. The prisoners there, if they've been good, can accept visitors from friends and family members, attorneys, or the occasional writer. The latter has to go through several rounds of forms and questions though. It took a few months for my research to be approved. You can get the forms at the library if you're interested in that route."

"Alright, thanks so much, Professor. You've been such a help."

"Be careful, Ms. Gold, if you decide to go looking for Eleanor. I don't know what happened to her, or why she turned to criminal super science, but she is one of the greatest minds of our age. Ruthless and logical in every way."

"Thank you. I'll be careful. And, I wish you the best in your new teaching position."

"Yes, ma'am. Have a good day."

The phone smacked into its receiver and Lona sat down in one of the kitchen chairs.

She thought about the Alchemist. About her keen eyes and wry smile. She thought about how, were it not for Lona herself, she would've got away—as she had so many times before. Lona was loathe to try and speak to this woman but, as she stared through the glass door to the patio where Andy died, she knew that she must.

"I guess I'm going to the library."

DISPATCH LEANED IN the doorway, twisting a pink dreadlock around her finger. She smiled at Awesome.

"Is he gonna make it?"

The scent of antiseptic rose from Awesome's palm as Christina dabbed at it with a soaked swab and her voice was cheery as she said,

"Yeah. Your healing factor is pretty high, Baron. You should be back at it in a day or two."

"Or whenever Stargazer says."

Dispatch laughed at her own joke and Awesome chuckled even as he examined the angry gash in his hand.

Christina readied the needle and thread.

"You said 'healing factor?'"

Dispatch laughed again as Christina poked the needle through his skin.

"Yeah. We got it from the comics."

"And the old cards. Remember the old Caped Crusader Cards? They always used to list whether the hero had a 'healing factor.' When Stargazer started the clinic, I worked with him to set up a grading system to help make triage more efficient. Someone with very little healing factor requires more time and resources. With you, I just have to clean this cut and sew it up and it'll be fine in a few days. But another Sheet, with a lower healing factor, I would apply some more hi-tech stuff."

"She's saying you don't need any Green Goop."

"Right. And the Green Goop is expensive. We don't have much of it so we save it for the folks who can't heal as fast. They need to get back on their feet. Not just for the city—"

And Awesome finished her thought, thinking of Opal and her son—

"But for their families, too."

"Right. They don't have the luxury of being laid up in the Guild hospital wing forever."

Awesome nodded.

"So where does this stuff come from?"

Stargazer appeared in the doorway just then and let Dispatch know her husband had come in from the field. She went off to find him and Stargazer came into the room and plopped down on the chair next to Awesome. It was Stargazer who answered Awesome's question.

"The Green Goop comes from a couple places. We have a guy in the Guild who sneaks us a few cases every year. We had a scientist helping us synthesize it but she's fallen off the grid. And, we have some contacts in the Super Science Black Market. That's where we got most of our equipment."

"Don't be so modest, Stargazer."

Stargazer shrugged and, under his hood, Awesome could see an embarrassed smile as Christina continued.

"He built a lot of this stuff. Including the vitals machine I hooked you up to when you came in."

"I just modified someone else's design, that's all. There's no way we could afford the ones they keep in the high-end hospitals."

Just then, Dispatch re-appeared in the doorway, this time with a tall, spindly man all in dark green. This was Nebula, formerly the Mist. His close-cut hair was heathered with gray and his fair skin had taken on a very red tint. Dispatch pointed at his ruddy cheeks as she addressed Christina.

"Someone's not used to the day shift. Didn't wear sunscreen."

"Yikes. I'll get you some hydro-gel. I'm just about done here."

Dispatch kissed Nebula gently on the end of his burned nose.

"Back to work, baby. Christina, don't be too nice to him, alright? It's his own fault."

She winked as she walked away and then Nebula turned to Awesome and shrugged.

"Better than Guild medicine, huh, Baron?"

Awesome turned toward Nebula again. Did everyone know he was Guild trained?

As if Stargazer could read his mind, he responded.

"News travels fast around here, man. Why do you think we all keep our identities a secret?"

Nebula laughed and Awesome nodded in understanding.

"It's better than the Guild, as far as I can tell. At least, I like this place a lot better."

"Did you live on Floor Ten?"

"Yeah."

Nebula chuckled at this.

"I tried to get out of it. The only way I could, though, was to get transferred out of Arc City."

"Were you a Double A?"

"Only for about six months. I was one of the lucky ones. The guy who was the Mist before me got shot up and I took his place up in Boston. I'd been serving under the Gray Gryphon before that and they went ahead and sent me up. After that, whenever I came back, I stayed on Floor Eleven."

"Is it better?"

"Not much. About one extra hook for your cape. After I was done with the Guild, though, I came right back here. Couldn't keep away, you know? I grew up here. I love this city."

"I get it."

"I know. I never knew your dad and I didn't really know Lightning. But I know how much Arc City meant to them. If you're following in their footsteps, and it seems like you are, then you're going to do well by the city."

"I hope so."

Awesome left the room a few moments later with Stargazer who closed the door behind him as Nebula started to remove his mask. As they walked, Stargazer pulled a bundle of fabric from within his pocket.

"Here, I grabbed some gloves for you. We should head out, man. It's getting dark."

Awesome slid the leather glove over his bandaged hand and started to follow Stargazer as they were interrupted. Dispatch leaned out of her office as the door to the garage opened and Lona Chang walked in.

LONA WAVED AT Awesome and Stargazer and pulled her backpack higher on her shoulder. She hoped she was right. She hoped she could do some good.

"Do you guys have a map?"

"What?"

Stargazer half-squinted at Lona.

"It's just this White Wolf problem. I was at the library and I noticed something. Do you have a map here? I'd like to see it."

Stargazer led them both through the Sheet Clinic and up a set of stairs into a long room with high windows. A big table stood in the middle, under a mountain of papers and files. The walls were covered with maps of the city and binders were stacked atop old filing cabinets. On the far wall, though, was what Lona had come for.

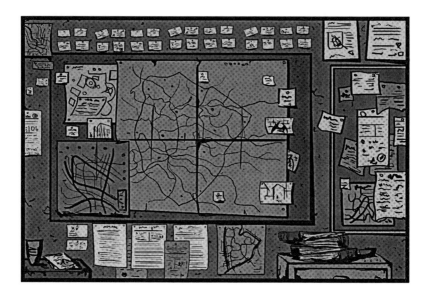

"You've got hits from all the major gangs here."

Stargazer sighed and crossed his arms as he approached the wall.

"That's right. We were trying to track everything but it's overwhelming. It's all over the map and these gangs are totally unpredictable. What've you got?"

"I was just leaving the library in Old Town. You know they have that big Arc City map at the entryway. The old one?"

As she spoke she took a hand-full of disused, red-tipped pushpins from the corner of the corkboard and began sliding them into the city map.

"I was thinking about The White Wolves. I saw they hit New Haven again. The thing is, the White Wolves have always been a disorganized street gang. Wanton destruction. Smash and grab. But not anymore."

She slid a few more pins into the map.

"What do you mean? They're still all over the place. Every neighborhood."

"No. They're not in *every* neighborhood. It just seems that way because it's such a good cross-section of Arc City. They're hitting the richest neighborhoods, the old neighborhoods, the poor neighborhoods—it seems like there isn't a pattern but there is."

She put the last pin in the map and looked at it. Dust swirled between the pins like eddies in a river. She took a blue, colored pencil from her bag and began drawing on the map, tracing a path that only she could see.

"When they arrested the Alchemist and Ironhide she had figured out exactly how long it took for Captain Lightning to show up in that part of town. Ironhide was even counting down—his job was to keep the Suits and the crowds busy just long enough for her to get away from the bank unnoticed.

She couldn't have been the only one to figure out response times. Whoever's in charge of the White Wolves now is staying ahead of everyone. The only way you've managed to grab any of them was by coincidence—just, right place, right time.

They're doing the same thing the Alchemist did. But they're not only accounting for the Guild—they've also been watching you and figuring out how long you take to show up. And, I think they aren't just leaving before you show up—they're making sure they're home safe before you ever get to the scene of the crime."

"Home?"

"Yeah. That map in the library—it's an old Arc City railway map. Every one of these hits is within one and a half miles of the old railway station. Actually, most of them are the nicest neighborhoods you can hit within that distance. They're only picking targets they can be completely clear of before you get there and then they're sending out whatever they've stolen on the old rail system. I think that's why their stolen goods aren't showing up on Arc City's underground market."

Stargazer and Awesome stared at the map—at the constellation of crimes.

"So they're part of a larger syndicate. They must be."

Lona nodded.

Stargazer grinned at Lona and clapped her on the shoulder.

"This is good work."

"Thank you."

He nodded to Awesome as he slid his gloves on.

"We'd better get going. If we stake out the old rail yards, figure out where they're getting in and out, we'll be able to get a head start on them."

Lona nodded at them both, flushed from the excitement of solving this puzzle.

"I need to get going too."

She watched as a Sheet strode down the hallway with a set of fighting sticks tucked under her arm, her bright red braids swaying as she walked.

"Wait—do you think any of these women might have an extra wig I could borrow?"

Awesome and Stargazer stared at her for a moment and then Stargazer nodded.

"I think we can find something for you."

Lona Chang

Minutes later Lona kissed Awesome and headed back down the stairs and out to the garage. She was proud and happy but also nervous about what was to come. She pulled her backpack closer and thought of her next errand.

ELEANOR WOODS SETTLED against the hard plastic back of her chair and stared across the table at Lona through red, rectangular-framed glasses. She wore a set of plain, black cotton, prison-distributed clothes and Lona remembered how brightly she had been attired at the bank—how stylish and cheeky she had seemed. Like the world was nothing to this woman, like she lived to resist it, to transform it. Still, even in her somber prison garb and no bright red lipstick, Eleanor Woods gave Lona the impression that she was in full control.

"Allison Starling, huh? Pretty gutsy."

Lona tucked a strand of silky black hair behind her ear and adjusted her glasses. She felt uncomfortable but knew Pythia must have Onyx Island under supervision and she didn't want to be recognized. She resisted the urge to adjust the wig and her mother's cat-eye glasses were far too strong. She peered over instead of through them.

"Gutsy?"

"Where did you even get her name?"

"I went to the library to get the formal visitor forms but, while I was there, I looked you up. I found your photo in an old Arc City University yearbook. There was your old lab and it listed Allison Starling as your long-time lab assistant. I thought, if I gave them the name, you might see me."

"Not bad. Did you say you were her daughter?"

"Yeah."

"Did you get a fake ID?"

"I made one."

"Made one?"

"I'm an artist."

"And the guard at visitor reception?"

"He was new. First day. He wasn't sure what he was doing and he fumbled with all the paperwork so much he barely even looked at me or the ID."

"That's lucky."

Lona felt herself blush. She was lucky.

"Why not just file a formal request?"

Lona got the feeling that Eleanor could at least guess at her reasoning.

"I don't have the time. The forms take weeks. I needed to see you as soon as possible."

"Alright, kid, what do you need to know?"

Dust kicked up then, around Eleanor Woods. Violet and silver, it swirled and branched off in several, vague directions like streams from a river. Lona shook her head. She didn't understand the branches but, as she stared at the woman across the table, Lona realized that there could be no skirting issues or dodging questions with Eleanor Woods. The woman was too sharp, too quick, too savvy.

"I need to know if you made the weapon that killed Captain

Lightning."

"Friend of yours?"

Eleanor had said it with a sarcastic smirk but her face changed as she observed Lona. Still, she said nothing and didn't change her tone when Lona answered.

"Yes."

"But they caught his killer. We do occasionally get news in here. Slip Shadow."

"Shadow Slipper. But—"

"But you don't think he's responsible."

"No."

"And why not?"

"Because Captain Lightning died in my arms. I saved a part of his damaged uniform and I took it to a scientist for his assessment. He's the one who referred me to you. He said it wasn't caused by an extra-normal human. It was caused by a weapon. It left a signature. A silver—"

"A silver ring around the hole. Through and through."

"Yes. So it is yours?"

"It's a project I worked on several years ago. Probably before you were born."

"Did you complete it?"

"No, I wasn't getting the results I wanted."

"And it was some kind of weapon?"

Dr. Woods shook her head. She seemed perturbed now. Insulted. Her brow was knotted and a scowl grew on her mouth.

"No. It wasn't."

"What were you making then?"

"I was working on a transversable bridge connecting two disparate points in spacetime."

"So—"

"So, I couldn't get it to work. The device was unstable. That design only worked in tiny blips. Minute bridges would pop up—then immediately destabilise. They would bore through whatever material the device had been aimed at, but only for a millisecond. I couldn't form a stable bridge."

"And the silver ring—"

"It's not silver. It's the signature of exotic matter, which should've formed the seal at either end. Instead it only left a—"

"A scar."

"Right."

"How far did you get with it? Why did you stop?"

"Allison Starling died in a lab accident."

"Oh. I—I'm so sorry. If I'd known—"

"No. You were clever. I can't fault you for that."

Lona sighed as she thought of the girl from the photo.

"After she died, I left the university and started the preliminary work for a new project. But, a couple of months later, I was recruited to work as part of a think tank. It was a different time. Right after the war. The think tank had excellent resources."

"Did you ever go back to your original work?"

"No, I started down a new path. But, when I joined, I had to hand over all my research."

"So—this think tank—"

"The way I understand it, there were a bunch of us in different places, working on different things but it all ran back to one, larger project. New research, new science was coming from that main project but I never got close to it."

"What were they doing?"

"I don't know. But my wife—" and here Eleanor paused to glance at Lona before continuing, "—my wife worked on the main project. She was a mathematician but really she just processed a lot of paperwork. We met when they transferred her to my department from that spooky old place."

"Spooky old place?"

"Yes. The building where they started the whole project. It was out in the country and Catherine always said it looked like an old castle. It was called—"

"Grayston."

Lona thought of all the buildings they had seen and particularly remembered the Grayston Community Center south of Arc City.

"That's right. It all started there. And it was called the Grayston Project."

"So what was the purpose of the main project?"

"I can't say."

"What do you mean?"

"I mean I literally don't know. Not even Catherine knew. Everything in that place was kept under wraps. We only knew what we were working on and, often, what we were working on was blacked out and redacted by the time we saw it. Still…"

"What?"

"Listen, I don't know what they did with my research. I had no idea they would try to use it. I haven't seen those original files in years. I never had an issue with Captain Lightning—"

"But you're the Alchemist."

"Yes. I am the Alchemist. Because when Catherine and I left the Grayston Project, I couldn't find work. I could never find work again. I tried to take my research with me when the project was being shut down and, because of that, I was blacklisted. No one would hire me. So, what else should I have done? Let my career—my research—die? What would you have done, if you were told you couldn't do the thing you love?"

"I'd do it anyway."

"So that's what I did. Sometimes what I did was illegal. Sometimes I had to fund my research with the money I robbed from banks or I sold tech on the Super Science Black Market. I never intentionally hurt anyone. I just wanted to live. I just wanted to work."

"So what happened to Grayston?"

"It's my understanding that it was mothballed. Whatever they were doing in there, they could never get it to work. But—"

"What?"

"You could talk to Catherine."

"Really? You think she would talk to me?"

"She will if you take her a message from me."

Lona looked across the table at Eleanor Woods. She saw, now, something familiar. Eleanor Woods, when she spoke of Catherine, softened. The violet dust around her eddied and rippled. Lona saw a woman determined. Determined to continue her work, to do something worthwhile, to create a life for herself when the world seemed against her, to reach out to the person she loved above all others.

"What should I say?"

"DUCK!"

Awesome did. A set of metal claws swooped over his head. Awesome kicked at the White Wolf's knee and he went down. Stargazer jumped on him.

Now, a long-bladed knife swiped at Awesome's head. He leapt back but tripped over the first man's bound body. He stumbled.

Stargazer's hands came alive with blue sparks and he shot the knife-wielding Wolf with a jolt of electricity. The man fell and Awesome cuffed him.

Now there were four left.

Awesome and Stargazer stood their ground on the old bridge. Maybe the oldest in Arc City. Two narrow lanes stretched from bank to bank, about forty feet above the rocky, rushing Coal Creek. It connected Willow Heights to Arc City's Southeast bank and its massive train yards.

Awesome felt a terrible sense of foreboding. Lona had been right—this place was the White Wolf headquarters. But neither Stargazer nor Awesome had expected to encounter a huge pack of them, getting ready to go out on the town. Now the Wolves were caught between turning toward home or carrying on with their intended purpose. Instead of either, they stood and fought. And, for the first time, Awesome understood how this disorganized street gang had suddenly become a major crime family. They had a new leader.

"There she is."

Standing on the opposite side of the bridge with a wolf mask, no—a real white wolf pelt—thrown over her head and shoulders. Pale arms and legs with red scars emerged from a mis-matched set of motorcycle leathers—all painted white.

She stood behind four of her henchmen and stretched out her arms. Suddenly, long, bone spikes emerged from her knuckles and jutted out over her pale fingers. She moved to the front of the pack. The wolves charged Awesome and Stargazer.

As she ran at them Awesome realized he'd seen her before. She'd been known as Claw and had always operated in Baltimore. Marvelous Man had fought her several times. Seeing her here, now, in Arc City, only confirmed what Awesome, Lona, and the Sheets had suspected. Their city was a magnet for crime. All it took was the death of their hero to topple the balance. How much worse would this get?

Awesome couldn't afford the time to consider it just now.

Claw stabbed at Stargazer, who dodged, leaping back. Awesome fell in next to him and landed a hard kick in the first Wolf's liver. He crumpled and went down with a whimper. Another Wolf, this one with a silver revolver, took aim at Awesome's chest and cocked but didn't see Stargazer's hands come to life. A blue jolt took that one in the head; his revolver clattered on the cement. Now it was Claw and one Wolf.

The Wolf charged. He was a big man but he was fast. He took a swing at Awesome and the big fist landed square on Awesome's jaw. Awesome ducked the next one as Stargazer brought his hands up again. But this Wolf was too quick. He thrust out a side kick and landed high on Stargazer's chest, sending him backward. Stargazer landed hard on the pavement and coughed.

Awesome took a swing now and it crunched into the big man's nose and Awesome almost celebrated but Stargazer's voice rang in his ears.

"She's running!"

Awesome glanced to the side of the big Wolf as he slipped another punch and saw Claw rushing back across the bridge. She held up a small device and glared back over her shoulder as she ran.

"Boom!"

Her scream was followed by an actual, ear-piercing boom as the east side of the bridge exploded.

Gray dust clouded the air. Awesome couldn't see a foot in front of him but he managed to catch the big Wolf's next punch. He grabbed the man's arm and slammed him into the ground, pulling a pair of cuffs and a beacon from the back of his belt.

Awesome looked across the bridge as the dust cleared. Claw was still standing there, cackling. Motorcycle engines revved in the near distance.

"You have to jump, Baron."

Stargazer was at his side but his breath was short and he leaned forward, his hands on his knees.

"You alright?"

"I think that jackass broke my ribs."

Over the hill, from the train yards, they saw motorcycles headed for Claw. She was going to get away. They would probably pack up and move to another neighborhood, maybe another town. Maybe they'd never be caught.

"I can't make the jump but you could. You have to do it."

Awesome stared across the gap. It was about twelve feet. The broken pavement thrust out toward the opposite bank in jagged spikes and, below, rushed Coal Creek. Awesome's head spun.

"I can't."

He looked across the gap at Claw who suddenly realized the Baron was considering actually coming after her.

"You have to, Baron. You have to jump."

Awesome breathed in and out and went back a few more feet. Now he could get a running start. He kept his eyes focused on Claw and knew that if he didn't grab her now, they might never get her.

His legs pumped. His heart thumped. His blood rushed. He ran as hard as he could and, just as he got to the gap, his heels came down and he skidded to a stop. His arms windmilled as he nearly fell over the edge.

Looking into the gap, his breath was short and his vision whirled and all he could hear was the sound of Claw riding away on the back of a motorcycle.

Awesome walked back to Stargazer who was cuffing the last Wolf they'd brought down.

"It's ok, Baron. It's ok."

"No, it's not."

Stargazer gave him a slap on the shoulder but winced and doubled over again. Awesome helped him stand.

"You ok? Can you make it back to the clinic?"

"Yeah. We'll take the slow way."

"What's the slow way?"

"I called Dispatch. She's going to come pick us up."

Lona Chang

Awesome nodded and stood with Stargazer on the broken edge of the bridge. They stared down into the rush of water and Awesome let out a long sigh.

YOU CAN'T FEEL guilty about this, Jones."

Awesome leaned into the sofa cushions. He had been running his hands over Tulie's head and ears as he told Lona about his afternoon, his confrontation with Claw, and his failure to overcome his fear.

"How can I not? Who knows what those Wolves will do because I couldn't catch them."

"You're human."

"I'm supposed to be more than human."

"Are you?"

Awesome sighed.

"Jones, you might have a tough hide, and amazing strength, but your heart is human. *That's* who you are. This fear is a part of you and so is overcoming it. You can do this."

"But will it happen in time?"

"It'll have to."

The wind blew outside. Dark clouds hid the stars.

"It's your turn."

Lona sighed. She had come home to find Awesome sitting at the kitchen table with his head in his hands while Tulie stared at him and whined. They hadn't got to talking about her day yet and now that it was her turn, she looked across the living room, to the armchair where she had dumped her bag and tried to assess what had happened.

"Just start at the beginning."

THIS WAS THE BEGINNING:

A woman's voice rang through the intercom attached to the brownstone building in Old Town.

"Yes?"

"Is this Catherine Ziegel?"

"Please go away."

"I have a message for you."

The woman didn't answer and Lona pressed the button to speak again.

"Eleanor says to put the kettle on."

Another couple of empty seconds passed and Lona considered turning back down the steps but, just as she made to move, the buzzer rang and the door clicked open.

Catherine Ziegel was, in many ways, exactly what Eleanor was not. Tall, lithe, and wan, she moved about the old apartment like a fairy creature. The lines in her face didn't seem to have been carved so much as lightly painted. Still, Lona thought the woman looked tired and drawn as she invited her guest to sit on the antique sofa.

Lona admired the plush piece of furniture before sitting.

"This is a Biedermeier isn't it?"

"Oh yes. You have quite an eye."

"More of a habit, really. I was raised in an antique shop."

Catherine offered Lona a glass of water, which she accepted. When the pleasantries were finished, Catherine took a seat on an elegant and exceptionally well-kept Rococo armchair.

"Please tell me—how is she? She won't let me visit her at all. She says it's too risky. Is she faring well? How did you come to speak to her?"

"She looks well. She seems steely but spirited—if that makes sense."

"Yes. Well, that's Eleanor. Have they taken away her lovely outfit?"

"I'm afraid so."

"She's always been such a clotheshorse. I suppose they let her keep the glasses—the red ones?"

Lona nodded.

"How do you know her? I'm sorry but I can't recall ever meeting you."

Sighing, Lona told Catherine most of the story that led her to that particular room on that particular day.

"Grayston?"

"Yes. Since the night Captain Lightning died, I've been trying to track down what he meant by that word and it led me here. Eleanor thought you might have some insight."

Catherine was still and silent for a long time. After a while, she stood and went to the window. With long, slender fingers, she touched the lace curtains and watched the street below.

"Project Grayston was a long time ago. I'm not sure how much I can help you but... I will do my best, Miss Chang. I began work at Grayston as a young woman. I have advanced degrees in math and biology but I was essentially used to process the information that came through the main program. I was checking and double-checking the numbers and then boiling it all down and giving my results to the superiors. Basically, I was a human computer and I worked in the main Grayston building—just south of the city.

Lona pictured the old, castle-like building, as Catherine continued.

"I honestly can't tell you what they were doing. The entire building was sectioned off and we were all under heavy security. We couldn't leave our sections or speak to anyone from any of the other sections. All the paperwork I received was redacted. It was just raw data. No names, no context. It was lonely and depressing but I was at least working in my field and, at the time, it seemed like we were all toiling toward some greater good. The war was over but nothing felt safe or certain and, in that time, I felt needed."

Catherine shook her head and let her hand drop from where it had been resting on the windowsill. She turned back toward Lona and sighed then sat again in her chair. The way she moved was like a feather, silent and light, but when her eyes met Lona's it seemed she bore a great weight. Lona nodded to her, signaling that she would help carry Catherine's burden, whatever it was, and Catherine continued.

"One evening, as I was leaving, I was just getting into my car when I saw a man—a fellow scientist—with his head against his steering wheel as if he were sick or distressed. I tapped on his window to ask if he was alright and he rolled it down and asked my name. His eyes were red and he'd been crying. It was the strangest thing. I checked his badge—which didn't have names or anything—just a code. But I recognized the code. Whoever this man was, he was working on the main problem at Grayston. Top level and top secret. He said, 'I'm not sure I can keep doing this. I'm not sure any of us *should* be doing this.' I asked him what he meant and he just shook his head. I told him that whatever it was, it would surely be alright. Oh, hell, I was so young and naive.

The next day, I was transferred away from the main Grayston Project. I supposed someone must have seen us talking and of course that was forbidden. I ended up at the branch where Eleanor was working and that's how we met and so on. After a few months, the entire Grayston Project was starting to wind down and Eleanor and I left before that happened—hoping we could get university jobs elsewhere.

But Eleanor refused to leave her research in the lab. She said it was just as much her right to keep as theirs. She snuck out several of her papers and I suppose they found out. She was blacklisted because of that. She never managed to get work in her field again. We moved around a lot but, in the end, we came back to Arc City. Our families both immigrated here when we were children and we could really never leave it."

Catherina sighed and looked out the window. A nostalgic smile came to her lips and Lona thought it a lovely, if all too brief, sight.

"Anyway, after a few years, out of the blue, I got a phone call. It was the scientist I'd seen crying. He said his name was Jacob Kawaguchi. He said, 'I violated my non-disclosure contract. I published a book and I wanted someone to know about it before they find me. It's called *The Dark Star*. You were in the program. You should know. You can help. It's too late for me."

Lona looked into the woman's pale, gray eyes.

"Did you help him?"

"I had no idea what he was talking about. I wasn't sure *how* to help him and—and I was afraid. After what they'd done to Eleanor's career, I had the feeling that we got off lucky—that it could've been so much worse. Violating the secrets contract? That seemed like suicide."

She smoothed the fabric of her skirt with shaky hands as she went on.

"Still, I did look for the book. The next day I went to my local bookshop and asked for it. They said someone had come in that morning—a security type, just like the ones who'd been watching us at Grayston—and bought every copy. I went to another store, and another. I drove two hours out to Kingston and tried a few stores there. All gone. That was it. The Grayston Project had covered it up—I was sure of it.

I asked about the publisher and got their information. They were a small press based in France. I called and they said they'd just been bought out. They were closing up shop. That was enough for me. I never even told Eleanor about the whole incident or trying to find the book or anything. I thought it might put us both in danger."

"But you're telling me."

"You seem eager to face the risk."

"So that's it? The key to what happened at Grayston was in this book and—it's gone?"

Catherine leaned into the soft fabric of her antique chair. She looked exhausted.

"I don't think it's necessarily gone. I asked the store clerks about the books. *The Dark Star* had been on the shelves for over a week. A few copies were sold."

"You never tried to track them down?"

"Of course not."

"But you think it might be possible now."

"Possible? Yes. But it's been years since the book's release. Who knows what's happened to those copies. You'd have to be the luckiest woman in the world to find one now. But, yes, I suppose it's possible."

Lona nodded.

"Thank you, Ms. Ziegel."

"Please call me Catherine."

"Thank you, Catherine. I really appreciate it. You've been very helpful."

Lona got up to leave when Catherine stopped her, said to wait, and went off into the other room. She returned a short time later with a little, velvet bag.

"You should take this."

Lona peaked inside and saw a small, golden box—exactly like the one Ironhide had intended to use to get away from the Guild.

"What—"

"It was my Emergency Exit. A one-way trip."

"But—"

"I won't be needing it now."

"What do you mean?"

"Eleanor didn't tell you? I'm dying, Miss Chang. The bank job was Ellie's last hurrah. She wanted to use the money to take me away. We always meant to travel but, once we were settled, we rarely left the city. I kept this box in case I ever needed to get away fast but I don't need it now. It's quite easy to use. Here, let me show you."

Catherine showed her how to dial up the coordinates and set a counter and then told her that, whenever she was ready, to open the box. It would count down from whatever time she had set before starting up.

"Thank you. But, Catherine, I'm so sorry. I never meant to take Eleanor away from you. She was robbing a bank and—"

"Listen, Eleanor always made her own choices. She took the risks and she liked it—maybe too much. She reveled in bucking the system. I often wish I were more like her though I think we balance one another well. But you—you remind me of her. And, honestly, that worries me.

You're walking into something dark and dangerous, Miss Chang. You need to be prepared."

Lona watched as gold dust popped into existence and swirled around Catherine. It spun away from her—not as multiple trails this time, but as one.

"Thank you."

She started to go once more and then again turned back to Catherine.

"I have one more question. I don't mean to intrude—it just seemed such a curious thing."

"What?"

"Put the kettle on?"

Catherine's mouth broke into a wide smile and she blushed and laughed a light, weightless laugh.

"Eleanor doesn't turn off, you know? Once she's working, she's like a hound on a scent. It's impossible to drag her away. She often left in the evenings to go to her lab and work on whatever problem was bothering her. Before leaving she always said, 'Put the kettle on. I'll be back before it whistles.' But, of course, she never was. It became a joke between us. Eventually it came to mean, 'I'll be late. But I'll be home.' And, even more than that it meant, 'I love you.'"

Lona smiled.

"Goodbye, Catherine."

"Good luck, Miss Chang."

LONA HUMMED AN old song as she wrapped her hands for boxing practice a few mornings later. What were the words again? They had just started to flow into her mind when Awesome came outside with two tall glasses of water.

"Thanks, Jones."

"You about ready?"

She nodded and stood.

"You've got a lot of power in your hands but your feet are still sloppy so today we should work on your movement. Go ahead and start shadow boxing."

Lona complied and was sweating before she knew it. Jab. Jab. Cross. Jab. Uppercut. Slip. Jab. Cross. Slip. As she threw, images from her investigation reeled in her mind. Catherine Ziegler. Eleanor Woods. Charlie Moss. Captain Lightning.

Andy Archer.

Grayston.

The old empty building.

She pictured the broken gargoyle staring at her.

Awesome squared up with her and held up a set of mitts. Jab. Jab. Cross. Her heart raced. She felt close to something—close to the solution? The truth? The danger? The end? The nearness of this nameless thing was like an invisible beast, puffing hot breath onto her palm, smelling her, sizing her up. Would she be ready for whatever came next?

"You ok?"

"What? Yeah. Yeah, I'm ok. Keep going."

"Alright."

Awesome turned to the side and bounced on his toes as he modeled the form. His movement seemed both precise and erratic. It was quick and unpredictable. Lona tried to mimic him. Her feet were slower but she began to understand the premise, the idea behind the movement.

A few minutes later, they stopped to take a break. Lona gulped her water but Awesome looked over the rim of his glass at her.

"Are you sure everything's alright?"

She wiped her mouth and sighed.

"Catherine was right, you know? In looking for the truth about what happened to Andy, we are walking into danger. Whatever The Guild knows or doesn't know—they don't want us on this. They're willing to set up an innocent man just to make sure everyone stops poking around. And, whoever really killed Andy, is still out there. Whatever Grayston was— or *is*—it's dangerous. This is bigger than I thought it was. It's bigger than an Agent and some crook getting caught up in a showdown. It's bigger than tracking down any single person. It's not just a mystery. It's deeper and more sinister and there are way more pieces than—than any dime store detective ever had to fit together."

"Lona, you aren't a dime store detective. You might've got your start reading all those Kraker novels but it's obvious you've gone way beyond that now. Real life stuff doesn't fit together the way novels or comic books do. Andy taught us that the first day he walked into our life. And now, with him gone, we have to find all these new answers on our own. But, look, you're smarter than the puzzle, Lona, and braver than whoever is hiding behind it. I can see it. Neima could see it. Your dad could see it."

Lona's fingers went to her chest where her father's key hung around her neck. The metal was warm now, taking up the heat from her body.

"You're a detective. And not because it's your legacy but because you have the courage, intelligence, integrity, and heart to know when something isn't right and to do something about it. You're a hero, Lona. You can do this."

She smiled up at him and nodded.

"Alright."

Lona held up her hands and they went back to work. Her bare feet padded on the hot patio stones as the day warmed up. She bobbed and weaved as they worked on defense. Then, they moved to grappling. Lona pushed when Awesome pulled and pulled when he pushed—using his own weight against him just as Ben had taught him. After a while, Lona went in to refill their glasses and looked up, out the window, when Tulie began barking.

Stargazer and Opal were standing in their patio. Concerned, Awesome asked,

"Everything ok?"

"Yeah. We've got something for you. I wanted to come by and give it to you before we take off for training."

"Hey, Stargazer."

"Detective."

"What? How did you—"

"Come on now, don't give me that look. I brought you something. Well, actually I brought two things. Baron's first. "

Stargazer reached behind his back where two small packages were clipped. He handed the first one to Awesome. Small and cylindrical, the object—wrapped in a black bag—fit perfectly into Awesome's hand. Awesome unwrapped it but still wasn't sure what to make of it. The object was a palm-length, black cylinder with a white tip.

"Here, it works like this. There's a safety and a switch."

Stargazer showed Awesome a small button, within a recess, on the side.

"Slide this up. Then press here."

As he did so, the cylinder shot out at either end, extending into a full-size cane at dangerous speed. Awesome held it aloft.

"It's lighter than the old one."

"But just as durable. It's a new metal—araneum."

"It must've cost you a fortune."

"Someone owed me a favor. Give it a swing, man."

Awesome held the cane out like a sword as Lona and Stargazer moved back. He swung and sliced, parried, and thrusted. The cane sang as it swished through the air.

"I gotta tell you, Opal loves the sound of this thing, man."

Opal smirked.

"It's true."

"Loves it. I almost couldn't get it away from her. I'm going to have to make her a new white cane, I think."

"You realize I can hear you, right?"

"Are you saying you want a surprise?"

"No, I just—"

"Yeah. You do. Maybe Christmas."

Opal crossed her arms and scoffed but she laughed under her breath.

"Oh, just give the Detective her present already."

Stargazer handed the larger package to Lona and she sat at the patio table to open it. As she pulled the nylon bag away, she became more confused than she already had been. Inside Stargazer's bag was a second bag.

"You're always carrying that backpack so I figured I'd make you something better. It's high-quality. Anti-rip, anti-cut. It's got a bunch of pockets. No, it's ok, go ahead and check 'em out."

Lona unzipped the first pocket and withdrew a light piece of clothing and, shaking it out, she found it was a beautiful, dark gray jacket. She stood and slid into it. The jacket came to her hips but the fabric felt light and flexible and she found that she could easily move.

"It has bullet proof panels in the chest and back. And it's an all-weather fabric. Cool in the summer, warm in the winter."

Lona started to thank him but Opal interrupted her and told her to check the bag again. When she did, she found a sturdy belt with clips like the ones Opal and Stargazer used and clip-on packs to go with it. Within the packs she found a flashlight—

"Super bright. Four-thousand lumens."

A set of binoculars.

A pair of thin, leather gloves.

"Those are just like the ones most of us use."

Finally, Lona pulled the last package from within the bag. She unwrapped it to find a mask and a gun.

"Don't worry. It's a stunner."

"It looks like the ones the Guild Squires use."

"It is one of theirs. I've modified it though. It only reacts to the Detective's touch—your fingerprints."

"How did you?"

"Opal took one of your glasses the last time she was here."

Opal gave a nod.

"The mask was Stargazer's idea. The gun was mine."

"Oh… uh…"

Opal must have sensed Lona's anxiety about the firearm. She was firm and serious when she spoke again.

"I get it. You never asked for one of these. But you're out in the field now. Maybe you aren't confronting street thugs or bank robbers or whatever but you're taking on the wrongs in Arc City in your own way. You need to protect yourself and a stunner is a good option—I mean, not for me. Can you imagine?"

Opal actually threw her head back and laughed then but Stargazer stepped forward and helped Lona hold the gun the correct way.

"We can teach you to use it. Just come down to the Sheet Clinic sometime."

Lona nodded and started to put the stunner down when she remembered she was still clutching the mask, all balled up in her clenched fist.

"The mask is just like Opal's. It's pretty minimal but it's durable and it'll stick to your face. It might not be as good as the Baron's but it'll do."

Lona spread the mask over her face and Awesome, accustomed to fitting his own mask, helped her find the suction so it stuck properly.

"I think your work on the White Wolves case was just the beginning. The Baron told me how close you are to tracking down Lightning's true killer. He's the one who called you the Detective and I think he's right. You've found your calling."

Opal stepped forward and put a firm hand on Lona's shoulder.

"What he's saying is, 'Welcome to the Sheets.'"

Stargazer nodded.

"You're a hero. You're a Sheet. You are the Detective."

LONA FINGERED THE key that hung around her neck as she stood on Julia's balcony. Though it was still morning, the air was hot and sticky. Lona looked across the street to the bagel shop, happy it was still in business. Lona decided to stop by before she went home.

The balcony door slid open as Julia came outside and handed Lona a glass of iced tea.

"So they're just going to close it down?"

Julia nodded. They had been discussing the museum before Julia went inside to get drinks.

"They're going to say it's for renovations. But the truth is that it's just not secure. They've already moved a lot of the most valuable pieces into collections for other museums or put them away for safekeeping. Even with attendance down, there's just no way to keep an eye on the collection and the people."

"What about everyone who works there? What about you?"

"I don't know. They're offering severance packages to most of us and some of the higher-ups are taking temporary jobs out of town. Verun is going over to Arc City University to work with their archaeology department. But I'm not sure what I'll do. Before she left, Neima paid up the rent here to the end of the lease and I have some money saved but..."

She trailed off and Lona watched her friend stare into her tea. Ice cubes swam in the amber liquid. Down the street, a horn blared. Julia sighed.

"I'll figure something out."

"You know you can always stay with us."

"I know. And I appreciate it."

Lona blinked as the dust around Julia flared and spiraled off into several different directions. She rubbed her eyes.

"You alright?"

Lona wiped at her eyes and then looked at Julia again. The dust was back to normal—a faint shimmer, barely noticeable.

"It's my ability. I'm seeing new things lately. I don't really know what to make of it."

"Do you think it's evolving? I mean, you're still just learning to use your ability. It could be changing, right?"

"I guess so."

"Did you tell Awesome about it?"

Lona nodded.

"I've been keeping track of what I see. Just taking notes. And I'm meditating—not just here, but at home too. I think I just have to wait and see what happens. I just— "

"Yeah, I miss her too."

A few minutes later, Julia got her work clothes ready. She still had two weeks before the museum officially shut down. Lona said her goodbyes and made her way down the stairs and out to the street. She walked across to the bagel shop and bought a full box—more than her usual one or two bagels—and thanked the shopkeeper who smiled and carried on with her business as though all of Arc City weren't closing down around her.

Lona got in the truck, pulled her new pack off her shoulder, and withdrew her notebook and pen. She made note of the dust she had seen around Julia and, when she was through, absently drew long spirals onto the page as she considered what it might mean. As she slid the notebook back into the pack, she noticed the cover of her father's journal. She rested her hand on the soft leather and sighed.

"I'm not giving up, Dad. I'll figure this out."

Finally, she started up the truck and pulled into the street. She turned toward home but found that Maple—the street she usually took— was blocked off. Man-sized potholes chipped the asphalt. Char marked the old, brick buildings, and several of the shop windows were shattered. She kept driving and then stopped at the next light. Now, up ahead, she could make out the sparkle of gold dust at the next intersection.

Lona turned there and tried to find the dust again. She focused. And, as she was focusing, she heard a POP as the truck tire burst.

She pulled over and parked, slid her bag on over her jacket and looked around. It was still daylight but she'd heard about carjacking traps throughout the city. It appeared safe.

Traffic was busy and she slid over to the passenger side and got out on the sidewalk and walked to the obviously flat, back tire. She knelt and examined it. Running her hands along the tread, she found a long nail sticking through and sighed.

"Where's the spare on this thing?"

She checked around the truck and finally under it and smiled when she saw the spare tire situated above the rear axel.

"Thanks, Andy."

"You alright there, Miss?"

She turned to see an older man behind her. He wore a velvet jacket in spite of the heat and flicked his cigarette into a little, pewter ashtray in his palm.

"Yes, thank you. I'm sure I'll be fine."

Though, this being the first vehicle Lona had ever owned, she wasn't actually sure. She walked back to the front of the truck, opened the glove box with a click, took out the manual and flipped through it.

"Yes. I'll be fine."

She muttered to herself as she read through the instructions and slid the manual into her inside jacket pocket as she went back to the ruined tire.

Some time later, she was finished.

With a heave, she threw the old tire into the bed of the truck and watched as a trail of gold dust went in its wake.

"Looks good."

The man was back. Lona turned and laughed as she thanked him.

"Thanks."

"If you like, you can use the washroom in my shop to clean up."

Lona looked above his head at the store's sign.

"Yes, alright. Thanks very much."

"Not at all, Miss. I could use the business."

He showed her through the store, past old lamps and skeleton keys, costume jewelry and carnival glass. Mr. Chang had brought Lona to shops like this when she was a girl. It was a junk store.

Just past several jars of old buttons, the man opened a door into a washroom and Lona went inside. Black dirt swirled down the man's pink sink with suds from seashell-shaped soap. She stared into the gilt mirror and found black streaks on her nose and cheek as well and remembered the messy afternoons she and Awesome had once spent at her pottery class downtown. Lona hadn't heard from Alex since she received Andy's mug. She thought of Andy again as she stared in the mirror. Her dark jacket touched the top of her thighs. Her pack was still snug against her back. She pictured herself with the mask, tried to see herself as the Detective—as Humphrey Langdon's daughter—as a hero, a Cape, a Sheet.

She pulled her curls back into a low ponytail before washing and drying her face then she set out into the store once again.

A clock chimed and a cuckoo sprang out of its face. Lona grinned as she remembered all of Mr. Chang's old cuckoos and wondered if he had found any of them in shops like this.

"You never know, Lona. Treasures can be found in the most unlikely of places."

Her adopted father's voice echoed in her mind and she realized how much she missed him as she heard herself reply to him now.

"I know, Bàba. I know."

She wandered through the store, past a vase full of marbles and several pairs of glittery high heels and stopped when she came to a tall bookcase.

"I have a full collection of Hyatt's House of Horrors."

Lona glanced back at the man who was now standing behind the counter, sorting through another stack of books. She walked past the case, and nearer the register to a display of oddities. She let her fingers linger on an old magnifying glass then picked it up and put it to her eyes. Through the lens, she inspected a monkey with brass cymbals, a bouquet of carved wooden roses, and a porcelain kitten. Smiling, she decided to buy the magnifying glass and walked to the register.

"I'll just take this."

"Excellent choice. I do love this old piece. Notice the carved bone handle."

She picked it up, inspected the handle, and then glanced through it once more. Through it she read the words, *The Dark Star.*

Lona dropped the magnifying glass but, with astonishing speed, the shopkeeper caught it.

"Are you quite alright, Miss?"

"Yes, thank you."

But her voice was shaking. She reached for the thin paperback within the stack of books he had been sorting.

"I'll take this as well."

"WHAT IS THIS, Roy? Why are we here?"

They sat in a little diner on the edge of what had once been a nice neighborhood. Roy glared at Awesome across the table. An Arc City Bolts baseball cap shadowed his eyes and he kept the collar of his jacket up in spite of the heat. A glass of ice water condensated in front of him and dripped onto the vinyl, checkered tablecloth. Awesome was reminded of the day he first met Roy, the display of his ability through cubes of ice, the thrill of meeting real heroes.

"It's a dark spot on the Guild's security grid. At least for now. Someone keeps shorting out our cameras in this neighborhood."

"What's going on?"

"Is Julia alright? Have you heard from her?"

"Sure, she's doing alright. Lona went over there this morning to work with her. I think she's fine. Why, Roy, what's going on?"

Roy took a long, deep breath and nervously bent at the bill of his cap.

"Have you made a decision about coming back to the Guild?"

"No. But—"

"Awesome, I can't hold them off. You need to decide or—"

"Or what? What's going to happen?"

"Pythia is going to crack down on the Sheets and you're going to be the first one on the list, Awesome."

"Because of the Echo?"

At the Echo's name, Roy noticeably flinched and Awesome realized that, even though he and Lona had discussed that night over and over, Roy probably hadn't talked to anyone about it since he became a full Agent. His part in the Echo's death had been minimal and swept under the rug and, as Awesome knew perfectly well, no one at the Guild particularly enjoyed dredging up the past.

"Because of the Echo and because you won't stop snooping around about Andy's death."

"Snooping?"

"We got him, Awesome. *I got him.*"

"Do you really believe Dave Estos killed Andy?"

"Who?"

"Shadow Slider, Roy. Didn't you look into the guy's file before you took him in?"

"Well, look, we got a tip that it was him, that he'd been bragging about it to some of his friends. We tracked him down. He put up a fight but as soon as we cuffed him, he confessed."

"And what's happened to him since then? Did he have a trial?"

"I—well—"

"Roy, they should've scheduled a Guild Tribunal. You should've been called as a witness since you're the one who brought him in. Is he still being held?"

"I don't know. Awesome, I'm bringing in a lot of guys lately. There's just so much. This city—"

"I know. Believe me, I know. But there's something going on with Andy's death. The Guild isn't saying everything they know and they're acting stranger than ever. The other Sheets—"

"See, this is the problem. You can't be a Sheet anymore, Awesome. You're not a Sheet. You're a Cape, or at least you should be. You need to come back to The Guild. These guys can't be trusted—"

"You don't know them. You don't know the Sheets."

"I know they're undisciplined and unorganized and—"

"And uncontrolled? Isn't that the real reason Pythia wants to treat all the Sheets like criminals? Because we aren't under her thumb? Roy there's something bigger than us going on here, bigger than a bunch of unregistered Agents trying to help Arc City. Andy was onto something—something he wasn't supposed to find—and now it seems like the Guild is trying to sweep it under the rug. What happened to Ironhide? Do you ever think about that? Did you ever look into it? He was never taken to the regular places. Where is he? What about Wildfire? What about the man who supposedly killed Andy? The Guild—or Pythia—is hiding something. Don't you want to know what that is?"

"Yeah, of course I do but—look, Awesome, it's not up to me. I belong to The Guild and I have to follow orders, alright? If I have to start bringing in Sheets then that's what I'm going to do."

"And if she orders you to bring me in?"

Leaning back in his chair, Roy sighed. Dark half moons underscored his eyes; his mouth was pale and dry.

"Awesome, I'm sorry, but if you're not with us, you're against us. I can't protect you."

Roy stood and brought his collar closer to his cheeks.

"I'm sorry."

He went out the door and, a few seconds later, Awesome heard his motorcycle roaring to life. Awesome watched out the window as the red taillights trailed away. He leaned back against the hard chair and stared at his half-drunk cup of coffee.

"Me, too."

Then he stood as well, left some money on the table, and exited the diner through the back door. In a few seconds, he wasn't Awesome Jones but the Baron. He climbed the fire escape to the top of the old apartment building next door and looked out at Arc City.

LONA SETTLED INTO the sofa and Tulie lay on the floor beside her, tapping her tail against the carpet. She had come straight home from the junk store. Now, with a mixture of hope and anxiety, she opened the well-worn copy of *The Dark Star*.

The Dark Star by Jake Knight

EXCERPT 1

In the land of Prinn, all the Wicks were brought forward to show their promise. They glowed brighter than the rest of the Prinneans. Their youth, though, made them unstable. Their Light was raw, undeveloped, and full of promise.

My job was to discover the Wicks who showed the most potential and assign them to the proper Houses. They were be trained according to their specific Light—be they healers, makers, shapers, conductors, etc.—they will go on to lead an incandescent life. Sometimes, though, the Wicks were too dangerous to live in Prinn. They were assigned to different Houses and I do not know what becomes of them.

I worked in the Chandlery. My job was important. It was

important not only to the good of the Wicks but to the entire land of Prinn.

At least that's what I always thought.

That was before I met Sola.

EXCERPT 2

Sola came into the Chandlery with another Wick—Valen. Valen was stronger, healthier, and his Light was a beautiful, golden gleam. All of us in the Chandlery knew immediately how incandescent Valen would someday be but it was only my superior, Fellow Adamas, who noticed Sola.

EXCERPT 3

Where had Sola come from? No one seemed to know. He wasn't from Prinn, nor from the surrounding territories, which Prinn protected. Sola wasn't even his Mother's Name.

"It doesn't matter what his Mother's Name was," Fellow Adamas said when I questioned him.

"Doesn't it?"

"Of course not. All that matters is that Sola is here. He has great potential."

"Still, Fellow Adamas," I argued, "wouldn't it be better if we took more time to understand who Sola truly is and where he came from?"

"It does not concern us. We're running out of time. The Luminary has decreed that the Nova is upon us and it is our duty to do everything we can to combat it. The matter is closed, Young Fellow," he said, speaking in a furious whisper.

The words from *The Dark Star* swam around in Lona's head. She opened her little notebook and began a list of terms: Prinn, Sola, Light, Luminary, Nova.

EXCERPT 4

"We are moving to a new division," Fellow Adamas said, his voice full of edgy excitement. He was packing papers into his bag and stopped to hand an inventory of the Wicks to one of the other Young Fellows.

"*We?* I'm coming with you?"

"Of course, Sola trusts you."

"Sola?"

"Yes. The Luminary has decreed that we are to have a new House—dedicated to my research. I have helped to design it."

"We're leaving The Chandlery?" I asked, hesitantly. The Chandlery had been my ambition in life. Studying the Wicks and helping them reach their full Luminance had been the most rewarding position I could have asked for.

"Yes, of course. We are moving to the old fortress at Prinn's Edge."

I pictured the fortress. The imposing stone structure, guarded by silent, stone monsters was not a welcoming image. I shivered at the thought. No one had worked from Prinn's Edge for many seasons and I wondered how I could possibly adjust to life there after The Chandlery.

"And the Luminary—"

"The Luminary has decreed that this is to be. And so it must be. But our new division is one of secret. The Torrens cannot know what we are working at or it could quicken the Nova."

"I don't want to leave The Chandlery, Fellow Adamas."

"Not even to become a Full Fellow?"

I confess, I nearly gasped at the prospect of achieving Full Fellow. Typically, one strove for many decades before reaching such a high status.

"Full Fellow?"

"A Young Fellow cannot be expected to work in such a division."

"But why? Why me? I'm sure there are more qualified Fellows."

Fellow Adamas, who had been a Full Fellow for three years already, stared at me through his spectacles and, after several moments, smirked.

"As I said, Sola trusts you."

EXCERPT 5

We had been at Prinn's Edge for three months when I found Sola crying under the desk in the examination room.

"You aren't supposed to be in here, Sola," I said. Sola almost never spoke and so I continued, "Are you alright? Come out of there; tell me what's wrong. Do you miss Valen? The Chandlery?"

Sola whimpered and wiped his eyes. He stayed in the shadows of the desk with his back against the wall.

"Valen," he said, nodding. "The Chandlery."

A deep and aching pain grew in my chest. I missed the

Chandlery as well and I felt for the boy who had endured far more hardship than I had

"We can't go back to the Chandlery, Sola. I'm sorry."

And, truly, I was sorry. But, if what the Luminary said was true, we had no choice. Fellow Adamas saw promise in Sola and we had to see it through. The child peered out from the shadows at me though, with pale blue eyes, rimmed in red, and shook his head. It was plain that he didn't understand.

"Sola, I must tell you something but it is a secret. Do you understand?"

Sola put his hand over his heart to show that he did.

EXCERPT 6

"You what?" Fellow Adamas was furious and his anger was terrifying. He shook with rage and tore at his white hair.

"I told him of the Black Radiance."

"You had no right. *He* has no right." Fellow Adamas swept the papers and glass testing vials from the table and all of it landed in a crash and crackle in the floor.

"He wants to be special. What's so wrong with letting him know that he is?"

In that moment, Fellow Adamas seemed to deflate somewhat. The lines around his mouth deepened as he grimaced. He took a seat on the work stool and buried his face in his hands. It was through his digits that his voice emerged.

"The Black Radiance is dangerous. Sola is dangerous."

"He's a little boy."

"He won't always be a little boy."

Tulie was pacing back and forth as she waited to go outside. When she finally started whining, Lona snapped the book shut.

"Alright, girl. I'm sorry. Let's go."

Lona took the leash from the wall and snapped it onto Tulie's collar then threw her jacket and pack on. She never left the house without it now, even to walk Tulie.

"I hope Jones comes home soon."

Tulie hoped so too. Awesome had been gone all day and she had felt Lona's anxiety as Lona curled herself into a tight ball on the sofa, turning pages all the while.

Lona Chang

The evening was warm but Lona's jacket was still comfortable. She felt exhausted. Lona wondered exactly how much of the story was true, how much of real life Kawaguchi had taken for his novel. All of it, though, felt immediately familiar.

Was Sola a real boy or just an allegory for what had happened at Grayston? He felt real. But, then again, how often had Lona sunk into a fictional world, fallen into the characters' lives as if they were her friends or family? Still, she sympathised with Sola. As soon as Tulie was satisfied, they turned back toward home and, after pouring herself a glass of iced tea, Lona was back on the sofa with her book. Tulie jumped up and nosed her head into Lona's lap.

EXCERPT 7

"Are you sure he's ready for this," I asked Fellow Adamas as I stared through the screen at Sola and the Torren. That one is dangerous.

"There's no point if it isn't dangerous," Fellow Adamas said. His words were part of a worsening trend. Fellow Adamas seemed to be sinking every day deeper into the world of his work. He barely left Prinn's Edge and, when he did, he was never gone for long. All that mattered to him now was bringing out the Black Radiance.

This Torren had been sanctioned to the Snuffers. He had used his Light to hurt others and he was to be punished—jailed. Instead, he was chained to a chair at Prinn's Edge, staring a little boy in the face.

I watched as Sola fearlessly approached the Torren. Unlike every trial before, he was now equipped with the knowledge that he might have the Black Radiance—that he might be the one to bring an end to the Nova—and he did not hesitate or flinch as he closed his eyes and let his Light emerge.

Lona turned the pages furiously. Stopping only occasionally to make a note. She underlined the words, "Black Radiance."

EXCERPT 8

"It's not working," I said.

"I know," Fellow Adamas said, looking defeated and old. His shoulders slumped as he made note of the day's findings.

"Sola will not possess the Black Radiance."

"We can't know that."

I looked at the numerals on the latest sheets. Everything we were trying, everything we had done so far, pointed to Sola never reaching his full Luminance. This was not an uncommon occurrence. Wicks didn't always achieve their full Luminance and, on that night, I realized that Sola may never achieve his.

"Perhaps he is not the one, Fellow Adamas."

Fellow Adamas sighed heavily, his face set like stone. He was not to be moved.

"Send Sola back to the Chandlery so he may be assigned to a House and made useful. I will continue working on the problem."

"What will you do?"

"I will revisit the Old Masters."

Studying the Old Masters was beyond the clearance of even the Full Fellows. The Luminary had forbidden it long ago. Some knowledge, the Luminary decreed, was not to be known.

"But, the Luminary—"

"The Luminary has given me full Rights and Privileges."

As much as I disliked the idea of Fellow Adamas uncovering some truth that should remain covered, I nodded in acquiescence and took heart in the idea that I would likely at least be returning to The Chandlery.

"Very well. I will—"

"You will be assisting me. The Luminary has decreed it."

EXCERPT 9

Over the next few years, I saw very little of Sola. He was sent back to The Chandlery where he was reunited with Valen who was, unfortunately, on his way out. Valen had always been tapped for greatness and he went through The Chandlery in a short time, ultimately being assigned to a high House. Sola, inconsolable without him, soon followed—using his Light where he could to get ahead.

Valen and Sola both did well and I fostered the hope that he would be able to put all thought of the Black Radiance behind him even as I was working with Fellow Adamas to find the key to unlocking his full Luminence and, ultimately, the answer to the Nova.

EXCERPT 10

Fellow Adamas glared back at me incredulously. What was it to me if the Nova came? What did it matter to me? Did I truly care?

But, though he spoke the words with much vigor and damnation, they had a hollow sound. I realized he might as well have been talking to himself. He no longer cared about the Nova or what it might do to Prinn. He cared only about the Black Radiance and how to bring it about. Fellow Adamas would find the answer or no one would.

At this point, Lona ran up against several pages of scientific jargon that, she supposed might have been of some value to an actual scientist but, written as it was in imaginary units of measure and non-existent elements, Lona had a hard time concentrating and ended up skimming through at least twenty pages while Tulie slept peacefully at her feet.

EXCERPT 11

> We spent day after day in the labs of Prinn's Edge until I was weary with the calculations Fellow Adamas never tired of presenting to me. The Old Masters had possessed an understanding of Light that dwarfed my own and even Fellow Adamas'. However, with every ancient text Fellow Adamas read, he grew closer and sank deeper into that world. The following calculations were used to predict (unsuccessfully) the strength of a Wick's Light if he or she were to reach Full Luminance:

Lona yawned and rose to make some tea. The sky was dark and she stared at her reflection in the kitchen window as the teakettle warmed on the stove. She pictured herself as a character in Kawaguchi's novel. She imagined herself wearing the long, white robes of the Fellows and walking through the halls of Prinn's Edge. Then, she pictured herself in a lab coat, wandering Grayston, looking for something or someone.

It was Sola, she knew. Sola was the key to all of this. But what did the rest of it mean? What was the Luminary? And what was the Nova and the Black Radiance? What did it all mean?

Her reflection looked back at her, tired and thoughtful. Would *The Dark Star* really be of any help in the end? Lona had begun this journey with only a name and the memory of the wounds in her friend. Those things had led her to the library, the outskirts of the city, a prison, and now a novel. Had she gone too far afield?

She remembered Catherine Ziegel's words, repeated from Kawaguchi on the night she had found him weeping, "I'm not sure any of us should be doing this."

The kettle whistled and she poured steaming water over a bag of ginger tea. She held the mug, Andy's mug, under her face and let the fragrant, moist air rise and settle on her cheeks. She musn't second-guess herself at this point, she thought. She would carry on and see if *The Dark Star* led to the truth. If it didn't, she would keep searching.

EXCERPT 12

Fellow Adamas handled the scroll with special tenderness. His gloved finger hovered, vulture-like, above the words as he read the ancient words and translated them to me as I transcribed.

"The Old Masters tell here of the first Black Radiance. It says that when the first Nova came and the Uneven Light—"

"Uneven Light? What could that mean?"

"Don't interrupt. Write."

I put my head back down and continued my duties.

"The Uneven Light warned Prinnelon (that's Ancient Prinn) that the Dark Star was brought upon them. The Dark Star was possessed of a unique Light—neither Even nor Uneven—and that Light was unleashed into the lands and thereupon consumed all that which was Uneven."

"But what—"

"Shut. Up."

"But, Fellow Adamas, this is all just a story. There is nothing of The Sciences here. It is only Wisp Magic—rushlight. The Old Masters may have wielded tremendous power but I'm beginning to believe they didn't truly understand the mechanics of what they were doing."

"Get. Out."

"What?"

"Out. Out! Get out now! Leave me to my work!" he screamed, his face red and horrible.

I took my bag and left the room. In retrospect, if I had known what would come of his studying, I would have refused to leave, I would have tried to stay his hand or, at least, I like to think I would have.

In truth, I'm not sure whether I could have ever stopped Fellow Adamas.

Now Lona turned page after page of the narrator lamenting his decision not to challenge his superior. He returned to his own lab, at the other end of Prinn's Edge and worked on earlier mathematical problems regarding the Light (which were described in detail) until one night he heard the clatter of a voltaic chariot and ventured across the facility to investigate.

EXCERPT 13

...but when I threw open the doors to what had once been the examination room, I found there Fellow Adamas and Sola standing over a prostrate Torren. His face had been marked with the Torren "X" brand on either side and should have shown red. Instead, he lay pale and lifeless on a stone table. His brands were a dull gray and no Light shone from his eyes.

"His Light has gone," I said, aghast. What had happened here? I wanted to think the Torren had arrived this way but I knew this to be a falsehood and could not make myself believe it. Looking at Fellow Adamas and Sola—who was now a young man, no longer a Wick—I knew that it was of their doing.

"He was a dangerous Torren," Fellow Adamas said. "He was to be punished."

"By you?" I asked, a fear suddenly growing in my heart and spreading throughout my body. I could feel my legs quivering.

"The Luminary gave me full Rights and Privileges. I have exercised them as I see fit."

"The Torren was bad," Sola said. "Nothing else was working."

"What have you done?" I whispered. I was terrified at the part Sola had played in the death of the Torren.

"He merely forced a disconnect."

"A disconnect? Between what?"

"Between the Torren and his Light. Sola snipped the cord between the Torren and the Light and now—"

"You what? Did you use your Light to do this, Sola?"

"Fellow, I thought you would be pleased. I thought you would be proud of me. Am I not special now?"

"Answer the question, Sola."

But it was Fellow Adamas who answered in his stead.

"Sola needed help. That's all. His Light is too weak on its own," and at this remark, Sola seemed severely injured. "Sola needed an additional tool to aid his Light and I have provided it."

I now saw, in Sola's hand, a glass lens, sharp-edged and raw-cut. I couldn't begin to understand what Fellow Adamas had done to amplify Sola's Light but I understood that it was wrong.

My mouth gaped open as I stared at Sola. His eyes were changed somehow. His Light seemed different, *he* seemed different. I wanted to believe otherwise and, maybe even that night I convinced myself that he was still Sola—still the boy who had come to us frightened and desperate to be special so many years ago—but it was not to be.

"I thought you would be proud of me. I thought you wanted me to be special!" Sola screamed. Then he turned on his heel and strode out of the room and out of Prinn's Edge.

Several pages passed as Lona read about Sola's disappearance, how he seemed to have faded into the shadows of Prinn, and how Fellow Adamas still had not stopped his research into the Black Radiance. The narrator, in spite of all his apparent reservations, stayed at Fellow Adamas' side as the Nova drew nearer and nearer.

EXCERPT 14

When I finally beheld Sola again, his face had been marked with the Torren "X" on either side and his Light had been completely changed. It was no longer the pure, unwavering light we had initially witnessed when Sola first came to us as a boy. It waivered, flickered, and changed in strength and vibrancy. Was Sola's Light even his own anymore?

It was impossible to speak to him. Sola had gone mad.

EXCERPT 15

The Luminary decreed that the Nova was nearer at hand

than ever but we had lost all hope of bringing out The Black Radiance in Sola. We could not even communicate with him. He had been held under guard but now there was a question of what to do with him. Fellow Adamas was set on his theories being correct. The only thing standing in the way of Sola's Full Luminence was Sola himself.

"He is casting the shadow," he said in a meeting with the Luminary.

"If he is casting the shadow, how can his Light be set free?"

"Sola must be dimmed."

"How dim?"

"Sola must go dark for his Light to shine."

I stood behind Fellow Adamas and said nothing. I was terrified of the Luminary. At the time, I also believed that I was afraid of the Nova. But, looking back, I realize that my fear was an excuse. I was letting dark work go forth through the shadows in the name of stopping the Nova but there must have been another way. I was blind then. I had lost my Light and didn't even realize it.

"Sola may not be extinguished, he is still under my protection and it is against the Old Ways," the Luminary said and I heaved a sigh of relief.

"But—" Fellow Adamas started.

"I urge you to find another way."

"Sola could be the Dark Star," Fellow Adamas said.

"Then we shall wait for Sola to go dark—if we have that much time."

EXCERPT 16

Epilogue:

When I left Prinn's Edge, it wasn't more than a shabby relic. No Fellows roamed the halls—except Fellow Adamas. A few Healers were assigned there and yet were not told of the danger into which they were going; they were guarded by Snuffers who, likewise, were ill-informed. Their entire purpose, the entire purpose of Prinn's Edge had been to bring out the Black Radiance in Sola. And, still, after all these seasons, that remained its sole purpose.

I visited Sola one last time before I left. He slept and, for an instant, I recognized the boy I had known when I, too, was young and hopeful. The instant passed, though, and like a cloud before the moon, Sola changed.

I wondered, as I watched him sleep, whether the tests Fellow Adamas was conducting now would make Sola better or worse but, in the end, I realized that it did not matter. Someday, Sola would be gone and his Light would become The Dark Star.

LONA LET THE flimsy back of the book fall shut. She looked again at the cover—a field of black with a pale, dead-looking star in the center. Running her fingers over the words, she thought about the novel's story and its eerie familiarity—like meeting someone once known but long forgotten.

While she was deep in thought, Lona heard the key in the kitchen door and Tulie jumped up, wagging her tail.

"He's back!"

Lona met Awesome in the kitchen and, when they exchanged looks, and each saw that the other was troubled and thoughtful, neither wanted to go first.

Finally Lona asked,

"What's happened?"

Awesome sighed, running his hand over his hair.

"It's Roy. He—"

BRIIIING! BRIIING!

The telephone exploded with dust as Lona turned toward it.

"There's something wrong."

She grabbed the receiver and held it to her ear. The voice on the other end was muffled, frantic, crying.

"They came for Neima. I hid. What's going on, Lona? Help me!"

"Julia? What happened? Where are you?"

"I'm in the apartment. Please come help! Please help me."

"We'll be there. We're coming. You'll be alright. We'll be there. We're leaving now."

The line went dead. Lona hung up and looked at Awesome.

"What's going on?"

Lona relayed what Julia had said and Awesome was already charging into the bedroom grabbing their bags and stuffing their favorite or most important things into them. Lona slid *The Dark Star* into her own pack.

"Get the box."

In two minutes they were out the door with Tulie at their heels.

Lona drove and listened while Awesome told her what he'd heard from Roy.

"They're targeting the Sheets? It doesn't make any sense. The Sheets are helping."

"Not according to Pythia."

"Do you think this is connected?"

"I don't know. But none of this feels right. When we get to Julia's, we need to contact the Sheets. We'll have to warn them. But—"

"But you think they're going to come for you first?"

"Yeah."

"What can we do?"

He shook his head.

"I can't go up against the full force of the Guild. That would be insane. But maybe…"

"What?"

"Maybe I go in and talk to Pythia."

"Pythia? What about some of the other Capes instead. Blue Buckler or Supersonic Sleuth? They seem like rational people."

"But Pythia controls all of them. Look at the hold she has on Roy."

"I don't know, Jones, I doubt she's going to be open to conversations at this point. I think talking to her is a last resort."

"Arc City is falling, Lona, and I can only imagine how much worse it would be around here without the Sheets. The Guild is fighting the wrong war. I don't get what they're so afraid of."

"The Nova."

The words came out of Lona's mouth quietly and almost unexpectedly. Her mind was still spinning around the story of *The Dark Star* but as she drove down the shadowy lanes, in and out of streetlights, she thought about the Guild, Pythia, the Luminary and Sola.

She told Awesome about her day, about visiting Julia, about the way home being closed off, about finding herself broken down next to an old junk shop and about how her ability led her to *The Dark Star*.

"So, you read the whole thing?"

"Yeah, well, basically. Some of it was kind of unreadable. But the story—"

And then she gave him an abbreviated summary of Sola's tale.

"And you think it's a parable about the Guild?"

"I don't know. Maybe. I think whatever's going on, Sola is the key. If he's even—"

Lona stopped suddenly. They were outside Julia's apartment and couldn't afford to sit outside and talk. Lona slipped on her mask then pulled her stunner from within her pack. When she was ready, she nodded to Awesome, who was also masked now. Tulie hunkered down in the floorboard as they exited without a sound.

Wordlessly, they got out of the truck and swept up the stairs toward Julia's apartment. They stopped at the door. It was already ajar. The wood around the lock was splintered.

Lona pushed inside with a creak and Awesome rushed in ahead of her. He swept through the apartment quick and fluid and Lona could tell his time spent in the field with Stargazer had paid off. His footsteps were silent around the overturned coffee table, broken glass, and smashed wardrobe and when he got back to her, he whispered.

"It's clear."

"But Julia—"

He shook his head.

"Could she be hiding?"

"I don't know; this place is a wreck."

Lona focused. She took a deep breath and closed her eyes. When she opened them, a trail of violet dust blinked, weakly, into existence. She followed it and the trail grew stronger. Soon, Lona was standing in Julia's bedroom, watching the dust as it flowed across the floorboards and into the wall.

"Julia? Are you in here? It's just us. Are you alright?"

They heard a shuffling behind the wall, then movement to their left and a shifting in the closet. Lona opened it up to find a panel in the floor sliding open. Julia emerged and Lona helped her out. They went to the bed and sat down together.

"What happened?"

"Someone was beating on the door. Really loud. I hid in the little room behind the false wall."

"The little room?"

"It's a post-war building. When we moved in, Neima told me that when people came to Arc City with their families after the war, they had false walls built in so they could hide their children if anyone tried to take them. When I heard the men bust in, I ran into the closet and slid into the little room."

"And they were looking for Neima?"

"Yes. They talked about 'The Psychic' and said 'she's an old woman—she couldn't get far.'"

"I guess they didn't figure on her preceding their arrival by a few weeks. Anyway, are you alright? They didn't find you?"

"No but—"

"What?"

"Lona, I think they were from the Guild. One of their voices—I remembered it from when I was working in the Guild cafeteria. I know Neima didn't really leave the Guild on good terms but—"

"Alright, we need to get out of here. We can explain on the way, but I don't think you're safe, Julia. I'm not sure any of us who left the Guild are safe."

"What? No, I'm not going anywhere."

Julia stood and started straightening the room, tugging at the covers so Lona was forced to stand.

"Julia, we have to. You can't stay here."

"I have the little room. I can stay."

"No, listen they might come back, alright? And if they do, they might look harder than they did this time."

Julia stood next to the wardrobe where she'd been righting the toppled over bottles of nail polish and lotion and buried her face in her hands.

"You don't understand, Lona. I can't. I can't leave. I can't leave the apartment."

"What?"

"I—"

She looked from Lona to Awesome who took the hint.

"I'm going to go keep a lookout. I'll let you know if I see anything."

But Lona knew they needed to be quick. Whatever Julia was holding back, whatever had convinced her she couldn't leave, Lona had to resolve it quickly. There was an urgency in the air—an electricity—that Lona felt but would be hard-pressed to explain. She simply knew they had to move.

"Julia, please tell me. What's going on?"

"I can't leave. I haven't left."

"What? You didn't go to work this morning?"

Lona Chang

"I didn't go to work...ever."

"What do you mean? I saw--"

Lona's voice trailed off as her mouth fell open and she realized what Julia had been trying to tell her. She answered her own question, piecing together what Julia was saying now with the way she had been acting the last few months.

"You haven't left this apartment since you came here. It was always one of your copies."

Julia nodded and rubbed at the scar on her chest as tears came to her eyes and slid down her cheeks.

"After what the Echo did, I stayed with Neima in the cabin. I was so sick. I was having the night terrors. I lived and I died and every single morning when I woke up, I remembered that a part of me was gone. I could feel the absence of it. I used to be five. Now I'm four.

At first, I was afraid to split at all. I was afraid of what might happen to one of my reflections if I left it alone for even a second—if I let it go into the kitchen by itself or let it use a knife or let it go for a walk. But then I became even more afraid, Lona.

I knew what it was to die. I knew that gray nothingness—the absolute nonexistence. I only felt it for seconds but I was terrified of feeling it again. And, if I died—if the *real* me died—there wouldn't be five or four or three. There would be none. I would die and that would be the end of my story.

So, I started sending my reflections out. It started at the cabin. My reflections went for walks with Neima. My reflections helped her make dinner. My reflection met with Roy when he came out to break it off with me.

Neima thought it would be good for me to come back to Arc City, to be around you, to be part of something bigger than myself and have a job and do things besides sit in the cabin all day. But she was wrong. Once we moved into this apartment, I never left. I split to go to your wedding, Andy's funeral, and every day that I have worked at the museum while the real me stayed here—safe.

But, today—today—I"

Lona threw her arms around her friend. Today Julia's apparent safety had been compromised. And, even though they had come for Neima, Julia—the real Julia—had been in danger. Lona felt Julia's heart pounding against her own chest.

"Julia, listen to me, it's going to be—"

She was interrupted as Awesome slung the door open. Through it, from the street below, she could hear Tulie barking.

"Two Suits are headed our way. We need to get out of here."

"HOW CLOSE ARE THEY?"

Lona pulled a bag from the closet and started tossing Julia's clothes in along with whatever threw out pops of dust when she looked at it—a journal, a necklace, a pair of old tennis shoes.

"They're on the sidewalk."

Awesome pulled the lace curtain aside and peered out again.

"I'll lead them off. You guys get down to the truck."

"But where—"

"I'll meet you on Baxter and 6th in five minutes."

Lona nodded.

"Be careful."

"You, too."

He charged out of the apartment and down the stairs. Lona zipped up Julia's bag.

"We need to go."

Julia shook her head uncertainly.

"Listen, Julia, the first time I ever met you, I was terrified. I was covered in the blood of a man who had been very kind to me and who had died protecting me. I was running for my life and I had no idea who I was dealing with when I found myself standing in a shabby little room in the Guild Hall. You smiled at me. Do you remember? You hugged me like we'd known each other for years and you helped me get cleaned up and you gave me some of your clothes. You helped me when I didn't know how to help myself.

I'm here to help you now, alright? You are stronger than this, Julia. You are braver than you think and you can do this. You have it in you to beat this. You're in danger and you need to leave this place right now. I'm here to help you but first you have to help yourself. You have to take the first step out of this apartment."

With a look of petrified determination, Julia nodded and took her bag from Lona who drew her stunner and moved toward the door. She opened it in a rush and looked outside. The hall was empty. Lona swept across the hall and looked down the stairs.

"It's clear. Listen, you can do this."

Julia took a deep breath. Lona saw that Julia was quivering but her jaw was set as she stared at the threshold.

"You can do it. Just take the first step."

Finally, a sandaled foot landed on the tile. Then another. Julia looked up at Lona who smiled behind her mask.

"Alright, can you make it to the truck?"

"I think so. Yes. I can."

With Lona leading, they descended the stairs and ran out to the sidewalk where Lona bolted to the truck. She threw open the door for Julia who jumped inside and was met by Tulie.

Lona Chang

As she started the truck, Tulie whined.

"It's ok, girl. We're going to go get him."

Julia held her bag on her lap with one hand and stroked Tulie's back with the other.

"And then what?"

Lona put the truck in gear and started down the street, glancing in the rearview mirror to check whether they were being followed.

"I don't know."

STUNNER SHOTS WHIZZED by Awesome Jones as he charged out of the building. One shot screeched past him and slammed into the window of the closed bagel shop, shattering the glass. He kept going, past the museum, past the defunct art gallery, past the coffee shop and the little seafood place that had closed down right after Andy died.

Bolts of silver light landed all around him but he kept going and turned the corner onto Staples Street, bounded onto a dumpster and then lept up and grabbed the fire escape ladder of a two-story building. He waited for a few seconds now, knowing that if the Suits lost him, they might double back and investigate the apartment again.

Finally, they appeared at the corner and he ran up the fire escape and across the roof. He stopped and listened for them on the metal stairs to be sure they were following before he scrambled onto the opposite fire escape and raced down the stairs.

At street level, he charged again, and headed out onto Baxter Street. The intersection at Sixth was only two blocks away.

TURNING ONCE AND then again, Lona took the truck on a winding path toward their destination, hoping they wouldn't run into any Suits on the way there. As Lona drove, Julia petted Tulie and stared out the window. And, in spite of her sense of urgency, Lona wondered whether the true Julia's experience was different than that of her copies, whether this was the first time she had really seen the city since moving back.

"What's happened to this place?"

Julia leaned her head against the truck's bench seat and watched the city go by. Lona shook her head.

"What's happened to the Guild?"

"I don't know."

Julia sighed.

"When I was there, I always felt like they were holding me back, or, like they didn't have time for me. Like they were always worried about something more important, whatever the next big threat was—the next thing they'd have to protect the world from. Whoever would've thought it'd be us?"

She laughed sourly and wound her fingers through Tulie's fur before continuing.

"Going after you and Awesome and Neima? What happened?"

Their intersection loomed up ahead and Lona braked and looked around but didn't put the truck in park.

"Get down. Just in case, ok?"

Julia did as instructed and pulled Tulie into the floorboard with her.

The street was still dark and quiet. The shops were closed. The apartments were black. Tall maples, up and down the street, wavered in the breeze amid the streetlights.

Lona rolled down the window and peeked outside, behind the truck. A blast of silver light screeched past her nose and pinged the heavy truck door, busting the mirror in the process. Two black Guild cars were headed toward them and two more Suits pursued on foot.

She heard a crack behind the truck. One of the old maples shook. At the sound of another crack, Lona turned to look over her shoulder.

Awesome Jones landed a hard kick—his third—into the tree. It finally toppled and lay in the road between the Suits and Lona's truck. Awesome ran toward them.

"Let's go!"

Lona threw the truck in park and started to scoot over as Awesome opened the door.

"We've got to—"

But before Awesome could finish, the roar of a motorcycle thundered up ahead and screeched to a stop in front of them. Lona's mouth dropped open as she stared at Photon under the streetlight. He leapt off his motorcycle.

"You should go on."

"But—"

"I can handle this. Please, go."

Lona reached into her jacket and un-holstered her stunner then checked her mask to make certain it was in place.

"No."

"Lona—"

But they didn't have time to argue. Another silver shot rang past Awesome's ear and he shut the truck door and ducked. Lona and Julia exchanged looks before Lona unslung her bag and opened it up. She withdrew a little gold box and handed it to Julia.

> "Listen, no one knows you're in this truck so just stay down, open this box, and press the button. It'll take you somewhere safe. It's already set. Catherine showed me how to set the counter and it's set for two minutes. So as soon as I leave, hold on to Tulie and open it up, alright?"

> "What? Who's Catherine?"

> "I'll explain later. I have to help Jones but we'll meet you later."

Lona added, *I hope*, in her mind as she leapt from the truck, slammed the door behind her, and went running.

AWESOME, PASSING IN an out of the streetlights, strode toward Roy who didn't look at all surprised to see him.

"I'm sorry Baron, but I have to take you in."

"Roy, I need to talk to you. Can we just get out of here?"

Roy shook his head.

"If you come peacefully, it'll look better. She'll be more lenient. Maybe you can still rejoin the Guild?"

"Why? So I can be like you? So I can be a clueless—"

But Awesome's teeth clacked together as a hard right from Roy landed in his jaw and he stumbled backward.

"I'm not coming with you, Roy."

"It's Photon now."

Awesome turned to leave and Roy tackled him, or would have, if Awesome hadn't rolled his old friend over, dumping him on the city street. A stunner shot screamed as it flew past his ear. It was the Suits. They'd exited their vehicles and were rushing toward him and Roy.

Their shot was answered by another. As he stood, Roy saw a woman in a long jacket and black mask wielding a stunner. Her autumn-colored curls were tied back in a low ponytail and came alight each time she fired a burst.

"Lona?"

"It's the Detective now."

Awesome threw a fierce jab and it barely grazed Roy as he got out of the way. Roy heaved a front kick, which missed Awesome. Awesome countered with a spinning hook kick, but also came up empty.

Down the street, Lona crouched behind a mailbox as six Guild operatives bounded toward them, breaking off—two for her, four for Awesome and Roy. She glanced back at the truck and hoped Julia had opened the box. She tried to peer into the window but a stunner shot slammed into the mailbox and it rang like a steel drum.

She popped up and fired two shots. They both went wide. She ducked again. Took a deep breath. Another stunner slammed into the pavement next to her foot and left a black scar in the cement.

Jumping out, toward the storefronts on her right, Lona focused and tried to rely on her ability. She aimed the stunner along a path of red dust, shot, then repeated the action. Two Suits dropped.

She grinned at her success then turned to her left and saw—

Awesome ducked, slipping Roy's furious hook. While he was low, he tried to sweep Roy's leg but Roy jumped. Roy shot a blast of colored light at Awesome but Awesome looked away, recognizing the setup Roy always used for that move.

"This is useless, Roy. I know all your stuff."

"Not all of it."

At that, Roy let loose a blast of hard, bright white light. A focused beam, Awesome had seen it in action in the woods the night the Echo had come for them. It was dangerous and, Roy was right,

Awesome had never sparred with Roy after his ability had come to full maturity.

Awesome launched himself behind one of the big maples. Roy's laser bored into it. Awesome reached behind his back as he ran from one tree to another, quicker than Roy could keep up, then reappeared just feet away from him, extending his cane as he came. Roy realized he wasn't the only one with new moves.

Roy aimed and shot. Awesome ducked and swung the cane, catching a piece of Roy's knee as he tried to jump back.

Awesome moved in again, ready to strike, as a stunner shot grazed his right leg. Only a partial blast, and with his tough hide, Awesome didn't go down but the feeling crept from his leg and was instantly replaced with a cold, tingling sensation. Awesome turned to look at the Suit who had shot him but instead watched as the Suit dropped to the concrete—hard—and Lona appeared behind him.

Awesome nodded to her before ducking under another blast from Roy.

Bobbing and weaving under Roy's blasts, Awesome thrust his cane and got Roy hard in the stomach. Roy doubled over. He fired another shot from his knees but Awesome stepped aside and it flew easily past him.

Stunner shots crashed behind him. Awesome knew Lona was engaged in a tough battle and, while he trusted her, she had never been in the field. He was worried. He had to get to her and they would have to get out of here together. Lona had been right. There would be no conversation with Pythia now; she only wanted him and the rest of the Sheets off the streets and out of sight. He couldn't allow that to happen. Neither he nor Lona nor any of the good people he'd been helping were going to end up in Claymore or whatever box Pythia wanted to throw them in.

Awesome swung again and Roy's legs went out from under him.

He held up his hand. Awesome lurched out of the way of another blast and raised his cane high above his head. He had Roy down and powerless. In the instant that followed, though, Awesome remembered that night in the woods, remembered the way his father's cane had crunched through the Echo's skull. His heart raced and his hand faltered. And, in that instant, Roy fired.

Just down the street a shot whizzed past Lona's cheek and slammed into the brick of the closed-down delicatessen behind her. She shot back but this Suit was quick. Something about this man was different. He, and his partner, weren't wearing the typical, single-breasted jacket the other Suits wore, their black coats were more military in style and double-breasted with plain, silver buttons.

The man ducked and the stunner round slammed through his black hat, which flew off his head and landed in the street.

Lona slipped into the dark alleyway beside the delicatessen and crouched behind a dumpster. The glowing charge meter on her stunner was at zero. She was empty. Lona put her back against the cold brick and listened in the darkness. Footsteps soon followed.

"You're under arrest. I'm taking you into custody for crimes against the Guild."

This Suit didn't seem at all like the others she had seen, met, and fought. He was louder, more open, more combative. She listened as his hard, rubber soles tapped against the pavement and then listened again to the chunk of something metallic. It sounded like he was reloading his stunner but when the cartridge slid in, it had a different sound—a higher-pitched whine.

Along her hand, Lona saw a faint sparkle of dust and groped on the ground until her fingers closed around an old tin can. She stood, as quietly as she could, and threw the can across the alleyway. The Suit shot at the sound. The can made a series of strange popping noises that let the Suit know he hadn't got Lona. When he looked around, he got a blast of Lona's super-bright flashlight in the eyes.

Lona Chang

He shot blindly toward the light but missed. Lona ran past him, almost out of the alley before she felt a strong hand grab her wrist from behind.

The other Suit. She'd forgotten about him. There had been two left.

"Not so fast. You're coming with us."

She would've cursed herself for not paying more attention—if she'd had time. Her heart raced as she went, automatically, through the motions Awesome had taught her.

Lona pulled her wrist against the weakest part of his grip as she turned inward, toward him, and, with the fingers of her other hand curled around the stem of the heavy flashlight, she threw a swift jab at his nose. It crunched. Blood gushed and he gurgled in pain even as he pulled his stunner from its holster.

Lona, quicker than this Suit had expected, stepped aside; she shot out her arm and thrust his gun hand downward. With her left hand, she started to grab the barrel and take it from the Suit but, as they struggled, the Suit from the alley approached.

His vision was still swimming but he aimed and took the shot. At the last second, Lona wrenched the stunner from her Suit's hands. The struggle moved them, only slightly, to the left. It was just enough. The Suit Lona had been fighting was now standing where she had been.

Bright, silver lights popped all over his torso. He screamed as tiny holes emerged in his double-breasted coat. He fell to the ground and grabbed at his flesh as it ripped apart and his body fell into a state of entropy.

Lona looked back at the Suit in the alley. She aimed the stunner she'd taken from the downed man and fired. She didn't wait to see whether she'd made the shot, though, she had to find Jones and get out of here.

AWESOME FELL TO the ground, unconscious. Roy rolled him onto his chest and pulled his X-cuffs from his belt, knelt, and slapped them on Awesome's wrists.

"Roy, you can't do this."

Roy rose to see Lona, masked, bruised, and dirty, coming toward him.

"Lona, look, just get out of here. I don't want to take you in but I will."

"Please, just listen to me. The Guild—"

But as she spoke, a stunner shot rang past her shoulder, barely missing her and slamming into the tree behind her.

"I'm sorry, Lona."

Roy raised his hand to fire a blast and Lona reached for the stunner she'd taken off the Suit who'd been shot. But, just as Roy's hand began to light up, he fell aside with an "Ooopf!"

Julia was standing over him, shaking the pain out of her hand from the punch she'd just landed. Tulie at her side, growled at Roy.

"What the hell is happening? Roy, what's happened to you?"

Roy looked up at her, dumbfounded. Lona stared at Julia, too. She seemed different, changed. Her eyes were dark, deep pools of black and she seemed wiser and more sure of herself than she ever had. A stunner shot whizzed past her head and still she stood over Roy.

Lona fired back but, with her focus more on Roy, Julia, and Awesome lying unconscious on the ground, her shot went wide and missed.

"When I met you, you were a Double A. A *sidekick*. You were miserable. All you wanted was to be special and important. And this is how you've gone about it? Betraying your friends? Not listening to the people who love and care about you? Don't you get it, Roy?

Lona realized, then, that Julia's hand was glowing with a brilliant, white light. No, not her hand. Something in her hand. The box.

Another stunner shot. Lona returned fire. Again, she missed. Could she get past Roy to Awesome?

Julia continued, obviously unphased.

"You were *always* important to me. You were always special. You were always loved—you idiot! How can you do this? How can you do this to your friends? To me? How can you just blindly follow orders—never questioning what Pythia wants or why? Is this what you wanted? Is this the man you always dreamed you could be? Look around you! Look at *yourself!* You're Photon now. You're Arc City's Cape. You *finally* made it, after all these years. Tell me? Do you feel special now? Do you feel important?"

Suddenly, as Julia's words washed over her, everything fell into place for Lona. The lonely boy. The dejected sidekick. The man who only wanted to be important—powerful. She understood Jacob Kawaguchi's message. She understood *The Dark Star* and what it was. She understood how Andy had died and what Awesome Jones would be walking into.

She had to tell Roy.

She had to get Awesome out of here.

She had to get them all out of here.

She charged toward Roy. Another stunner shot whizzed past and grazed Lona's right arm as she ran. An icy numbness spread through her arm. She was cold all over. Her feet stopped. Her vision tunneled; darkness encroached from every angle. With her left hand, she raised her stolen stunner and aimed at the approaching Suit even as she tried to scream at Roy, tried to tell him what she had realized. It was so important. He had to help Awesome. He had to know.

"Roy, please, you have to help Awesome. Roy, it's—"

But her last words were sucked away as she fell into a world of white light. Had she said the words she meant to say? Had Roy heard them? Julia's arms closed around her. She felt Tulie's hot breath on her face.

Everything went black.

EVERYTHING WAS BLACK.

In the darkness, Awesome heard a faint voice. Familiar, he thought, but like a voice in a dream, it seemed inhuman, unnatural.

He tried to move his arms but he couldn't. He tried to move his legs but he couldn't.

Gradually, he opened his eyes. Unfocused, black blobs moved before him, occasionally murmuring.

He blinked, shook his head. In a few seconds, his vision cleared.

Awesome Jones was in a big, round room. On the floor was a mosaic, decorated in stars and planets. In the center of the room, Awesome looked down and found the Earth at his feet. He also found that his wrists and ankles were bound, with hi-tech straps, to a sturdy chair.

He tried to move but couldn't.

His breathing echoed in the big, round room.

Two men in dark scrubs and surgical masks moved in front of him. One pushed a metal cart, the other walked behind the first, slowly.

Now, Awesome saw, from across the room, another man. A big man. A huge man. His chest heaved as he breathed. An inhuman glow emerged from under the hood, which was pulled low over his downcast head. He stood like a statue.

Something about this man, about his very presence, put Awesome on high alert. His heart thumped in its cage and Awesome tried to slow it down, tried to calm himself so he could pay attention. Pay attention and get out of whatever and wherever this was.

His questions regarding the place and purpose of this round room, though, were soon answered.

A familiar, earthy voice began to speak. Awesome looked across the room to the person in dark, indigo robes. His vision was still blurry but, as the voice spoke, it cleared.

> "Awesome Jones, you stand accused of high treason against the Guild. You have blatantly disregarded our laws and customs. You wore a Cape without explicit permissions. You have caused unrest, fear, and damage to property and persons. You acted with others like yourself in a conspiracy to undermine the important work done here—work done in the name of The Greater Good."

Awesome watched as Pythia spoke, flanked by six other figures, all in black robes. Meanwhile, the huge man with glowing eyes stood off to the side, as if waiting.

> "You are hereby found guilty. Your sentence will be carried out immediately."

The men in black scrubs moved toward him but stopped when Awesome filled the room with his voice.

> "A trial by one's peers? Is this what you meant, Pythia? Is this what happened to Ironhide? Is this what happened to Dave Estos?"

She didn't answer.

> "You just pronounce sentence and the problem goes away

forever and neither the public, nor the other Capes, have any say, any ability to act, not even any knowledge that this is going on? You say you're acting on behalf of The Greater Good but the people you're protecting are ignorant of your existence— let alone what's going on here!

"And what would you have me do?"

"Give them a say."

She scoffed.

"They're not children, Pythia. And they're not *lesser* than you. They're human beings and they deserve a say in how they're governed and how the people protecting them police the streets. What could be so important that you have to work in the darkness, passing judgement in the shadows of the Guild Hall?"

"Look around you, Mr. Jones. Arc City is a microcosm of what will happen the world over. Thanks to various advances, the population is booming and the blood stream has become diluted. Those with abilities are more common and more numerous than ever before. And how many of those extra-normal humans do you think are worthy of the Cape? How many would even want it? How many would take up that burden when it is all too easy to simply turn one's power on those around him? When one can take what one wants by force?

We are being overrun, Mr. Jones. The world is falling out of balance. It is up to me to restore that balance. The gifts we were given are meant to be rare and pure and put to the purpose of spreading good and protecting the innocent."

"The ignorant, you mean."

"You asked what was so important. You now know. The world is at stake."

"And you're going to deal with the problem one person at a time?"

"If we have to, yes. And we will set an example, if necessary."

"And I'm the example?"

"No, you are a test."

"So I'll be put to death and then what?"

Pythia made a face that might have been a mix of confusion and disgust—were she capable of those emotions—which Awesome doubted.

"Mr. Jones, you ought to know better than anyone that the Guild does not condone lethal use of force and I do not pass a sentence of death."

One of the men in black scrubs removed the cover from his cart to reveal a sterile tray of tools. A syringe. A bright, shining scalpel. Two long tubes and two metal circles. He passed the syringe to the other man in scrubs, who moved to stand behind Awesome's back.

Pythia spoke again.

"You will be separated from your ability."

"What?"

"Your sentence will be carried out by the Hand of Justice."

At the sound of his name, the giant man raised his head and stepped forward. He walked with a heavy, mechanical motion toward Awesome. His feet came down hard, like metal, and Awesome saw, under the robes, that they were metal, as was one of his giant hands.

"When you wake, your sentence will be complete. Do not fear. You won't feel a thing."

And, just as Awesome felt the jab of a needle in the back of his neck, the giant man stood above him and removed his hood, revealing his mottled face.

"The Echo—"

SOME MONTHS AGO:

The older man stood in a clearing in the woods. A man in a double breasted coat held an umbrella above his head while several other men, identically dressed, strapped the subject onto a gurney and opened the door of a large, medical van.

The older man examined the ground around him, the ruined trees, the deep gouges in the earth, the scorch marks here and there. The blood, diluted with rainwater.

Everyone had been cleared away except the subject. The older man's mind went round and round. The possibilities were primed. Was he ready?

A high-pitched ring cut through his thoughts and the sound of the rain tapping against his umbrella. A suited man pulled a small phone from his jacket pocket, spoke for a few seconds and then approached the older man.

"Excuse me, Doctor. She wants to speak with you."

The older man held the phone to his ear and the other voice immediately spoke.

"Dr. Kivi, Can it be done?"

"I don't know yet. I'm preparing to inspect the subject."

"Your lab is waiting for you."

"It's a long drive to Grayston, Pythia."

"Will he make it?"

"Who can say?"

"You can."

"I can't. Not yet."

"It will work, Doctor. We need him. We need the Hand of Justice."

She hung up.

"We're ready to go, Doctor Kivi."

"Yes, alright."

The older man—Doctor Kivi—climbed into the back of the van and sat on the bench beside the gurney. He peered down at the huge man strapped to it. There was barely any of him left. His face was smashed but he had been unrecognizable long before that. The older man leaned in and looked closely at the bloody mess of flesh.

"Well, Sunny, here we are again."

Doctor Kivi took the Echo's beautiful, well-shaped hand in his own. It was still warm.

"LONA! Lona!"

Lona opened her eyes at the sound of Julia's voice. Her vision was hazy but she recognized her friend's shape.

Lona blinked, confusedly.

Tulie was licking her face.

She bolted up and rubbed her eyes.

"Where's Jones? What happened?"

Julia's face became clear and Lona realized she was lying on an old, blue sofa. Dawn was just breaking through the windows, filtering through lace curtains.

"I don't know where he is. You were hit by one of those stunners and you went down. I'd already started the box and as you were going down, I pulled you into the light with me and Tulie. I'm sorry, I couldn't get to Awesome."

Lona stood and, woozily, sat back down.

"Have you seen a phone?"

"Yeah, there's one in the kitchen. It's old but it's got a dial tone."

"Alright. Help me get in there."

Julia helped Lona stand and then pulled her arm across her shoulders. They padded through the old house, the dusty hardwood creaking under their feet. The pages of an outdated calendar waved in the breeze from the open window. A painting of blue irises was framed and hung on the far kitchen wall. Julia helped Lona take a seat in a hard kitchen chair and then handed her the phone.

"Lona—"

Lona was dialing.

"Yeah?"

"Where are we?"

SOMEWHOW, AWESOME WAS still awake. Was he supposed to be awake? He broke into a cold sweat as he struggled against the straps that held him to the heavy, metal chair.

The Echo's face—and yet not the Echo's face—loomed over Awesome. The eyes—Evangeline Jones' eyes—were gone. They had been replaced by glowing, green orbs. Metal plates ran from the Echo's forehead, down the left side of his face, and onto his jaw. In and out of the plates were wires and tiny lights.

What remained of the Echo's head had been shaved and Awesome could see the twisted way his remaining skin came together. On the left side, there was no skin. Only metal. Shiny and blinking, the plate that covered his cranium threw Awesome back to that night, that fight, that final blow.

But it hadn't been final at all.

The Echo—now the Hand of Justice—was staring down at him with new eyes. They appeared void of life. Lit only by electricity, it seemed as though there was nothing behind them.

What had they done to him?

Awesome's heart raced as the Echo approached and he heard the flick of a knife behind his back. Awesome let out a gasp as cold metal brushed against his left wrist and the straps fell away.

"Close your eyes, Baron."

A warm hand touched his own and his fingers were wrapped around two objects: a knife and his own, fully retracted cane. Before he could consider his sudden change in circumstance, he shut his eyes against a searing light and cut his other hand free then knelt to slice at the straps around his ankles.

"It's time. Let's go."

Awesome opened his eyes and saw Roy, in black scrubs, his surgical mask removed, standing beside him. Awesome stood. He made ready to attack the Echo as Roy shot another blast of light at Pythia and the men surrounding her but the Echo did not move. He stood, instead, like a statue—his face blank, his eyes unmoving.

Roy took off running and Awesome followed.

"Roy, why did you—?"

"It was Lona. She said it was the Echo. I had to find you. Come on, we've got to get out of here."

"Where are we?"

"The basement of The Guild Hall."

The men around Pythia threw back their robes. Underneath were the double-breasted suits he had seen on the street. They pulled their stunners—or what had seemed to be stunners—and aimed. Shots slammed into the wall and floor around Awesome and left tiny holes in their wake but Pythia screamed at them.

"Careful! Don't hit The Hand. And don't kill them. Stun only."

Awesome and Roy raced through the room as Roy threw blast after blast of light at the Suits.

"Who are these guys?"

"Elite Squires. They're new."

Lona Chang

Two of the Elites jumped in front of Roy and Awesome as they ran for the door. Roy let forth a blast of laser, clipping one Elite as he tried to leap away. Another Elite aimed his stunner at Awesome who charged in, disarmed him, and thrust his cane, between he and the Elite so it landed just under the man's chin—hard. As he toppled backward, Awesome threw a hard kick at the man's gut and he went down. Awesome turned to see Roy land a right hook in his Elite's jaw. The man groaned and doubled over.

"Let's go."

Roy led the way out the door and Awesome found himself in a long, dim hallway with concrete walls and floors. Stunner shots screeched past them as they raced out the heavy door at the end of the hallway. Awesome held it shut as Roy tried the elevator.

"It's on lockdown. All the elevators and exterior doors aren't going to work. They'll have the lobby loaded with Suits, too."

"Can we take the stairs?"

Roy kicked at the door to the stairs but it wouldn't budge. Finally, he traded places with Awesome and burned the hallway door handle while Awesome ripped the door to the stairwell off its hinges.

They ran into the stairwell and turned back toward the door.

"Shield your eyes."

Awesome did and Roy aimed his hand at the door and shot a hot blast of light at the whole thing until it glowed red.

"That'll give us a little time."

They raced up three floors and past three landings with no sign of exit until they came to a door.

"This lets out on the training level. There's another set of stairs at the other end."

Awesome remembered the stairs he was talking about. He, Roy, and Julia had hidden in that stairwell one night and eaten stolen ice cream while they listened to Silver Starling singing in the hot tub after her training session. But there was no time now for reminiscence. He was running.

They careened around the corner and into the hall of specialty training rooms. They were all empty and Awesome wondered what time it was—how long he'd been trapped here. He stared into the dark windows as they passed and suddenly slid to a stop.

"Turn them all on."

"What?"

"Turn them on. Everything."

Roy followed Awesome's direction, twisting dials and pressing buttons until all the rooms were whirring with ice storms, high wind, flashing lights, and gunfire. Last of all the Shadows—the programmable sparring partners who'd knocked Awesome around day in and day out when he was in training—came to life.

Now, Awesome flicked out his cane and, swinging it like a bat, he shattered the thick glass in room after room as they made their way down the hall. The space behind them was a hurricane of snow, rain, wind and rubber bullets.

At the end of the hall, they slammed the door behind them and Roy superheated the handle.

They raced past the poolroom, through the locker rooms, and into the stairwell.

The next floor up, several regular Suits, who Awesome recognized, shot stunner blasts down at them from halfway up the next set of stairs. Roy and Awesome ducked into the third floor and ran through the cafeteria.

It was nearly empty. Two newer Capes who must've just come in from the night shift were sitting at a table drinking coffee and talking while one of them inspected and set his own broken arm.

Awesome blew past them and hoped they wouldn't follow. Roy nodded to the youngest of them as he went past.

"Jackson."

"Morning, Mr. Photon!"

"It's Roy!"

Roy called out the words as he ran and the young man nodded again, blushing.

"Mr. Photon?"

Almost breaking into a laugh as they turned out of the cafeteria and raced down a back hallway, Roy gave Awesome a shrug. They turned into one of the old, forgotten courtyards, ran past a pond full of electronic fish, and skidded into another stairwell.

"This one should take us all the way up."

Awesome recognized it as soon as he was in. No one ever used the old stairwell. It still had the original building's railing in it and the steps were wood and carpeted and they creaked as Awesome and Roy pounded up them. These stairs—because they were never occupied—were the ones Awesome had always taken down to breakfast from his own tenth floor room.

Several minutes and ten flights later, Awesome and Roy burst onto the roof of the Guild Hall.

"Well, now what?"

DAWN WAS BREAKING over Arc City's skyline. The city, Awesome thought, was still beautiful. The air was still cool and clear and he wished so much that he wasn't here—that he was at home, with Lona, instead. He hoped he would be soon.

Awesome looked around. In all their time at the Guild, Awesome had never come up to the roof. It was broken into two sections and had a second, higher landing toward the front of the building and little parapets all the way around it. Awesome ran to each side and peered over. His stomach turned as the world spun below him. Still, across the alley, there was a slightly lower building. They might be able to reach the fire escape if they took a running jump.

"Seriously?"

Roy looked out over the edge.

"Yeah. I just—I'm not sure if—"

But Awesome didn't have time to finish his thought. The door to the roof blasted open and a mix of regular Suits and Elite Squires rushed through the opening.

"Photon, Baron—put your hands up and drop to your knees. You're under arrest."

Awesome and Roy exchanged looks.

"I'm sorry I got you into this, Roy."

"I'm not. I was acting like an ass."

"Yeah."

Roy laughed.

"Put your hands in the air!"

They did.

The Suits approached with handcuffs at the ready. But, as soon as they hesitated, Roy's hands came alight and a brilliant flash erupted on the roof of the Guild Hall. Awesome extended his cane and swept the closest Suit's feet out from under him. He swung again, crashing into the knee of another.

A shot whizzed past his head. Then another. This one was louder, brighter, more dangerous. It slammed into the parapet behind him and swiss cheesed the old stonework.

Roy threw a laser blast at the Elite guard who'd fired. His hand sizzled and the gun clattered against the roof. Awesome swung his cane like a golf club and sent the gun flying to the next rooftop.

Another Elite fired. His shot slammed into the Suit who happened to be charging at Awesome. The Suit stopped short and screamed as holes emerged on his chest and belly. Awesome stared at the Suit, wide-eyed, and caught him as he went down.

"Andy..."

Now, Awesome understood. Andy had run afoul of Pythia's Elite guard and had paid the price. Just like Roy and Awesome were about to—if they couldn't get off this roof.

He glared at the Elite who'd fired the shot.

"Was it you? Was it you who killed Andy?"

The man stopped in his tracks. A star-shaped scar adorned his hand, which Awesome noticed as the Elite raised his altered stunner and aimed.

"We were under orders."

"Pythia's orders?"

The man raised an eyebrow as he shot. Awesome rolled away from the flash of the Elite's gun as Roy took aim and blasted the man in the face with dazzling light. The Elite rubbed his eyes. Awesome screamed and started to charge the man as several more Suits poured out the door.

"Too many. We have to jump."

Roy had Awesome by the wrist and was pulling him toward the edge of the building as at least twenty Suits rushed onto the roof.

"What's that noise?"

The whirring thump of helicopter blades suddenly pounded in their ears and they turned to see, from the west side of the building, a big, black heliplane rising above the parapets of the Guild Hall. Awesome shook his head.

"We're finished."

Roy threw another laser beam at three Suits who were shooting at the heliplane. The plane's guns whirled around and fired stunner shots back at the Suits. Roy shouted over the noise.

"Whatever it is, it's not a Guild plane."

The cargo door opened. Stargazer, Nebula, and Opal leapt from within.

Stargazer shot hot, blue blasts of electricity at the Suits. Nebula cloaked as a Suit took fire. The Suit wheeled around—surprised—then found Nebula standing behind him. The Suit went down.

Opal tore through Suit after Suit with her cane. She was fluid, quick, strong. And, as a group of six men barreled toward her—she opened her mouth and let loose her mother's sonic scream. The men clutched their bleeding ears and fell to their knees, their guns dropping to the rooftop.

Then, suddenly, Stargazer was shouting as he laid down cover fire for Awesome and Roy.

"Let's go! Come on, Baron! Photon!"

Running, Awesome watched as a Suit took aim at Stargazer. He tapped the Suit in the temple. The man yelped and fell. His gun went off, barely missing Stargazer's head.

They raced to the edge of the roof.

Opal finished clearing out a path for them and took a running leap back into the plane. Stargazer waved to Nebula.

"Nebula, let's go!"

Nebula threw a punch at a tall, lanky Elite and then disappeared. He reappeared just in front of the plane and started the run-up for his jump. His cape billowing in the breeze, he started the run—and was cut down. Awesome turned and saw that it had been the Elite's gun.

Roy saw it too and shot a laser blast at the Elite. The man ducked and backstepped and shot his modified stunner again. The blast whizzed past Roy's ear. Roy fired again and this time caught him. The Elite fired a last blast and as he tumbled backward. The blast went wide—almost clipping the plane.

Roy and Stargazer stood suddenly together. Laying down cover fire as Awesome rushed to Nebula's side. Nebula clutched his left arm as he winced and breathed in quick puffs. The pain, Awesome realized, must be excruciating.

"Come on, Nebula. We have to get you out of here."

"I don't think I can—"

He turned white and passed out.

Without another word, Awesome heaved Nebula onto his back and stood. He went to the edge of the roof and looked over. The world spun. He took a few steps back. Roy and Stargazer were still laying down coverfire but Stargazer gave him a nod.

Awesome took a deep breath and felt the weight of his injured comrade on his shoulders—felt the weight of all his friends, all of Arc City, on his shoulders—as a familiar switch flipped. It ran through his body like electricity.

He took off running and, at the edge of the roof, leapt toward the plane. He soared through the air—easily—and landed with a thud inside the plane. Opal helped him lay Nebula down as Stargazer and Roy bounded in and the cargo door closed.

"We made it."

Roy wiped the sweat from his brow and then looked down at Nebula.

"Oh, no. Will *he* make it?"

Then, from the front, Dispatch called out,

"None of us will if we don't get out of here now! Stargazer, get up here and take the comm."

She piloted up and away from the Guild Hall as Stargazer ran up to the front of the plane to join her.

Nebula screamed in his sleep. Opal shook her head as she knelt on the floor of the plane next to him.

"His arm isn't right. It's falling apart."

Awesome knelt and threw back Nebula's cape. Nebula had always worn old-style hand and arm wraps. The strips of sturdy, gray and green cloth wrapped around his knuckles and wound tightly all the way up his forearms and yet, in spite of the layers of cloth and skin and sinew, little, silver-rimmed holes ran all the way through. Awesome could see the floor of the plane through them.

"I need a knife!"

Stargazer clipped off the large tactical knife from his boot and tossed it back to Awesome as Dispatch flew them up, over Arc City, and then southeast, into the pink sunrise.

Awesome unsheathed the knife and sliced at the strips of cloth as Roy looked across the two of them to Opal.

"Won't we be followed?"

"Not if we can get Nebula back up."

"What do you mean?"

"He can throw a cloak around the Shooting Star."

"The what?"

"Well, the Shooting Star III, actually. This thing we're in."

"What happened to the first two Shooting Stars?"

Stargazer called from the front,

"You don't want to know. How's he doing, Baron?"

Awesome had finally cut away the strips.

"It's bad."

Under the cloth, around the silver-rimmed holes, Nebula's veins were turning black and stiff. They wobbled and fought away from each other, trying to reroute themselves. All the while, Nebula's flesh was going mottled like grey patchwork.

Suddenly, Nebula disappeared. Roy exclaimed,

"What—"

"He's still here."

Awesome had his hands on Nebula's shoulder.

"His ability's going haywire."

"Get him up!"

This came from Dispatch and was followed with,

"Eddie! Eddie! Get your ass back here!"

Nebula suddenly reappeared. His lips moved weakly.

"Zoe..."

His eyelids fluttered and Awesome winced as he watched the darkness spread further up Nebula's arm. Awesome remembered the way Andy's body had looked. The way his flesh was gray up to his neck when his wounds had been in his gut. This would spread. Nebula's body would fight against itself and what it did not understand until there was nothing left of him.

"We're going to have to take it off."

Roy nodded. Opal agreed. The two of them held Nebula down as Awesome took one of the cloth strips and made a tourniquet high on Nebula's arm. Opal wadded up another strip and thrust it in Nebula's mouth as Awesome set his own jaw.

It would have to be quick and precise.

Suddenly, the plane shook. Then again.

"What's going on?"

"Your Guild friends are here. Baron, you've got to get him up!"

Roy glanced out the window and saw Sunstreak soaring through the air beside them. She threw a ball of fire toward one of their propellers and the shot went wide as Dispatch maneuvered.

"You've got to get him up, Baron."

Opal shook her head.

"If we shoot a stunner at her, she'll fall out of the sky. Baron, you're going to have to do this and then we're going to have to wake him up."

The plane shook again.

"Just do it. Do it!"

Awesome brought down the knife and sliced between ruined and healthy flesh. He sawed at the bone with as much strength as he dared until it came through the other side. The arm fell away and black blood pooled beneath it. Roy moved closer and fired an intense, focused beam into the wound, cauterizing it instantly. Opal was moving too. She pulled a first aid kit off the wall and grabbed from it a syringe with a long, thick needle then knelt beside her friend.

"I can hear his heart. I'll do it."

Without another word, she rammed the needle straight into Nebula's chest.

Gasping, Nebula shot up. His breath came out in hot, ragged gasps and he looked down at his arm.

"Thanks."

Awesome nodded.

"Sure thing."

Dispatch called out from the front.

"I'm really glad you're all ok back there but I need a cloak around this thing yesterday!"

The plane shook again, more violently now.

"Well, why didn't you say so?"

"I think I just did!"

Nebula slammed his remaining fist against the metal floor of the plane. In a second, everything around Awesome was a pale shade of violet and his vision was cloudy, as if a mist had fallen around them.

"Thank you!"

"Is this what the world looks like to you when you're invisible?"

"No. This is what the world looks like when I'm not. Where are we going?"

Awesome shook his head.

"I don't actually know. How did you guys even know where I was?"

Opal smiled her smirk of a smile and patted him on the back.

"We got a phone call."

"A phone call?"

"Yeah, from the Detective."

LONA STOOD AT the kitchen window, gripping her cold cup of coffee as Julia turned the pages of *The Dark Star*.

"What are you humming?"

Lona didn't realize that she had been humming until then.

"An old song, I think. It's stuck in my head."

Closing the back cover, Julia flipped back through the skinny paperback and sighed.

"Wow. Once you know it's the Guild this Kawaguchi guy's talking about, it seems kind of obvious."

Lona said nothing and watched out the window. The front lawn, complete with a little stone path that led up to the porch, was overgrown and morning glories twisted up the weatherbeaten fence that surrounded the front of the house. Beyond that was a field of sunflowers and, beyond that, the treeline. Maples, white ash, black cherry, cottonwoods, and elms surrounded the property.

"So the Guild is headed up by Pythia—the Luminary—and she was using Guild scientists to monitor extra-normal children—especially war orphans—just in case one of them had some special ability. That must be where Hawthorne started. I heard about that place when I first came to the Guild. And then, one of them did have a unique power—the Echo or Sola or whatever his name really was—and she wanted to harness his ability to fight the Nova."

"I think so."

"But what's the Nova?"

"We are."

Tulie rubbed her head against Lona's thigh. Lona reached down and ran her fingers over Tulie's soft coat.

"Anyone—anyone who has a special ability—who isn't part of the Guild is Pythia's problem."

"So, the Echo—"

"What have we always done with super criminals? Lock them away. And, sometimes they escape. Or sometimes they get back on the outside and go back to their old life. Or sometimes they hurt people while they're in there. This way, Pythia can avoid that problem by taking their abilities away forever. Somehow she's found a way to harness the Echo's power."

"But he had to kill people to take their ability. And then—I mean, he'd be incredibly dangerous. Even more dangerous than he was already."

"I know. But I think they must have found a way to—"

Lona stopped as the trees and then the sunflowers in the field suddenly wavered and rippled as though blown by a mighty gust. She narrowed her eyes and watched. The morning glories shook, the grass pressed against the earth, and gold dust exploded into her vision and swirled through the yard.

"What—"

A heliplane and the sound of its engines suddenly popped into her world. She peered through the front window and saw Dispatch at the helm. She ran outside, onto the porch, as the propellers spun to a stop and the cargo door opened in the back.

Then, Awesome came out and around, propping Nebula up, helping him walk. Roy and Opal followed with Stargazer and Dispatch bringing up the rear. Stargazer was holding a metal case and Dispatch carried a first aid kit. Now Lona saw that Nebula's left arm was missing, Roy had a black eye, and Awesome was covered in dark blood. Lona frowned at Awesome, worried.

"It's ok. We made it out, at least. Thanks to them—"

"And I still have a pulse. Thanks to your husband."

"And me."

"And my wife, yes."

Opal cleared her throat.

"And Opal and Stargazer and Photon."

Dispatch crowed and clapped Nebula on the back.

"Come on, baby. Let's get you inside."

Julia opened the door for them and Awesome led the way inside but Stargazer stopped on the porch and looked around, back at the sunflowers, the trees, and, in the distance, the mountains.

"What is this place?"

"It was our friend's. He left it to us when he died."

"It's beautiful."

"I know."

She looked out at the field. The sunflowers gently waved in the breeze, their black and yellow heads bowing and bobbing and following the rays of the morning sun. Birds were singing. Pale clouds drifted across a fresh, blue sky. This place seemed as far from Arc City—as far from their problems—as they could get. And, at least for now, they were safe.

"Thank you, Stargazer. Thank you for saving Awesome's life."

Stargazer put a gloved hand on her shoulder.

"I promised I'd bring him back safe, Detective."

She smiled and he continued,

"The Baron is important. If the Guild is going to wage an open war on Sheets, or criminals, or anyone who just doesn't want to play by their rules, we're going to need him. And you."

They went inside and found Nebula lying on the sofa while Dispatch cleaned him up. Julia and Roy were talking—finally—in low voices by the empty fireplace and Opal was speaking into the kitchen phone.

"No, I'm not sure when I'll be home. Make sure he does his homework. Tell him I love him…"

Stargazer joined Dispatch and Lona wandered into the kitchen where she found Awesome making a pot of coffee.

Awesome turned at the sound of her footsteps and saw her there in the morning light.

That smile.

She fell into his arms and they stood together, as one, for a long time. He breathed in the smell of her as she pressed her face against his chest.

"What happens now?"

THE SUNFLOWERS WATCHED and followed the sun as it rose and fell over Andy Archer's—now Awesome and Lona's—home. The day was warm and the old farmhouse, in spite of the number of people in it, was quiet. They sat in groups in the kitchen or the living room. Nebula slept for a while in a bedroom and dust motes floated through the air as he lay dreaming. Dispatch, Stargazer, Awesome, and Lona opened the case Stargazer had brought and inspected the discarded arm. Lona told them about the gun. About Eleanor Woods and her work. About Grayston. About the Echo.

"If Pythia is using these Elite guards to protect the Hand, then the guns were probably originally meant to put him down if whatever procedure they'd done didn't work."

"You mean—"

"I mean, based on what you two said, the Echo is like some kind of robot now. He's blank. But, when they first brought him back, they couldn't know whether he would stay under their control. They're just feeding him the abilities of these criminals and he could've been more dangerous than ever. They had to find a way to put him down permanently if need-be."

"And the man—or one of the men—who shot Andy—I saw him on the roof. He said he was following orders but—"

"But Pythia wouldn't give that order, even at her worst she wouldn't order Andy's death."

"So who did?"

Lona shook her head.

That night, after a dinner Lona made from the canned and dry goods she found in the pantry, they all sat together around the big, farm table. Awesome made and poured coffee or tea or water and they were quiet, the house was quiet, the night was quiet as Lona spoke again.

She told them about their friendship with Andy Archer. She told them that, even though he was the hero of Arc City and maybe the greatest hero of his age, when he got too close to the truth—he died. She told them what she speculated—that Andy recognized something strange about the way the Echo's death had been dealt with, that he must've gone to Pythia with questions and was rejected, that he must have investigated the Echo's past and the Guild's secret divisions and that he must have, like Lona, found Grayston. She guessed that he went into the basement of the Guild, found the Hand of Justice and Pythia's private sentencing room, and was shot by the Elite Squires.

"He escaped the same way you two did. But he could fly."

"And he chose to fly to us."

"And give us a message."

Lona took a long look at her hands and at the other hands around the table. Some were paler or darker. Larger and smaller. Older and younger. All of them were battered from the work they had done that day.

"Andy wasn't just a cape, or an Agent, he was a hero. And, he was our friend. He introduced us to a new kind of life, a life of sacrifice and danger but also one of considerable reward.

He helped both of us see that we could do more than we had ever done, that we could be more than we had ever been. He believed in us and because of that, we believed in ourselves. And, to the very end, he was looking out for us, warning us, preparing us. He loved us. He loved us as though we were his own children, his own family. That's why we're sitting here now—because of his warning and because of his love.

He saw something on the horizon. He saw the setting of his sun and the dawning of a new one. The world is changing. The Guild has operated in secret for centuries. It has acted as a guard for the innocent from the shadows. But I think the time for that is coming to an end. Pythia has lost control. She's not going to sit by while we, or anyone else, openly oppose her. She will wage war."

A quiet swept over the kitchen as Lona's words settled around them and collected like a snowdrift, absorbing all other sound. Lona and Awesome and their two sets of friends, brought together by choice and adversity and the will to do what was right, sat in quiet for some time. Finally, it was Julia who broke the silence with her voice.

"What can we do?"

"I don't know. I wish—"

And then there was a knock at the door.

THE MAN ON their threshold was very tall and very slender. He had dark brown skin, flecks of white in his beard, and inhumanly gold eyes. Intricate tattoos dotted his cheeks and bald head and they moved, along with the deep creases around his eyes, when he smiled at them all.

"Hello. I am the Raven. May I come in?"

Julia squinted at the man.

"Uhh—I'm not—"

He stepped a little to the side then and revealed to them his companion.

"Neima!"

She wore a long, white dress and her hair—having lost all remnant of its reddish hue—was the same, snowy color. But it was still Neima.

> "It's alright. He's with me. I left in search of my mentor. But, unfortunately, he has left this world. Instead, I found the mentor of my mentor. He has been very kind. He helped me break through the spiritual block I was experiencing. We've come to help."

The two travelers came in from the night together and stood in the softly lit living room looking ethereal and wise and out of place among the dusty old tables and overstuffed sofa. Awesome closed the door behind them and, when they were all settled, the Raven spoke again.

"I must correct Neima slightly. We've come to *ask* for help."

"What? How can we—"

"Lona, do you have your father's journal? Did you bring it with you?"

She nodded and reached for her backpack, realizing then that it must have been the Raven who sent Awesome's uniform and her father's journal.

"You—"

"Have you broken the code?"

"Not yet. I've been trying but—why?"

Lona pulled the book from her bag and flipped through it.

"Because, Lona, it's the key to saving everything."

The picture of Lona's younger self fell from between the pages and, when she turned it over, dust exploded from her father's words.

ABOUT THE AUTHOR

Originally from Appalachia, AshleyRose Sullivan lives, writes, and paints in Los Angeles with her husband and their many imaginary friends. Her work has been published in places like The Rumpus, Barrelhouse, and Word Riot and her novels, Awesome Jones: A Superhero Fairy Tale and Silver Tongue are available from Seventh Star Press. She can be found at ashleyrosesullivan.com

Also available from AshleyRose Sullivan in print and eBook!

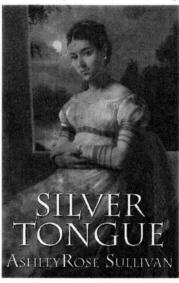

The Colonies lost the Revolutionary War. Now it's 1839 and the North American continent is divided into three territories: New Britannia, Nueva Espana, and Nouvelle France where seventeen-year-old Claire Poissant lives.

Claire has a magical way with words—literally. But a mystical power of persuasion isn't the only thing that makes her different. Half-French and half-Indian, Claire doesn't feel at home in either world. Maybe that's why she's bonded so tightly with her fellow outcasts and best friends: Phileas, a young man whose towering intellect and sexuality have always made him the target of bullies, and Sam, a descendant of George Washington who shares the disgraced general's terrible, secret curse.

But when Sam's family is murdered, these bonds are tested and Claire's special ability is strained to its limits as the three hunt the men responsible into dangerous lands. Along the way they cross paths with P.T. Barnum, William Frankenstein and other characters from both history and fantasy as they learn the hard way that man is often the most horrific monster and that growing up sometimes means learning to let go of the things you hold most dear.

CPSIA information can be obtained
at www.ICGtesting.com
Printed in the USA
FFOW03n1441110218
44944687-45218FF